Donated by
Floyd Dickman

SKY CARVER

SKY CARVER

by Dean Whitlock

Clarion Books · New York

Clarion Books
a Houghton Mifflin Company imprint
215 Park Avenue South, New York, NY 10003
Copyright © 2005 by Dean Whitlock

The text was set in 11-point Meridien Roman.

www.houghtonmifflinbooks.com

Printed in the U.S.A.

Library of Congress Cataloging-in-Publication Data
Whitlock, Dean.
Sky carver / by Dean Whitlock.
p. cm.
Summary: Thomas, a talented wood carver, discovers that he can also do
weather magic and undertakes a journey that could lead him to hone that skill
and save his village from drought, or perhaps to a completely different destiny.
ISBN 0-618-44393-2
[1. Fantasy.] I. Title.
PZ7.W59167Sk 2005
[Fic]—dc22

2004017819

ISBN-13: 978-0-618-44393-2
ISBN-10: 0-618-44393-2

QUM 10 9 8 7 6 5 4 3 2 1

To Sally and Ross,

who make it all fun

Thomas Painter turned the spoon in one hand, knife poised in the other. The hard, buttery wood glowed in the light from the small back window of the storage shed. He bit his lower lip, then drew the point of the blade along the grain one way, then back, etching a fine line from bowl to grip. He felt a pleasant surge of anticipation at what Aunt Singer would say when she saw it. This was no ordinary spoon he was carving for her. Its bowl was the mouth of a fanciful fish. Its broad head tapered smoothly down the handle to a flaring tail. He had followed the natural grain of the wood, a pear-wood branch rescued from the kitchen fire.

I am a good carver, he thought. Someday, people will call me that—Carver. Just like Aunt Dora; everyone calls her Singer for her voice. Someday, he thought.

Smiling, Thomas put the spoon down on a keg of linseed oil, then ran the edge of his carving knife over a fine stone and carefully stropped it in the palm of his hand. As he felt the fine edge slide over his skin, he dreamed again of changing his apprenticeship. He was thirteen, almost fourteen, old to be a new apprentice. But he could already carve. And he would never be much of a painter. He wrinkled his nose at the constant stink of pine spirits and burned pigment there in the shed. He buried his nose in the bowl of the spoon and inhaled deeply the smell of freshly shaved pear wood. If only he could smell this wood scent all day. Uncle Piper had plenty of other apprentices. There must be some way Thomas could change trades. But no, Uncle Piper would never agree. Not for Thomas Painter. The name said it all, he thought bitterly.

He glanced into the dark corner to the right of the window, at the back of the rough post supporting the end of the wall. So far no one had noticed the twining vine he was carving up the length of the post. A slight smile returned to his lips. He picked up the spoon and began to slice tiny shavings from the surface of the tail, adding detail to the ribbing there. Soon he was lost in his work again, and almost happy.

Suddenly, the door to the shed banged open. A voice snapped. "Thomas! What the blazing mages are you doing?"

Thomas looked up, blinking as his eyes focused back on the world. His cousin Dora Painter, Uncle Piper's shop boss, stood in the doorway, fists on her hips, staring at him as if he had two heads. The stare became a glare.

"Aunt Singer asked me to carve her a spoon," Thomas said. "At breakfast. Remember?"

"That was four hours ago," Dora growled. "What are you carving it out of? Stone?"

Thomas winced. "Better than stone," he said, holding out the spoon in an attempt to distract her from the time. "It's pear wood. It won't chip like her old one."

Dora's eyes widened as she noticed the shape of the spoon. She strode between the kegs and sacks of painting supplies and snatched it from Thomas's hand. "Great mages!" she exclaimed. "Mother asked for a spoon, not a . . . a . . ." Words failed her. She threw the spoon down.

Thomas jumped up and went after it. "If you do that, she won't have anything," he said angrily. "I'll have to start all over."

Dora grabbed at Thomas's arm. "You'll do no such thing. She can get another one from Joynter."

Thomas dodged away and came up holding the spoon. It was still in one piece. "See," he said, "it's still whole. Joynter's spoon would have broken."

"So what? You could get three of them in the time you've wasted on that . . . that useless bauble." She snatched the spoon again.

"Hey!" Thomas cried, lunging for it. "Give me that!" Dora held the spoon above his reach and stalked out the door. Thomas followed, still trying to grab his spoon. "Joynter's spoons are ugly," he snapped. "Ugly and clumsy."

"They work," Dora retorted, striding along the landing toward the back door of the shop.

"They break."

"They're cheap."

"You're right about that!" Thomas shouted. "They're cheap! Ugly and cheap!"

"Well, you can just tell that to Joynter," Dora said. "He's here right now." She jerked open the shop door and shoved Thomas through.

Uncle Piper looked up as they came barging in. Joynter's sharp face peered around Uncle Piper's wide bulk.

"What's this?" Uncle Piper said, frowning at both Dora and Thomas. Joynter merely deepened his perpetual scowl. Thomas's outrage dissolved under their combined glare.

"I found him hiding in the storeroom," Dora said. "Whittling on a spoon."

"I wasn't hiding," Thomas said. "Aunt Singer asked me to make her one."

"Yes," Uncle Piper agreed slowly, shifting his irritation to Dora. "I heard her ask."

"Well, he's wasted all morning on it," Dora replied. "Look." She held out the spoon.

Uncle Piper stared at it, and his face drooped a little in disappointment.

"He must have been sneaking away to work on that ridiculous thing for days," Joynter grated, his voice as sharp as his face.

"I have not," Thomas protested. He grabbed the spoon back from Dora.

"Hah! Who's the woodcrafter here?" Joynter demanded. Thomas bit back another retort. "You're a painter, boy, not a joynter. He needs discipline, Piper."

Uncle Piper puffed out his cheeks. "Well, Thomas," he said, "what do you think your father would say, eh?"

The remark made Thomas even more angry. Uncle Piper always called up the memory of his father.

"Fetch in a sack of the umber, a jug of pine spirits, and a keg of oil," Uncle Piper ordered when Thomas didn't reply. "Mix it up. Then come back here for your punishment when I've finished with Master Joynter."

"Yes, sir," Thomas muttered.

"And give me that . . . spoon."

Thomas handed it over and turned away, not wanting to see what Uncle Piper did with it. He still heard the clack as it landed in the wood box. Dora gave him a shove, then went over to join in the conference with Joynter. On the big central table were sheets of sketches for the new town hall, the biggest project to come into the shop since Thomas could remember. The planning and construction had consumed the crafters of the town for well over a year. They had all promised the mayor it would be finished before summer. Time was running out. On top of that, it hadn't rained for months. Dry weather made construction work easy, but this was the second year in a row. Last year's harvest had been scant; this year's looked to fare even worse. Tempers were stretched thin.

Knowing that didn't help Thomas's mood as he hauled supplies to Dulci. She was his cousin, too—Dora's little sister—and though she was a year younger than Thomas, she was far better at mixing and matching colors. And at line and balance and brushwork, and at portraiture and landscapes—in fact, all the apprentices were much better than he was at anything that had to do with painting. And that worried Uncle Piper almost as much as the designs for the town hall, because Thomas's father had been the best painter ever to have lived in the town. People carefully cleaned his murals to preserve them. They treasured his portraits. There was magic in his work, they all said.

Uncle Piper, though skilled with a brush, fell far short of his brother's talent. He was quite content with that, actually. What bothered him was Thomas the Younger. Uncle Piper—everyone in town, in fact—expected him to be as good as his father. Even better. But he wasn't. Middling good was the most polite way to describe it, but truth to tell, he lacked all talent.

Truth to tell, he didn't even *like* painting.

But he was born a Painter, only child of the great, the magical, Thomas Painter. And so he must be a painter.

Grumbling inside, he helped Dulci mix a bucket of thick mustardy umber paint, almost gagging at the smell of the newly opened jug of pine spirits. Joynter and Uncle Piper continued their conference over the central table. Dust danced in the light from the high windows on the north wall.

Finally, Joynter gave the table a hard slap. "All right, then," he snapped, "do it your way. But do it quickly. I need those panels."

"They'll be ready," Uncle Piper assured him, following toward the door.

Still complaining, Joynter stalked out.

Uncle Piper turned, scowling. "Come on, then," he growled. "There's work to do."

He kept them at it for another half hour before finally calling the midday break. Thomas's stomach was growling as loudly as Uncle Piper by then, but he held back till the others had left. Then he darted over to the wood box. The spoon was gone. He looked into the dying morning fire on the hearth. There was nothing left but ember and ash. His heart sank.

He stood there a moment, too disappointed to move. He squeezed back angry tears. Why couldn't Uncle Piper see? Shoulders sagging, he went out the back door and found Uncle Piper waiting on the landing, seated on a pair of upturned kegs, bagpipe draped across his lap.

"So, Thomas," he said. "Is the paint mixed?"

"Yes, sir," Thomas replied dully.

"And the panels? Did you get them sealed?"

"Yes, sir. They were done yesterday evening. Dulci put the base on them this morning."

"By herself."

"Yes, sir. Aunt Singer—"

Uncle Piper held up a big hand. "I know, I know. She asked you to make her a spoon. And you spent all morning on it."

"I wanted it to be a good one," Thomas said. Anger, and the memory of the ashes, made his voice catch.

"I'm sure you did. But judging by what you managed to do in one morning, I'll venture you could have whipped up something plain, and just as useful, in little over a moment. And then you could have got on with your real work." Thomas shrugged. Uncle Piper grumbled in his throat. "This is a busy time, Thomas," he said. "What would your father say if he found you working on bits of wood?"

Thomas looked down. "I don't know," he muttered, "but I imagine you'll tell me."

"Don't get cheeky," Uncle Piper warned. "Your father was an artist, and he would have told you that art takes work. It takes attention. It takes practice. You can have all the talent in the world, but if you don't practice . . . Now think about it. If you put half the effort into your painting as you did into that spoon, you'd be well on your way."

"To what?" Thomas retorted. "Whitewashing the mayor's new privy? I'm no good at painting, Uncle. You know that."

"Nonsense," Uncle Piper growled. "You just haven't come into your talent yet, that's all. Some people take longer."

"How long did it take my father?" Thomas demanded. "When did he show his talent?"

Uncle Piper shifted uncomfortably. They both knew the answer: Thomas the Elder had sketched his first portrait at age three, and it had been good. It still hung, proudly framed in walnut, in the front room of the house.

"Your father was special," Uncle Piper admitted. "But look at your mother. She didn't come into her talent till she was grown. Didn't even know she had it till after you were born."

"And it wasn't fowling," Thomas said. "It was completely new."

"It was mage talent," Piper said, almost disdainfully. "That can pop up anywhere. Look at her sister, your aunt Zarah. The same talent showed up in her later."

"But not fowling," Thomas insisted. "Her family were fowlers, but her talent is different."

"Zarah is still a fowler. And your mother would be, too, if she hadn't . . . Anyway, I didn't mean you were exactly like her," Uncle Piper said irritably. "I just meant you were a late bloomer, like her. You haven't come into your own yet. And when you do, you'll show your father's side. I'm sure of it. You're a Painter."

"But I'm not a *painter,*" Thomas argued. "I don't even *want* to be a painter."

"That's because you haven't tried!" Uncle Piper snapped. He threw up his hands. "Bah, listen to me—I sound as sharp as Joynter. Would you rather have him for a master, boy?" Thomas looked up hopefully, but Piper hadn't meant it as a real question. He grumbled on. "You'd soon lose your interest in wood under his sharp nose, eh? Now come on—I promised your father I'd watch over you, and that meant teaching you the craft. You're a Painter. That's all there is to it. You go eat. And here—" He reached into his apron and pulled out the spoon. "Give this to your aunt Singer."

Thomas stared at the spoon in amazement.

"Well, take it," Uncle Piper growled. "I'm not going to let you waste a whole morning's work, am I?" Thomas took the spoon, and Uncle Piper shifted the bagpipe under his arm. "Tell her I'll be in in a moment."

"Yes, sir!" Thomas said gratefully.

"Hmmph," Uncle Piper replied through his mouthpiece. As Thomas turned away, he added, "You're still to be punished for skipping the morning's work. After you eat, you can clean out the privy."

"Yes, sir," Thomas said. Holding the rescued spoon, he didn't mind such light punishment. Come to think of it, cleaning the privy was far better than mucking with paint.

Two

With two quick wing beats and a twist to her tail, Raven swooped into a strong updraft and soared high above the four crows in her little escort. Croaking with glee, she peeled sideways, half tucked her wings, and arrowed down through their midst. They scattered like squawking black confetti. She loved spring and its bright mix of sun and cloud over still-warming land. It created thermals and breezes that made flying a joy.

The crows regrouped and chased her, cawing raucously in laughter and crow imprecations. Crows were such fun, she thought. This whole mission was fun. Off on her own with four freewheeling companions. Away from Penalla, her moody mistress mage, and the dark little cloud that had hung over Penalla's head for weeks, making Raven and all her charges quite miserable. Raven turned a barrel roll and croaked a few jeering imprecations of her own back at the crows. Then she swooped down to startle a man in a flatboat on the river below, flapped past the town at the base of the upper falls, and soared up and up the face of the cliff on a friendly breeze. The forest of the high reach stretched before her, bright green with new leaves, laced by the river and streams and the winding trails used by loggers and tappers, hunters and trappers, and the few others who lived here in the forested heights at the foot of the mountains.

One in particular Raven was after: Nuatta, sister to her mistress mage. This sister was a mage herself, a weather mage, and was much in demand in the towns along the layered reaches of the River Slow. But she was a crotchety woman and preferred to live in solitude in the forests of the high reach, coming down below the upper falls only when the need for her talents was great. If the current dry spell went too long, for example. But that wasn't why her sister had sent Raven out to find her. Raven's task was much more interesting.

Now Raven led the crows up the first stream to the left of the river. Flapping steadily, with only an occasional prank at the jostling crows, she followed the stream till it was little more than a brook. Just where it became a freshet, there was a small clearing. In the clearing was a steep-roofed cabin. With a curt croak at the crows, Raven soared higher and took a long look. This was it, Nuatta's home, just as Penalla had described it.

Calling again to the crows, Raven swooped down among the crowns of the trees, out of sight of the clearing. Cawing and laughing, caught up in a new game of tag, they ignored her.

What a pain crows are, she thought. Might as well expect poetry from a pigeon.

She landed to work on her spell. Making them understand her was easy enough; making them obey was harder. She had been Penalla's apprentice for three years, and she had learned quickly at first. In fact, she had done so well, Penalla had rewarded her just last year with a special gift, a small black enameled feather on a silver chain. She wore it always, the only thing that changed with her from human to raven, a feather on her breast. But Penalla had also set her to more complicated tasks, and the spells had gotten more difficult.

Concentrating on command, she muttered a few words to reinforce her spell, then ordered the crows to stop playing and shut up. *Kakk*ing grouchily, they flapped toward her. She formed a vision of an angry Penalla plucking their tail feathers if they failed in this mission. That shut them up, though they still fluffed disgruntledly as they landed beside her.

Wait here, you mouse-brained louts, she commanded. *Be ready to fly fast when I call.*

They shifted nervously on the branch as she dropped off and continued toward the clearing under the canopy of trees. It was clever flying, swooping below the branches, dodging saplings and vines. She took a moment to enjoy it. Finally, she lighted on a branch just out of sight of the cabin and pushed the tip of her beak through the curtain of leaves.

The clearing was empty; the slab-sided cabin was silent. It was hard to believe anyone was there. Raven listened carefully and watched for any movement. She heard a nuthatch laugh a few trees over and contemplated sending it in close to look in the cabin's two small windows, but decided against it. Nuatta, if she was there, might notice odd behavior from a bird. After all, her sister was a bird mage, and they didn't get along. Raven began to worry. If Nuatta was gone, or Penalla had been wrong about her sister's habits, this could be a long wait. The blasted crows would be trouble.

Then the door to the cabin opened and Nuatta stepped out. She was thinner and taller than Penalla, and her hair was silvery gray, but the dark eyes and long nose matched her sister's exactly. Raven cackled with relief, then ducked back into the leaves when Nuatta stiffened and looked sharply around. Raven huddled in the shadows, hardly breathing, till she heard the cabin door close. Carefully, she pressed one eye against the curtain of leaves. Nuatta was walking toward the brook, where a small dam made a pool at the center of the clearing.

Nuatta stopped at the edge of the pool, pulled off her boots, and dipped her toe into the water. Frowning, she looked up. A small cloud had just gone over the sun, and a larger one was drifting up behind it on the breeze. She reached down to her side and drew what appeared to be a branch from a loop on her belt. The branch was straight, silver as her hair, and tipped with a spray of silvery green leaves shaped almost like raindrops. Raven watched avidly as Nuatta held it up. With a slight wave, Nuatta broke up the small cloud and sent its pieces flying away on a sudden gust of wind. With two sweeps, she pushed the larger cloud off toward the mountains, where it swelled and rained briefly, shrinking as it went.

Raven blinked in admiration. Nuatta might be a real witch of a person, but she was certainly a powerful mage. This could be more dangerous than she'd thought. Raven looked at the disappearing cloud, now little more than a mist over the mountains. She wondered if maybe she hadn't apprenticed herself to the wrong sister. But no, her talent really was birds. Weather working was impressive, important magic, but it wasn't for her. She liked being a bird. Nuatta might be able to control clouds, but she couldn't fly like one.

Raven watched with growing anticipation as Nuatta carefully set her wand on a bench by the pool. Then she took off her shirt and unwrapped her kilt, draping each neatly over the other end of the bench. Finally, she stepped into the pool. Raven tensed on her branch. Nuatta paused, splashing water up onto her legs, then her body. Slowly, she eased herself into the water and lay back. Her silver hair floated around her head like a cloud. She closed her eyes.

Silently, Raven dropped off the branch and flapped as fast as she could toward the pool. Her wingtips brushed the grass in the clearing. Heart pounding, she beat, beat, beat her wings, gaining speed, adjusting her angle, rising just a little. She soared over the bench and, with a quick scoop of her beak, snatched up the leafy wand.

In a moment, she was past the pool and rising sharply to top the trees at the other edge of the clearing. But it was hard work, with the wind now at her back and the air already warm. There was nothing to give her lift except her own muscles. Straining, she flapped harder. She heard splashing and a sharp cry behind her, and caught a glimpse in her wide side vision of Nuatta pulling herself angrily from the water. Raven flapped as hard as she could. Suddenly, a cold gust of wind blew up from nowhere, and she knew with a sinking heart that Nuatta had power even without her wand. But the gust came straight from Nuatta, below and behind, and actually helped to lift Raven over the wall of trees. Croaking with relief, she leveled off and dipped below Nuatta's line of sight.

Now she pulled as hard as she could for the waiting crows, sending the command to fly. Cawing like idiots, they obeyed. Instantly, a cold wind gusted their way. Raven croaked a wild curse and ordered them to shut up, to fly away, to scatter. Instead, they bunched behind her, cawing in fright. She cursed again. Looking back, she saw blasts of wind beat along the tops of the trees. Heavy clouds were forming at the top of Nuatta's hill, spreading out in search of the wand. She thrust out her head and flew for her life.

Still the clouds grew, blowing straight toward her, and only then did she notice the wisps of cloud that puffed from the tip of the wand. They left a trail leading straight to her. She shook her head, but that only made more cloud. She looped and curved, drawing big spirals of mist in the sky. A sudden swirl of black storm cycloned out like a tentacle, grasping at her. Panicked, she flew right back into the midst of the crows and stuffed the wand into a gasping beak. With a *kak* of dismay, the crow took one look behind and doubled his efforts. Removed from Raven's magic, the wand stopped misting. The other crows finally scattered. The clouds spread out, forfeiting strength to seek more widely.

On and on she led the crows, wings aching, breath burning in her chest. She had never flown so hard before. The crow with the wand started to tire, and Raven called another one over to carry the silver branch. Grouchily, he obeyed. They were all tired now— crows lacked a raven's stamina—but Raven didn't dare take the wand yet. Weather wasn't her talent, but the wand would respond to anyone with magic. Even washover magic would signal Nuatta and lead the clouds on.

She looked back and saw with relief that the clouds were slowing, breaking up. Her little caucus was finally getting out of range. Without the wand to focus her strength, Nuatta couldn't raise more than this squall. Not over such a wide area, nor so far away. Tired by the chase and the effort of magic, Raven allowed herself to slow down, but she kept a wary eye on the clouds. And when one of the crows tried to land to rest, she flew over and pecked at his tail.

That was a mistake. Pushed beyond their limits, the other crows shook off her command and came to their brother's aid, mobbing her with indignant cries.

All right, you half-fledged dolts! she said, backing off. *If you want to stay here and risk the clouds, that's fine. Just give me the blasted wand. I'll take it to Penalla by myself.*

Kah! they jeered. *Come and get it!*

And they swooped off, finding energy in defiance.

Outraged, Raven tore after the one with the wand. Startled by her unexpected burst of speed, he dropped it, but another one swooped in and snatched it out of the air before she could recover. The others laughed at her and chased their brother, turning it into a game of toss and catch. Seething, Raven flapped after them. She tried catching whichever one had the wand, but he always managed to flip it to a companion just as she got near. Then she tried catching the wand, but one of them always managed to scoop it up just ahead of her snapping beak. They were back over the river with their game now, approaching the sheer drop of the upper falls. Far behind, clouds were still coming, but even more slowly and breaking apart as they came.

Controlling her anger, Raven stopped chasing the crows. Instead, she simply matched their speed and flew alongside, not too close, ignoring their antics. That did the trick; with no one to tease, they slowed and, one by one, dropped out of the game. Then they crossed above the edge of the cliff and felt the spray from the tall waterfall below. Some people at the top were winching a bundle down the long stone face to others at the bottom. There was the mill and the village far below, and the newly plowed fields beyond, the river winding lazily between them into the distance. Raven and her band had leagues yet to go. The crows began to grumble.

Suddenly, Raven swooped sideways and snatched the wand. The crow squawked in outrage. She croaked a smart reply, proud of herself. He'd never noticed her drifting closer. But before she could flap away, another crow blind-sided her, soaring up from below to snatch at the wand. She tried to twist away; he twisted after and gave her a jar that shook feathers loose. The wand tore from her beak.

Give me that! she commanded, beating at him with her wings.

What do you mean? he squawked back indignantly. *I don't have it.*

Well, then, who does? Angrily she scanned the skies for the other crows. But they were all flying away in a huff, and not one of them had the wand. Heart plummeting, she looked down. There was the wand, twisting and falling, its leaves flapping as it went. And right below it, standing at a vee in a path from the village, was a boy leaning on a wheelbarrow.

With a croak of despair, Raven dove.

Three

Thomas set down the handles of the wheelbarrow and wearily wiped his sleeve across his face. Scooping and shoveling five months' worth of wet dung had proved harder than he'd expected. He waved futilely at the flies. They seemed to prefer his head to the now-empty barrow. The composting pits had buzzed with great swarms of them, fired up by the spring sunlight. His own private cloud had followed him back, landing on his ears and nose and hair, crawling around happily in his sweat. He swatted and missed again.

The meal had been a disappointment. Aunt Singer was still working when Thomas came in from his talk with Uncle Piper. Linen was a town specialty, and Aunt Singer was one of many weavers who supplied the river merchants with cloth. She was supposed to deliver six bolts of white linen to the wharf that evening, to be shipped downriver to the dyers, and was hard-pressed to finish the order. She glanced at his spoon, thanked him with a vague remark about "how interesting" it looked, then went right back to weaving.

Grandmother Weaver, too lame in the hands to work more than an hour a day, had managed to throw together a meal, but the meat was cold and the bread was burned and the cabbage was old enough to be half pickled in its own juice. Thomas grabbed a chunk of bread and a quick mouthful of meat, then went right to the shed to get the barrow and shovel. He attacked the privy with a fury that sustained him all the way to the pits and as far back as the road.

Now, faced with the imminent return to the paint shop, he succumbed to resentment and slouched against the barrow, letting his eyes follow the rutted lane as it wandered down the riverbank, away from Wanting Town. His parents had gone that way ten years ago, following his mother's vision. Her sudden show of talent as a seer. He couldn't remember it really—he'd been only three at the time—just that suddenly she had changed, and then she had gone downriver. Along with his father. He could hardly remember their faces; they were just two silhouettes who sometimes walked through his thoughts. Walked in and away, shrinking with distance and time. Following some mage who was supposed to train her newfound talent, leaving him stuck here with Uncle Piper, who thought Thomas's future was to be a painter.

Thomas slapped at the handles of the barrow. He'd given up wishing his parents would return. Now, when he let himself think about it, he was glad they were gone. Having the great Thomas Painter here to watch his son try to paint—that would be far worse than Uncle Piper's bullheaded nagging. He just wished his father's reputation had disappeared with them, leaving him free to get out of the paint shop. He had his knife; he could carve for his living— trade spoons for food, even barter passage on one of the flatboats heading downstream.

But no. No one wanted spoons carved like fishes. He'd have to carve something else, something better. He slipped his hand into his belt pouch and touched the small nut-sized elm burl there. He ran his finger over the half-carved shape, a sleeping cat. It would be a gift for Dulci on her birthday, an amulet to bring luck. People would pay for work like that. And for useful things like candlesticks, decorated boxes, quaichs, and festival bowls. And chair backs, door panels, beam ends to cap the joinery of new homes. And he would carve figurines, large versions of the little amulet, animals of all kinds. Full-sized statues, even, so perfect they'd look alive. Mayors. The Barons. The Duke himself. All he had to do was start walking downriver.

No, he thought again. That's what my father did; walked away and left everything behind. Everything undone. I'm not like that. I owe Singer and Piper more than that.

Still, the path drew his eyes. Thomas tore his thoughts from his father and his duty, let them wander back to all the wonderful things he would carve. He stared dreamily at nothing while the flies buzzed unnoticed around him. Unconsciously, his hand moved from the pouch to caress the handle of his knife.

Suddenly, out of nowhere, a falling branch grazed his head. It bounced lightly on his shoulder and slid down the front of his shirt. Without thinking, he caught it. Then a harsh croak from right above startled him even more. He flinched as a huge raven swooped past his face. Feathers brushed his cheek. Talons grabbed at his hands.

With a cry, Thomas threw himself back and struck at the bird. Croaking harshly, it soared off. He watched it, wondering what could have made it act so strangely. It seemed angry. Its croaks sounded almost like curses.

It swooped on him again, stabbing at his face with its sharp black beak.

"Hey!" Thomas yelled. "Get away, you blasted bird!" The anger and frustration he'd been hoarding broke lose. He whipped it with the branch.

A puff of mist burst from the leaves on the branch, but Thomas didn't notice. He flailed again, striking the raven's wing this time as it flapped heavily around his head, grabbing and pecking. He flailed again and again, and each time more mist sprang from the branch, until both he and the bird were enveloped in a thin damp fog. He swung blindly, carving a swath through the fog and landing a solid blow on the raven's head. It squawked and flew off, trailing mist as it clawed its way up out of reach.

Thomas waved the wand in a parting threat, slicing off blocks of cloud. Only then did he notice what was happening. He stared at the clouds, drifting away now on a growing breeze. He stared in amazement at the white wisps still leaking from the branch. He waved his free hand through the dissipating fog, feeling the dampness as it swirled around his fingers.

He studied the branch. It appeared to be just that, a branch torn from a tree. Though now that he looked closely, he could see that the leaves it bore were odd, shaped like tears, almost, and so fresh they seemed to pulse with green. The scar on the end was fresh, too, yet the bark where he held it was worn by long handling, smooth and silver, while the rest of the branch was gray and rough and very much alive.

Wondering, he looked back up, searching the sky for the raven. It was soaring high above him now, and there was a small flock of crows nearby, milling about nervously. Upstream, dark clouds were blowing over the lip of the high reach on a strengthening wind, converging toward the birds. The raven soared off downstream as if in retreat, followed by the crows.

Thomas watched, puzzled—the raven, the crows, the clouds. The branch. He looked at it again. He gave it a little shake. The leaves fluttered and emitted a tiny bit of mist. He waved the branch. Again, just a tiny mist from the leaves. But the wind was suddenly stronger, and the dark clouds drew together to form a single towering thunderhead that shadowed the sun.

Thomas regarded the cloud, then the branch. Hesitantly, feeling a little foolish, he lifted the branch and waved it at the cloud. Puffy bits swirled out from the cloud's leading edge. His mouth was suddenly very dry. He swallowed and lifted the branch again. This time, he made a single slash through the air. A line drew through the cloud, splitting it cleanly.

Thomas studied what he had done. Then he slashed again, and another line cut through the cloud, another piece split off. He swung the branch in wide arcs, drawing curves and loops in the cloud. He sliced off pieces and shaped them into circles. He stretched one into an oval. Then he added a tail. Then eyes. Then fins, and suddenly he had a fish—a fish that looked a little like a spoon, but still a fish.

Grinning, Thomas made another fish, and then a tiny school of cloud fish that seemed to wriggle in the currents of the air. He shaped a bird from the darkest part of the cloud. It made him think of the raven, but he couldn't see it anywhere, so he went back to making birds and then sheep, and now a face with an open mouth and clouds of laughter.

Thomas stopped then. He lowered his arm, realizing how tired it suddenly felt. It was even shaking a little. He rubbed it and took a deep breath, watching the sky as the clouds slowly tried to un-shape themselves. His mind felt a bit like that.

Then someone coughed.

Thomas turned. To his astonishment—and dismay—a crowd of people stood in the lane to the town. Staring at him. Staring at the shifting clouds, too, but mostly at him. And the look in their eyes chilled him. It wasn't a look of anger or fear; it was a look of awe. It made Thomas feel very exposed and uncomfortable. Embar-rassed even. It was a look that expected something of him.

The person who had coughed was none other than the mayor, appearing flushed and somehow satisfied. Beside him, sharp and lean in his dark-red tunic with the bull-and-knife emblem, stood the local baronsman. And then Thomas saw Ruel Baker and Silas Joynter and Carla Miller; it seemed as if half the town had come to watch him. His heart sank; Uncle Piper was there too. But even he looked awed instead of angry. In fact, he was smiling.

Uncle Piper pushed forward through the crowd, his smile growing as he came. He was absolutely beaming as he lumbered out past the mayor and came to stand in front of Thomas.

"You see, boy," he said gruffly, "I told you it'd come."

"Sir?" Thomas stammered, feeling totally confused.

"Your talent, Thomas," Uncle Piper explained. He waved up at the sky. "I told you you were a painter, eh?"

Thomas was dumbfounded. He tried to protest; it hadn't been painting. Uncle Piper just shook his head, and behind him the crowd agreed. Thomas caught snatches from the blurred mutter of their awed voices. "Painter . . . fantastic . . . magic . . . like his father . . ."

"But you know I can't paint," Thomas finally managed.

"Nonsense," Uncle Piper growled happily. "You're a Painter, aren't you? You just didn't have the right brush."

"Speaking of which," the baronsman said, stepping forward, "where did you get that?" He pointed his sharp chin at the branch, as if he didn't quite dare put his hand too near.

Thomas looked at the branch, which still seemed to pulse with life in his hand. "I don't know," he said. "I mean, it fell on me. I was standing here. . . ." He was suddenly aware of the wheelbarrow, and the flies.

But the crowd didn't notice. They muttered again, nodding sagely. "From the sky . . . laid on him . . . magic all right . . . destiny . . ."

"I guess it's a wand," Thomas said. He held it out, hoping someone would take it. They all edged back.

"Well, obviously, in your hands it's a wand," said the mayor with a large smile. "And more important than its source would be its function. I wonder, and I imagine everyone here is wondering, for it's a question that certainly would come to the mind of a thinking man in these dry days . . ." He paused importantly, speaking more to the townspeople than to Thomas. "I wonder if it can make rain."

Again there were nods and muttering from the crowd, and Thomas knew why: the drought. Every time it clouded over, people watched the sky hopefully, but the clouds always passed by in the distance. There had even been talk of hiring a weather mage, but people were suspicious of mages. Besides, the cost for such service was steep.

Now the mayor smiled at Thomas with a great many teeth. The crowd took on a new look. Their awe became need; expectation became a demand.

"How about it, lad?" the mayor urged as Thomas hesitated. "Do you think you can paint us a rainstorm?"

"I . . . I don't know," Thomas said, trying to avoid everyone's eyes. "I've never done this before."

"Don't worry, Thomas," Uncle Piper said. "You were born to it, eh?"

"Perhaps this will help inspire you," the baronsman said. He held up a gold coin, and Thomas's breath skipped. It was a talent, stamped with the Duke's profile, new and polished and bright in the returning sun. And worth a full month's work by a journeyman. "Make it rain and this is yours," the baronsman promised.

"Well," said the mayor, "there's the charm, eh? Honest pay for honest work. And a very kind offer from our Baron, as I think all would agree." Again he turned a bit to address the crowd behind him. "Friends," he spoke, "fellow citizens, what do we say? Shall he try it?"

A great mutter of ayes came in response.

"Well, then, it's unanimous," the mayor said happily. "Go to it, lad."

"Remember," Uncle Piper encouraged, "it's just like painting."

If that's what it is, Thomas thought, it's going to be a very dry year.

But he didn't dare say that with everyone looking at him so hopefully. Swallowing hard to clear the lump from his chest, he turned from the staring faces and looked up. The clouds were all drifting away, shrinking as they went. The afternoon sun shone clearly in the growing expanse of empty blue sky. Thomas looked at the branch, wondering how he had ever made it work. His hand was clenched so tightly around the bark that his knuckles were white. He swallowed hard.

Right, he thought. We all need this.

Steeling himself, he held up the wand and moved it. The clouds seemed to pause.

Heartened, Thomas moved the wand more briskly. He reached out with it, trying to herd the clouds back. Amazed, he saw them stop, even swell a little. He swung the wand again, trying to remember how he had slashed at the raven. With horror, he saw the clouds split in two as he sliced through the air. He heard muttering behind him.

Moving the wand more gently, he managed to coax the clouds back together. Then he stroked them toward him, as though he were brushing paint across a canvas. Hesitantly, the clouds came. Bits and swirls kept leaking off the edges, and he fought to hold them together. Almost in spite of what he did, they formed into one mass and drifted slowly overhead. He began to feel a little hope. He had stopped trying to paint, had stopped moving the wand at all, just held it up in his outstretched hand. The clouds came of their own accord, as though drawn to a beacon. They thickened and darkened. The wind increased, dry at first, but then damp and heavy. Mist leaked from the wand. Droplets formed on the tear-shaped leaves and dripped on Thomas's hand. The cloud billowed, looming suddenly into a dark, anvil-headed tower.

There was more muttering behind Thomas, but now it had a tinge of fear. Thomas felt it too: a sense of dread at the power made real by that pile of dark cloud. The air seemed to thicken. The wand tingled uncomfortably in his palm.

Then streaks of mist shredded from the cloud and started to fall toward the ground. The crowd gasped. Even Uncle Piper muttered a gruff curse of surprise. Thomas felt his heart soar. He clenched his hand and thrust the wand as high as he could reach.

Pain burst in his palm, as though the wand were covered with a thousand pins. A hot wind whipped his face. The cloud pulsed, swirled, and fountained upward, sucking the mist back into its guts. Thomas's hair stood on end. With a sizzle and crack that stung his ears, lightning jabbed down from the cloud and struck the ground at the edge of the river, not ten paces away. The light blinded him. Instantly, a booming roar of thunder deafened him. The ground shook. Thomas fell to his knees, eyes squeezed shut in pain.

Just as suddenly, the sharp pain in his hand ceased, replaced by a dull, burned feeling. The hollow in his ears filled with ringing. More slowly, the bright blindness began to fade. He became aware of hands on his shoulders, a voice mumbling, tinny and scared beneath the shrill ringing in his ears. Blinking tears from his eyes, Thomas could just make out Uncle Piper's face, close to his own, eyes wide with fear and concern. Thomas wiped his eyes with his left hand and nodded, trying to show he was all right. He struggled to his feet, with Uncle Piper's big hands on his shoulders doing most of the work. He stared through the fading dimness. The mayor and the baronsman were dark shapes, one blocky, one gaunt. The rest of the crowd was a blur.

Uncle Piper said something, then had to shout when Thomas shook his head dumbly. "Best put that down!" he yelled, and Thomas realized he was still clutching the wand, arm stiff now, holding it out from his body as if it could bite. Quickly but carefully, he brought his hand down to his side. He would have thrown the wand to the ground but was afraid of what might happen.

"Well," the mayor said, then shook his head and spoke more loudly. "Well, it's obvious the lad has power."

"I'm not sure I'd call it talent, though," the baronsman said sourly, pocketing his coin.

The mayor was of stouter stuff. "Of course he does," he insisted smoothly. "How else could he make the wand work at all, eh? Eh, friends? Now is not the time to give up, to relinquish the possibilities, the great potential inherent in this lad, our young friend here, young, uh, Painter, and his marvelous and powerful wand. We'll have our rain yet, fear not!"

There was a general mutter of approval, and one or two people even gave a weak cheer.

"And how do you plan to do that?" the baronsman asked. "He needs a master to teach him."

"How about that weather mage upstream?" Silas Joynter put in. "Nuatta. Maybe she could train the boy."

"Well, well, let's not be hasty," the mayor said, rushing over their words. "There would be some cost. Considerable cost. These mages, you know, they can be a greedy lot, my friends. And haste burns talent. Now is the time to come together to consider alternatives that suit all—"

"Zarah," shouted someone deeper in the crowd. "Ask Zarah."

"Aye, Zarah," another agreed, and other voices chimed in.

"Certainly, splendid idea," said the mayor stiffly. "I couldn't agree more. With Zarah's advice, and some careful consultation among ourselves, and with the reasoned advice of the baronsman here, I'm sure we can find the best path for young Painter, a path to bring out the strength and talent that will lead to a bright, rainy future for both him and our town. To Zarah!"

Clapping his hand on the baronsman's shoulder to draw him along, the mayor strode back through the crowd. It closed behind him, an excited swirl of chattering people. Thomas marched stiffly in their midst. He felt numb from the eyes down, unable to fight the pull of his neighbors. The wand still stung his hand. He held it carefully before him so it couldn't so much as twitch. Despite that, faint mist still trailed from its tear-shaped leaves. Right now, the thought of training to be a mage filled him with dread. All he wanted was to go someplace quiet, with a block of wood and his knife. But no one asked what he wanted.

Four

arah lived near the flume that drew water from the river into the mill pond. That meant marching right through the center of the town, past workshops and homes and the new town hall on the common, then more shops and homes. All of them were filled with people who came out to gawk at the crowd and stare with surprise at Thomas. A goodly number followed along, so it was quite a parade that finally emerged at the upriver end of the road and skirted the mill pond to reach Zarah's low, rambling home. The wall of the high cliff loomed in the background. Thomas felt trapped between the gray stone and the marching crowd.

Zarah emerged from one of the many sagging coops that straggled out from her small house like a string of mismatched beads. She had her bright skirts hiked up, and a small flock of pullets clustered around her thin ankles like chicks around a mother hen. Baron Strutter, her boss rooster, dashed over to swagger back and forth in front of them, clucking a challenge in aggravated tones. Zarah Fowler was Thomas's aunt on his mother's side. But she was also a hen witch, with a small bit of the talent for divination that had appeared first and so powerfully in her older sister.

Now, as though she had foreseen their arrival, she watched with a complete lack of surprise as the parade scattered chickens around her dusty yard. She wiped her hands calmly on her apron as the crowd drew to a jumbled halt around her. She smiled a quick greeting at Thomas and Uncle Piper, then turned her attention to the mayor, who stepped forward and cleared his throat importantly.

"So," she said, cutting him off. "You're here." She glanced up at the westering sun as if to add, *Finally*.

"Yes, ah, a good day to you, Fowler," the mayor said, his entrance spoiled. He cleared his throat again. "A most extraordinary event has occurred, one that brings us here—"

"About Thomas," she said, looking past the mayor at Thomas. He smiled back sheepishly and shrugged.

"Yes," the mayor said impatiently. "As you have rightfully divined, about Thomas Painter. He—"

Zarah's quick eyes, bright as a hen's, lighted on the branch that Thomas still carried stiffly in his right hand. "He has found a wand," she stated, cutting the mayor off again.

"He has not only found a wand," the mayor said loudly, trying to regain control of the conversation. "He can use it."

"In a manner of speaking," muttered the baronsman.

"But he lacks training," Zarah said, giving no indication that she'd heard the remark.

"He came near to fry us all with lightning, Zarah," Uncle Piper put in.

"Of course," Zarah said, in tones that meant, *What did you expect?* "It's a weather wand."

There were noises of amazement throughout the crowd, and Thomas had to bite his lip to control his smile. Zarah's strongest talents were observation and a quick wit.

"Quite right," the mayor said, almost shouting now. "It's a weather wand!" He took a breath and steadied himself. "It has been a dry time for our village," he said quickly. "A weather mage would be most welcome."

"But expensive," Zarah put in.

"Yes, quite," the mayor agreed. "Young Painter here could be our savior if . . ."

"If he could use the wand."

". . . if he could bring rain," the mayor finished with heavy emphasis. "We have seen him paint clouds onto the canvas of the sky, and even draw lightning with a brush stroke of the wand, so obviously he has some talent. For all this, he was not able to create rain." He paused, but Zarah merely raised an eyebrow to show he should go on. Frowning, he did. "We have come to hear what your own talent can divine for his future. Should we, at great expense I'm sure, send for an accomplished mage to bring the rain we all so desire, in the faint hope she would also train the boy to guard the skies over our fair village in years to come? Or, as more pragmatic minds might suggest, should we find some safe haven nearby where he can practice and come into more full powers on his own?"

"Or should he throw the wand into the river before he burns down the whole town?" the baronsman put in sourly.

Zarah stifled a smile. "That's three questions," she said, "but there are many more possibilities. Many, many more."

She gave Thomas a searching glance, but he could only shrug again. The stinging in his hand was fading, but the wand still tingled, the echo of its power still rang in his ears. Could he really control it? Did he want to? He didn't know what to say.

"I will do what I can," Zarah said, finally. "But what we find may not be what you are looking for."

"I'm sure," said the mayor, "that a reasonable solution—"

"It's not a matter of reason," Zarah said coolly. "Now step back. Give me some room."

She shooed her hands at the crowd, as if they were a flock of unruly hens. Like hens, they shuffled and clucked uncertainly, bumping and milling about as she walked through them to her little house and went inside. A moment later, she reappeared, carrying a short, coarse broom in one hand and a small beaded bag in the other. Thomas smiled proudly when he saw the broom. Its stick was a twisty shaft of briar, with a top knob shaped in a very reasonable likeness of her rooster, Baron Strutter. He had carved it for her last year.

Zarah shooed the crowd again, herding them into a large circle that gave her room to work. She swept the center of the circle clean of feathers, chaff, and droppings, then turned the broom over and used the comb on the bust of Baron Strutter to draw a broad circle in the dirt. In the center, she drew a smaller circle, about three hands round. Then she divided the outer circle into sixteen slices and drew an angular rune in the middle of each.

"Come here, Thomas," she called. "Not you," she added, as the mayor tried to step forward with him.

"I stand as representative of the town," the mayor protested, "to ask the question that—"

"It's Thomas who can use the wand," Zarah snapped back. "He'll ask the question."

Nervously, Thomas stepped forward.

"Hold this," Zarah said, handing him her broom. "And," she added quietly, "think hard. What do *you* want out of all this, eh?"

Then she reached into her beaded bag, brought out plump kernels of dried barley, and laid three in each wedge of the circle, right on the rune. Her lips moved soundlessly as she placed the grains. That done, she looked around distractedly, glared with some impatience at the crowd surrounding them, and pushed her way through to scan the rest of the yard. Her chickens scratched and clucked, pecking at gravel, bits of grain, and each other. Zarah darted forward and scooped up one of them, a plump young hen with black-and-white banding and gold flecks in her eyes. Then she came back and stood by Thomas.

"Are you ready?" she asked, very seriously.

He nodded and fixed his thoughts on his knife, and the feel of wood changing shape in his hands. What *he* wanted.

"All right," she said, and then to the crowd: "Be very still, all of you. Keep your minds still, too, if you can. And if you can't, think about this boy and this wand. That's all, just the boy and the wand."

She cast one long look around at them all, then stepped into the circle, carefully avoiding the lines, the barley, and the runes.

She rubbed the hen's neck and stroked its bright little comb, crooning some soft tune that seemed to calm it. Then she placed it in the small central circle, stepped back out, and took the broom from Thomas.

The hen stood uncertainly a moment, looking around with quick tilts of her head. She took a step forward. The crowd shifted quietly, everyone trying to see which way the little hen would go. She eyed them back, turning completely around in little steps that took her all the way around the edge of the inner circle. Suddenly, she noticed the three barleycorns in one of the wedges and darted forward to snap them up with three quick pecks. Clucking happily, she looked around and spotted another trio of barleycorns. She cut across the wedges, here and there, back and forth, pecking up barley to reveal the runes scratched beneath. Zarah, head tilting this way and that, scratched each rune in sequence in the ground at her feet. Finally, the little hen wandered away from the circle, leaving five of the runes still covered. As she approached the crowd, it parted in awe to let her pass through, then closed in again, all eyes on Zarah.

She stared down at the runes she had scribed at her feet. Humming the same tune she had used to calm the hen, she touched the carving on her broom to several of the runes, considering. She circled the first, fifth, ninth, and eleventh. Looked up briefly at the uneaten barley in the circle. Considered two others in the line at her feet. Scratched out the seventh, and—very slowly, as if not quite certain—also the tenth. Then she stood very quietly, looking down at all her scratchings with such attention that she seemed in a trance. Thomas had never seen her so still.

"Well?" said the mayor finally, when it seemed the whole crowd would burst.

"Thomas must leave here," Zarah said, not looking up. The crowd shifted forward, heads craning to hear.

"Leave, Zarah?" Uncle Piper stared at her, stricken. "Did you say leave?"

"Of course she said leave," the mayor replied. "It's obvious: He must leave until he learns to master the wand. For the safety of the town, and all."

"But he's too young," Uncle Piper complained.

"His father was only two years older when he became a journeyman," Zarah said quietly.

"But where will he go, eh?" Uncle Piper persisted. He stepped forward and took Thomas protectively by the shoulder. "Who'll go with him?"

"No one from here," Zarah replied. She pointed at the scratched-out tenth rune. "Not the weather mage, either."

"Of course not," the mayor said, with evident relief. "That decision would not be at all to our advantage. The cost, the uncertainty, the strain on the boy's loyalties—"

"But where?" Uncle Piper repeated. "He can't just go live in the forest."

"No," Zarah agreed, looking up for the first time, to stare intently at Thomas. "Not to the forest, not upstream to the high reach. He will go downstream, alone, soon. Very soon."

Thomas's heart skipped, half ecstatic, half dismayed. He had dreamed of leaving, of changing his trade, but not to become a mage.

"So the boy is to get his training downstream," the mayor said, putting on a bright voice. "Yes, that makes good sense. There are more people, of course, from whom to receive advice and direction as he grows into his powers. It will broaden his horizons, add maturity. And of course, there's plenty of room between here and Lowing to practice safely"—Lowing was the next town downstream—"while still giving us the benefit of any positive effect he may work on the weather. The runes have decided, my fellow citizens. A good plan. And when the boy returns—"

"He will go farther than Lowing," Zarah said, touching the carved beak to one particular rune. "Much farther." Then she began to sweep out the runes. "As to when he returns . . ." She paused at the very last rune, then swept it away too. "It doesn't say."

"Well, it must give some indication—" the mayor began, but Zarah cut him off again.

"Three things," she stated sharply. "It shows me three things, and no more. First, he will leave, quickly and alone. Second, he will go downstream, a long way downstream. Third, he will deal with power. All the rest is crossed by that last."

"Crossed, Zarah?" Uncle Piper asked worriedly. "You mean cursed?"

But Zarah didn't answer at once. She was staring at her broom, mouth open as if frozen in reply.

"Zarah?" Uncle Piper said.

Zarah tore her gaze free and glared all around. "I don't know what it means!" she snapped. "It's confused. Turned moonwise. Shoved down a privy and covered with dung, for all I can read it. And you," she added, turning on the mayor, "don't you confuse things any further trying to turn this to your greedy ends. Leave Thomas to his own fate. You want rain? Pay for a weather mage!"

The mayor puffed out like an indignant fowl. "I certainly hope *you* don't expect to be paid, not after such an unsatisfactory reading as this. The town came to you in honest need, asking merely some direction—"

"And got it," Zarah retorted. "Honestly—and freely—for Thomas's sake. And I'll tell you one more thing, you overstuffed capon: If he doesn't leave, you'll be very, very sorry. All of you. Now get out of my yard. And you in the back, take that hen out of your tunic right now!"

Zarah advanced on a man at the edge of the crowd, brandishing her broom. He gave one frightened look and dashed off, dumping a rumpled chicken behind him as he went. Some of the others laughed, but most were muttering among themselves and eyeing Thomas with real concern. The mayor tried to rally his supporters.

"Nonsense," he sputtered. "The ravings of an old hen witch, a mage sympathizer. The boy should stay nearby and—"

Suddenly, Baron Strutter crowed a loud challenge and attacked the mayor's ankles. At the same instant, Thomas felt a tug at his wand. He spun, and there was the little banded hen who had read his fortune. She pecked his hand and made another snatch at the wand. All the other birds began to squawk and flap around the yard, darting at full tilt among the legs of the startled crowd. Hens erupted from the coops, cackling and hopping, some flying at head height among the now-fleeing townspeople. It was a rout.

A half dozen chickens joined the banded hen, pecking and squawking as if Thomas were a fox in the coop. He clutched the wand against his chest and beat at them with his free hand. Zarah dashed over, sweeping them aside with the broom. Then, just as suddenly, it all stopped. The crowd disappeared around the mill. The chickens settled down and acted like chickens. A few last feathers drifted to the ground. Slowly, Zarah lowered her broom. She stared at it strangely, then peered suspiciously at the now-docile rooster pecking at her feet. Looking up, Thomas saw a big, dark bird take wing from the roof of her farthest coop and swoop into an updraft. It soared swiftly above the looming cliff and into the scattered clouds.

Five

Zarah told Thomas to leave right away. She came over that very evening and drew him aside. For some reason, she had brought her broom.

"Here," she said, holding it out beak first. The carved rooster squinted sternly at him. "Do you see anything . . . odd?"

He looked at her in surprise, then studied the carving closely. "No," he said slowly. "Is it cracked or something?"

She sighed and lowered the broom. "No."

He waited, a little worried. She stared at nothing.

Finally, she looked up. "Do you remember the runes this afternoon? The chosen ones?"

"Some of them," he replied.

"The tenth rune?" She watched him intently.

"You crossed it out," he said.

"It was crossed by the seventh, but that's not always . . ." She paused, lips pursed, and glanced at the broom handle again. "The tenth rune was Mu," she said. "The Mistress. Sometimes the Mage." She looked right at him. "Sometimes the Mother."

Thomas swallowed. He had thought of his mother a lot that day. "What was the seventh? The rune that crossed it?"

"Kni. The Blade. Sometimes Iron, but in your case I think Blade is correct, yes?"

Thomas flushed and briefly touched the handle of his knife.

"The pairing was crossed, so I scratched out Mu," Zarah went on, "but then . . ." Again she paused and looked away. "Then this spoke to me." She held out the broom handle. "Baron Strutter here opened his mouth and said 'Mu.' He said it three times, in fact, the windy old fowl." She looked at the carving and shivered.

Thomas stared at her in awe. "A real seeing!" he exclaimed.

"Yes, well, when a piece of wood starts talking, it's either magic or madness, but right now I can't tell you which. I suppose it would help if I knew what it meant. Mistress, Mage, Mother; maybe all three. And what does it have to do with that knife of yours? And why is it so important, it made a woodcarving speak? Feh!" She swept at the dusty ground in frustration. "What good is talent if you don't know how to use it?" And then, in a change that left Thomas swimming, "Leave tomorrow, as soon as you can."

He promised he would.

But the next morning, the mayor came to give him a private speech about duty.

"Your talent is a gift, as surprising and unexpected as the wand itself, a gift to the town, my young lad; a gift to all your friends and neighbors so in need of the cooling draft of rain in these dry and troubled times." And so on.

And Thomas promised again that he would leave right away, and would not forget the people who were depending on him, and would be sure to return as soon as he could call up the smallest shower.

And that was what he told the many others who came by to wish him well, or simply to stare in awe at the wand and ask what it felt like to be hit by lightning. He made many promises.

But he didn't leave right away, because Aunt Singer said she wouldn't let him. Eventually, she gave in to Zarah and the mayor, but she insisted that Thomas couldn't leave without a good cloak for traveling, and took up another day and night weaving and sewing it for him. Uncle Piper moped about the paint shop, playing mournful airs on his pipes. Dulci was awed and a little jealous. Only Cousin Dora seemed pleased to see him go.

For Thomas, the time passed in fits and starts. He had dreamed of fleeing the paint shop for so long, but the thought of actually leaving, and for who knew where, was still hard to take in. He could hardly believe the wand had won him his chance. He gathered together a small bundle of food and went around the shops to say goodbye to his friends. He finished the cat for Dulci and then carved a little dog for Dora, just because she made it clear she wasn't expecting anything. The wand he wrapped carefully in a piece of clean white linen and laid at the top of his bundle, along with his whetstone and a couple of small blocks of pear wood.

He hardly slept the last night and rose before dawn, to find Aunt Singer and Uncle Piper already up, breakfast ready, his new cloak laid at his place. Now, comforted somewhat by its weight, with his bundle hanging from his shoulder and his knife at his side, he finally felt ready to go. They set out together, passing silently through the familiar streets in the gray dawn light. At the town gate, he turned to say goodbye. And found there was nothing he could say. He tried clearing his throat, but it didn't help.

Uncle Piper seemed to be having the same trouble. "Well, Thomas," he finally managed, "I have to say I'm proud of you. I knew you'd be a great painter, but never this." He put his big hand on Thomas's shoulder and looked right into his eyes. "Come back to us as soon as you can now, eh? And not just for the rain and all. We'll miss you."

A huge lump rose in Thomas's throat. He nodded and mumbled, "I will," embarrassed by the way his voice broke.

"Well," Aunt Singer said brusquely, "you're off, then, and on your own. It's time you had this."

She drew from her sash a locket hung on a silver chain. The locket itself appeared to be bronze, or even gold. It had a simple design of looped whorls worked on both sides. She laid it in Thomas's hand, where it settled with more weight than he expected.

"Your mother and father left it for you," Uncle Piper said gruffly. "They said you should have it when you came of age. I guess that's now, eh?"

From his mother and father . . . In the two days of preparation, no one had mentioned that last leave-taking, when his parents had gone forever. Thomas stared at the locket, not sure if he wanted it.

"Go on," Uncle Piper said, "open it."

Reluctantly, Thomas did. And there inside was a tiny portrait of a family, man and woman and toddler. He knew without being told that these were his parents, the faces of the silhouettes that sometimes stalked through his dreaming. And he was the child.

"Your father painted it," Uncle Piper said. "Did it the day before they left. He . . . he was that good."

The painting was more than good; it was perfect. Tiny as it was, the faces were crystal clear. You could see the resolve in his mother's eyes, the intensity in his father's grip on her arm as she held the lad tightly to her. Thomas stared and stared at the painting. He had forgotten what his parents looked like. Seeing them now was confusing. The faces looked right, but the feeling they brought wasn't clear at all, a mix of sadness and something harder. It jarred with the sharp anticipation of his departure and left him almost numb.

Aunt Singer reached out and closed the locket where it lay in Thomas's hand, then draped the chain over his head and tucked it all under his tunic. The locket settled against his chest, a cool weight on his heart. "Keep it safe," she told him.

"I . . . I will," he stammered. "Thank you."

"Don't thank me, thank your mother and father. Now, you'd best be leaving." She grabbed his shoulders and pulled him into a tight hug but let go quickly and stepped back, as if afraid to hold him any longer.

Uncle Piper tried to say something, then just nodded his head and smiled. Thomas found himself nodding back. But when Uncle Piper settled his bagpipes under his arm, Thomas blurted out, "You're not going to play, are you?"

"He is," Aunt Singer said tartly, "and I'm going to sing. And if that's going to embarrass you, you'd better start walking quickly."

Thomas gave them both a last, strained smile. Aunt Singer began the tune, an old farewell she had used often as a lullaby.

Uncle Piper came in on the second line, the notes from his pipe lifting between her words with the effortless harmony of their shared talent. Thomas felt his eyes burn and turned quickly, striding out the gate and along the path, with only a last wave over his shoulder so they wouldn't see his tears, which he found far more embarrassing than their song.

By noon he was several miles downstream. His heart was wonderfully light, but he was already feeling a bit footsore. Now he regretted delaying. If he'd left when Zarah had said, he would have been able to take passage on the flatboat carrying Aunt Singer's cloth and the other goods from Wanting to the markets downriver. The next boat wouldn't come upstream for two weeks or more. Thomas could only hope to find passage at Lowing or the next town below. He couldn't imagine walking all the way to . . . wherever he was going. The mayor and the baronsman—everyone in the town, in fact—expected him to find a mage as soon as possible and begin his training. And he had every intention of doing just that. A promise was a promise. But Zarah had said he would go much farther than Lowing, and she couldn't see when he'd return. He might be going all the way to Dunsgow at the river's mouth.

I might go there anyway, he thought, just to see the world's largest city and the great sea and maybe even Duke Kovac himself.

But this was the way his parents had gone, downstream. Much, much farther than Lowing. So far that they had never returned.

He shook off the thought. It was sunny and he was on his way, free of the shop, his own boss for the moment. He was hungry, so he'd stop and eat, no matter what time of day it was. Maybe he'd do a little carving. There was no one to tell him not to, no one to say he wasn't a carver. He stood in the middle of the track, struck by the thought.

"Carver," he whispered, then more loudly, "*Carver*. From now on, my name is Carver."

With a smile so big it almost hurt, Carver turned aside, found a comfortable-looking lump of ground by the riverbank, and plopped down, slinging his bundle onto the greening grass beside him. The sun was bright and he was warm under his new cloak, despite a lingering coolness in the air. He took off the cloak and laid it down for a seat, then opened his bundle and carefully set the wrapped wand to one side in order to reach his food. First, though, he took his empty water bottle down to the river.

Drinking his fill, Carver topped off the bottle and squatted by the water's edge, watching the current lead the way downstream and trying out his new name. A rustling noise broke through his reverie. Turning, he saw a big raven digging through his bundle, scattering food as it dug its beak inside.

"Hey!" he shouted, springing up. "Get away from there!"

He scrambled up the riverbank, scooping up a stone and flinging it as he ran. The stone went wide, but the raven hopped into the air and flapped away, croaking angrily as it disappeared over the line of trees on the other side of the road.

The raven had dug out most of Carver's food and scattered it on the ground, along with his carving wood and tinder pouch. Strangely, it hadn't eaten anything. Suddenly, Carver realized the wand was gone. He looked frantically at the spot where the bird had disappeared, then remembered it hadn't been carrying anything when it flew away. He searched more carefully and found the wand under a fold of his cloak, still safely wrapped. He must have accidentally covered it when he went to get water. It was the wand the bird was after, he was sure of that, just as he was sure this was the same raven that had attacked him when the wand had first dropped on his head. He wondered if the bird could somehow sense the magic.

Frowning, Carver repacked his bundle, then sat and ate some hard cheese and dried fruit and a bit of dark bread. When he set out again, he kept watch for the raven. He discovered that there were a lot more birds around than he had ever noticed before. And there were moths and butterflies and flying beetles—everything that flew caught his attention, along with a good number of squirrels, quick and scrawny from the drought. But he didn't see the raven.

Still, Carver decided, it was too much to hope that the bird had gone for good. For whatever reason, it wanted the wand badly enough to try to steal it. He was half tempted to let the bird have it, if only to see what it would do with the thing. But he couldn't risk the wand; he had made his promises. He would have to fend off the raven.

When evening came, he purposefully chose a stopping place near a large tree, just before the track wound a little away from the river along the edge of a wide, fallow field. He lit a fire with his flint and the back edge of his knife and, after a small dinner, worked happily for a while on a bit of pear wood. Several times, he said the name Carver out loud. Then he caught himself at it and laughed. Twice he brought out and unwrapped the wand to inspect it. Then, as the twilight deepened, he reluctantly put away his carving and settled down to sleep. The end of the wand protruded enticingly from the open bundle.

Darkness came on full and his little fire burned low. Eyes closed, Carver listened carefully to the night around him. He had never slept outside before. The cloak kept him warm enough, and the ground was not much harder than his pallet back home, but the sounds were very different. He was glad Lowing wasn't too far ahead. He should reach it by midday tomorrow; then he could see if there was a boat.

There was a rustling in the tree above him. Carver started, then quickly made a snoring noise and rolled onto his side with his back to the bundle, hoping it looked natural. He let his breathing slow again and tried to relax. All he could hear was the shrill peeping of spring frogs in a wet spot downstream, almost drowned by the rush of blood in his ears. Then he heard it again: a faint rustling as something moved through the budding leaves overhead. There was a light swish and a faint tap as something came to rest on the other side of his bundle. Straining to breathe naturally, Carver felt more than heard the noises move closer: the rustle of a twig, the shift of cloth on cloth. Then he felt a pull on his hand and sprang up.

The raven was there, tugging madly on the wand. It beat its heavy wings and tried to fly, still gripping the linen in its powerful beak, but Carver had tied the other end of the wrapping to the inside of the bundle. And he had pulled a length of yarn from the hem of his new cloak and tied that from the bundle to his hand. Just as the raven realized his trick and let go to fly away, he tossed his cloak over it, then fell to his knees and grabbed it through the mass of wool.

The heavy beak clamped on Carver's fingers and he yelped. Despite the thickness of cloth, it hurt. More carefully now, he encircled the squirming, squawking body in the loop of his arms, then folded the cloth around it into a neat bag.

"Hah!" he crowed. "I've got you now, bird."

To his amazement, the raven cursed him in clear, croaking speech.

"Let me go, you blasted muck brain! I can't breathe in here!"

Six

Raven struggled frantically, fighting for air in the heavy folds of the boy's cloak. Her wings were squashed against her sides, her head pushed down against her breast, half choking her. It was dark and close and suffocating.

"Let me out!" she croaked, and tried to bite his hand again through the thick wool.

"Right, right!" he said, voice muffled by the folds of cloth and the wild beating of her own heart. "Just hold still!"

He began twisting and turning her inside the cloth, and she struggled even harder.

"Stop, you fur-brained wingless monkey! You're crushing me!" She choked on wool.

But suddenly her head was free, and she gulped in a great swallow of cool, fresh air. She relaxed for an instant, then realized her wings were still pinned by the cloak and started struggling again, trying to free them. She glimpsed the boy's face, stupid with amazement in the flickering light of the dying fire. She croaked angrily and jabbed her beak at his eyes.

Dodging, he held her at arms' length, but he didn't loosen his grip on the cloak.

"Hey! Try that again and I'll cover you back up," he threatened.

"Not before I blind you, Monkey Boy!" She lunged at his face again.

"I mean it!" He slapped her beak aside and pulled a thick fold of cloth back over her head.

"No! Stop!" she croaked, shaking her head furiously against

the heavy wool. "I'll stop. I'll be quiet! Uncover me!" Trembling, she forced herself to be still and even added "Please."

He was silent, and it was all Raven could do to lie quietly with her face covered like that, but finally he said, "Right. That's better." And he freed her head again.

She glared at him but restrained herself from taking another peck at his ugly brown eyes. He stared back warily. Gradually, her heart slowed and she regained some composure. She stretched her neck to get the feathers back in place. Instantly, his grip on the cloth tightened.

"Calm down!" she snapped. "I'm just trying to straighten things out. You've got me all ruffled the wrong way, you flat-faced oaf. Let me go."

"No," he said. "You'll just fly away." He said it so reasonably, she immediately wanted to peck out his tongue.

"You're right about that one, Monkey Boy," she muttered, but she stopped squirming.

They stared at each other for a moment while she tried to summon an owl or even a whippoorwill—any night bird that she might be able to use as a distraction—but blast it, there just weren't that many birds who flew at night, and she couldn't calm down enough to control the spell anyway. So she just glared at him and imagined what she'd do to his muddy eyes and whey-colored skin if she ever got loose.

Then he asked, "What's a monkey?"

"A monkey? How do you know about monkeys?"

"I don't," he replied. "You just called me one, though."

"It's a dirty little fur-covered dung-eating boy-shaped lip-faced wingless piece of—"

"Right," he said, cutting her off. "I guessed it was something like that." They glared at each other again. Then he continued, "Why are you trying to steal my wand?"

"*Your* wand?" Raven croaked indignantly. "It belongs to—" She broke off. She had almost said "Nuatta." That wasn't going to do, not if she wanted Monkey Boy here to let her go and give her the wand. He was obviously much too honest to appreciate the truth. She took a deep breath and forced herself to be calm again; to be clever like a raven. "It belongs to my mistress," she said, mimicking his reasonable tone. "I didn't steal it; I'm trying to rescue it."

"Who's your mistress?" he asked then.

"My mistress," she said haughtily, "is the great mage Penalla, mistress of the clouds, the rain, the wind, and all the powers that shape the weather. Including lightning," she added threateningly.

The boy didn't seem impressed. "Is she the mage who lives in the forest on the high reach above Wanting?" he asked.

"No," Raven replied. "That's her sister, Nuatta, who is very jealous of my mistress's power, which is why she stole her wand, which my mistress sent me to get back."

"And you dropped it on my head?"

"I didn't drop it, Monkey Brain!" she snapped. "It was the stupid crows!"

"What crows?"

Raven settled her feathers again. Somehow she had to get this oaf to let her go. "Nuatta is a bird mage," she said, building on her house of lies. "You people get them mixed up because they look so much alike. Penalla, my mistress, she's the weather mage. And that's her wand, which I am supposed to take back to her. She's going to be very angry at me if I don't get it back to her soon," she went on, which was certainly no lie. "To punish me, she puts me in a heavy sack." She looked pointedly at the folds of cloth trapping her body and trembled like a wren.

The boy frowned. "I'm sorry," he said, "but I'm not quite ready to let you go. How is it you serve a weather mage against a bird mage?"

"It's a long story," Raven muttered.

"We've got all night," he pointed out.

Blast, this boy was irksome! "Right," she said. "You see, I was apprenticed to Penalla, to learn the secrets of her magic, and—"

"You have weather talent?" the boy cut in.

"Of course I do!" she snapped.

"So you're a person? Not just a bemagicked bird?"

"Of course I'm a person!" Raven snapped. "Do I sound like some kind of trained parrot? '*Bra-ak*, pretty boy, pretty boy!' Is that what you thought?"

"What's a parrot?"

"It's a bird, dolt! And I'm a person! Right? And I'm Penalla's apprentice because I have weather talent!"

"Tell me, what's it like with Penalla? Is she a good mistress?"

"I can tell you all about her just as *soon* as you let me go," Raven offered.

"*If* I let you go," he retorted. "Finish your story and I'll decide."

Bristling, Raven continued. "I was apprenticed to Penalla, and was starting to learn a few things when she and her evil sister got in a big fight. Oh, it was awful: lightning bolts, rain, hail—it took everything to hold off the huge flocks of vultures and crows that Nuatta had summoned. My mistress won, of course. Nuatta had to fly for her life, but in the battle, she turned me into a raven. Then she sent some of her crows to sneak in—"

"Hold on," said the boy. "She turned you into a raven? How did she manage that? I thought mages couldn't directly bemagic you unless you allowed them to."

"Of course," Raven said, thinking wildly. "But I've always wanted to fly like a bird, and so, in my heart, I was secretly hoping that someday I might be able to talk Nuatta into turning me into some kind of bird. She's a bird mage, so she knew that. It's the kind of thing mages know, anything about their talent. So to get even with her sister, she turned me into a bird. And that's the story."

"That's not all the story," the boy said. "What about the crows and the wand?"

45

"Oh, that part." Raven cleared her throat. "Several weeks after the battle, my mistress was getting ready to set out on a journey. She had been called downriver, by Baron Cutter himself, to conjure up some rain. So she was taking her bath in the stream below our tree—"

"Your mistress mage lives in a tree?"

"Of course she does." Raven gave him a beady glare. Monkey Boy was blasted smart. "A weather mage has to live out in the weather, doesn't she?" And before he could think too much about that, she hurried on. "She put her wand down before she got in the water, of course, and this gang of crows swooped down out of nowhere and snatched it up. They were up and away with the wand before my mistress could even blink."

"What about you?" the boy asked. "Why didn't you chase them?"

"Why do you think they dropped the wand?" she retorted. "I chased them for hours, days it seemed, first catching one, then another, but they kept tossing the wand back and forth. Finally, just before they reached the high falls, I caught the last one and gave him such a thrashing, he dropped the wand. And you caught it. And if I don't get it back to my mistress, she'll cook my goose for good."

She stopped talking and watched the boy, wondering if maybe she hadn't embroidered the tale just a little too much.

He frowned at her, then nodded slowly. "Right. I'm going to let you go. But," he added firmly, "I'm keeping the wand. If you want your mistress to get it, you're going to have to take me to her. If you fly off, I'll go my own way. If you attack me, I'll break the wand and burn the pieces, and you can carry the coals to her." He shrugged and smiled. "But if you lead the way *and* tell me what it's like to be an apprentice mage, everything will be fine. Right?"

"Right," Raven sullenly agreed. "Just let me out of this filthy thing."

The boy began uwrapping the cloak, and she jumped free as

soon as she could. She hopped away and stretched her wings as wide as they would go, then immediately set about preening her feathers. She felt rumpled and abused, but it was such a relief to be out of that woolen cage! She kept one dark eye on Monkey Boy as she smoothed her tail feathers and pinions. He wanted to carry the wand? Fine. Let him be the one to deal with Nuatta if she caught up with them. Maybe he didn't notice the thin clouds that had started to hide the stars, but she did. The wand's mistress was getting closer.

The boy wrapped himself in his cloak, threw a couple of sticks on the coals, and sat down across from her. "I'm—" He cut off, and a big oafish grin spread slowly across his face. "My name is Carver," he said. Then the dolt repeated it: "Carver." He smiled at her, waiting. She glared back in silence. "Tell me, then," he said pleasantly, as though he hadn't just nearly suffocated her, "what's she like, your mistress mage? Does she teach you well? Do you like working with weather?"

"It's better than being trapped under a cloak," Raven grouched.

"Well, you can hardly blame me," he began, but Raven turned her back on him and flapped up into the tree.

"Hey!" he cried, jumping up. "You promised—"

"Keep your head on, Chicken Wits," she croaked. "I'll tell you in the morning." Besides, she added to herself, I didn't *promise* anything.

She watched closely as the boy lay down, but he didn't give her any chance to break even imagined promises. He tucked the wand back into his bundle, tied the bundle tightly shut, and drew it up under his head for a pillow. Muttering a few more curses, she stuck her head under her wing and tried to sleep.

Raven took great pleasure in waking the boy at first light by dropping twigs on him. To her great disgust, he came awake bright-eyed and cheerful. He did share his bread and cheese for breakfast, but when he finally packed up and started walking downriver, she chafed at his slow pace. She flew ahead and waited, flew ahead and waited, flew ahead and waited. At one point he offered to let her ride on his shoulder, and she gave it a try. But then he started asking questions about being a weather mage, and she had to make up a lot of quick lies. Being an apprentice bird mage, she could talk truthfully about the working of magic at least, and she cobbled up embroidered descriptions of how her mistress prepared for her magic without actually describing the magic itself.

"Before calling up any really big storms, she has to be completely prepared. She doesn't eat for at least a day, and she has me paint designs all over her body with henna and woad."

"What kind of designs?" he asked.

"I can't tell you. They're secrets only a weather mage can know. There's a powerful ban laid on every apprentice to keep us from telling anyone but another weather mage."

"But I have weather talent," he countered. "I'm supposed to be looking for a weather mage to apprentice to. Besides, I thought you couldn't be magicked directly unless you—"

"Of course you can't!" she snapped. "When you become an apprentice, you swear a powerful oath to obey your mistress in every way. You agree to let her bemagic you."

"What's the oath?"

"I can't tell you; it's part of the oath not to tell anyone the oath."

"But I have weather talent."

"Ha!" she cawed. "You can splash a few clouds around? Almost get yourself fried by lightning? You don't know that's weather talent. It could be washover magic. Your real talent could be something else entirely."

"Really?" He seemed pleased at the idea. "I might not have to be a weather mage?"

"Don't you want to be a weather mage?"

"Not really," he admitted.

"Then why in the blazing mages won't you just give me the wand and be done with it!"

He frowned. "Because I promised the mayor. Not just him—I promised the town. My aunt and uncle. It's a duty now." His voice dimmed, as if he had just realized something. Then he shook it off and smiled that irksome, reasonable smile again. "Besides, you make her sound so interesting, I really want to meet her."

Raven croaked in disgust and flew away for a while.

Shortly after midday they reached Lowing, where two side streams joined with the River Slow. The town itself spanned the river. The steeper side was surrounded by pasturage for sheep and goats, which provided wool for a fulling mill; the other was surrounded by newly plowed fields of grain to feed a gristmill.

They were on the grain side and had to get across the Slow to go up the other stream. Again Raven cursed the clumsiness of walking. For her, it was a minute to cross the river and an easy hour's flight to reach Penalla's roost. The way Monkey Boy moved, they wouldn't get there till next morning. She glanced nervously at the sky upriver, not sure if the clouds actually were darker there or if her imagination simply made them more threatening.

She told Monkey Boy she'd meet him on the other side and flew high above the town, watching as he passed through the outer buildings and the archway in the old wall. But then he went wrong and turned away from the river. Muttering curses, she swooped down and landed on his shoulder again. The close sides of the narrow street made her even more touchy.

"What are you doing, oaf?" she snapped. "The river is that way!" She grabbed his ear and pulled his head in the direction she wanted him to go.

"Ouch!" he exclaimed, batting at her head. "I know where I am."

"Then what the blazes—" She stopped suddenly when a potful of night soil came flying from an upper window and splattered in the gutter at the center of the street.

"Phew!" the boy said. "That's rank."

Raven blessed the fact that ravens can't smell and croaked a few choice names at the girl still leaning out the window. Then she turned back to Monkey Boy.

"You're supposed to be going to the river to find a ferry, remember?"

"I know," he said, "but look."

He pointed up at the beam ends that projected from the walls of some of the buildings. They were carved in a mix of animal faces and symbols, each indicating the nature of the shop inside.

"So?" she said.

"They're really well done. This town must have an excellent carver."

While Raven grouched on his shoulder, he wandered on, pointing out this carving and that carving, until she grabbed his ear again and threatened to rip it off if he didn't head for the river right away and get himself across it.

They finally reached the docks and found the ferry, but when they started to board, the ferryman held out his hand and demanded two copper deeds to take them across.

"I don't have any money," Monkey Boy said. "But I can work."

"No fare, no ferry," the man replied, rubbing at his lank beard with a heavy, callused hand. Raven fought down the urge to peck out his eyes.

"I can barter," the boy offered. "I've got bread and cheese and a couple of apples."

The man snorted, then pointed at Raven. "How about the bird?" he said. "Is it worth anything?"

The boy looked round at her and smiled. "Oh, he's a real treasure," he said. "He's a magic bird, given the power of speech by a great mage upriver."

Raven glared. Magic bird! She was a mage, not some enchanted sparrow. And the dolt couldn't even tell she was a girl!

"Phaw!" the ferryman exclaimed. "Magic, my auntie. Trained, maybe."

"Have it your way," the boy said congenially. "Would you like to hear? If you'll ferry us across, I'll make him speak."

Raven croaked indignantly. It was bad enough being taken for a boy, but she was blasted if she was going to perform for the hairy oaf. She raised her wings, but the boy put his hand to her feet before she could fly off.

"Stay still," he said. "It's our only way across."

She settled, glaring at the hairy boatman. He laughed at her and said, "Why not? Make it speak, lad, and I'll take you both across."

"All right then," the boy said happily, and he held his arm in front of Raven. "Come on," he said. "Jump on."

Grudgingly, Raven obeyed.

"Now, what's your name? Tell us your name, boy."

Boy, was it? She croaked some coarse gibberish, then messed his sleeve. The ferryman laughed uproariously.

Monkey Boy took a deep breath and visibly calmed himself. Then, with a shrug and a smile to the ferryman, he forged on with his act. "Say my name now, Raven. Say 'Carver.'"

"Why?" Raven replied clearly. "I thought your name was Monkey Boy. Monkey Boy, Monkey Boy, Monkey Boy," she chanted.

The ferryman roared again. "Fine!" he exclaimed. "Very fine! Come on board—the bird has earned your fare. Tell me," he added, as the boy carried her on board and settled in the center seat of the small blunt-ended boat, "what's it mean by 'Monkey Boy?'"

Carver glanced sideways at Raven, but she only chuckled at him. "It's a kind of hairy little boy-shaped animal," he said. "From a story."

The man snorted, but it was still half laughter. "Like a brownie, eh?"

"Yes," the boy agreed.

As they made their way across, Monkey Boy rinsed his sleeve

in the river while the ferryman tried to get Raven to speak again. She obliged by calling both of them every epithet she knew and a few she made up on the spot. The ferryman laughed all the harder, and when they landed, he offered the boy a silver skill for her, fifty times the two-copper fare. The boy pretended to consider it. Raven nipped his ear to make him leave.

"You're no fun, Raven," he said with a grin as he walked away. "Don't you want to know how much you're worth?"

"Worth more than you, dolt," she snapped. "At least I can tell a girl from a boy."

He gaped. "You're a girl?"

"That's right, clod head."

"Blazes, I'm sorry," he said. "I just assumed . . . the way you talk . . ."

"Keep it up, Monkey Boy, and you'll have to wash the rest of your shirt."

He grinned. "It was an honest mistake. Anyone could have—"

He gave a satisfying squawk as she nipped his ear and flew off.

She led him upstream well into the evening. The next morning, the sky was low and gray, as though it might even rain. She woke him early and croaked at him to hurry. Clouds meant Nuatta.

The hills rose steadily, and two hours of brisk walking brought them to the falls that separated the upper reach from the high reach on this stream. Raven showed him the half-hidden trail— more handholds than path—that wound up the steep cliff beside the tumbling water.

Monkey Boy studied it doubtfully. "I thought Penalla didn't live on the high reach."

"What?" Raven tried to remember what she had actually told him. "I meant not above your town," she said, then added quickly, "It's not that much higher here, anyway. It's just a ridge of the high reach that sticks down between two rivers. Anyway, the most powerful mages all live on the high reach. I figured you knew that. Everybody does."

"I didn't," the boy said, still eyeing the cliff nervously.

"Well, they do," she snapped. "There's more magic on the high reach."

"Why?"

"There just is!" She clacked her beak at him. "Are you going to start climbing or not?"

He took a deep breath and blew it out in a sigh. "Right." He finally started to climb.

Raven flew above him, swooping down now and again to point out a better handhold.

"I can do this on my own," he snapped, waving her away. "It's not all that steep."

At which point his foot slipped and he slid five feet down the slope in a spray of dirt before catching hold of a root. Disgusted, Raven flew to the top to wait for him.

Finally, he pulled himself over the lip and sat panting on the rocks, dipping water from the pool at the top. Raven waited as long as her patience would permit, then flew to his shoulder and nipped his ear.

"Will you stop that?" he snapped, batting at her head. Grumbling, he started around the pool, only to halt again at a side path that angled down the hill in the direction they had come.

"Hold on," he said. "Where does this path go?"

"Downstream," she croaked impatiently.

"Downstream? You mean down to the stream?" He turned on her incredulously. "Do you mean to tell me I could have come up this path instead of that . . . that . . ." He chopped his hand up and down as though he were carving a cliff face.

"That's the long way," Raven protested. "The cliff is shorter."

"Maybe for you!" he exclaimed. "Blazing mages, Raven, you really are a birdbrain!"

Shaking his head, he continued past the pool and around the next bend in the stream. Then stopped dead when he saw Penalla's tree.

Chuckling at his expression, Raven flew off his shoulder and raced ahead. She soared happily to the top of the tremendous tree and was met by a great chorus of caws, quacks, cackles, chirps, tweets, twits, and to-hoos. Wings of every kind rustled on the branches, as though they were leaved with birds. And there was Penalla, stepping out of her door to stand on the veranda of her roost, twenty feet over the boy's head. Croaking a greeting, Raven swooped down to land on her special perch at the edge of the veranda.

"You have the wand?" Penalla demanded, her voice cracking in excitement.

"Yes, mistress," Raven replied. "The boy is bringing it to you. He thinks it's yours."

Penalla gave her a sharp glance, then turned and regarded Monkey Boy, who was still standing open-mouthed at the bend in the stream. Raising her right hand, she waved her own wand, a brilliant black eagle feather. Instantly, a hundred of the largest birds flew down to grab the loops and lines on her kirtle and carry her down to the ground.

Raven flew down after her. "You probably shouldn't have done that," she muttered as she landed on her mistress's shoulder. "I told him you were the weather mage."

"What?" Penalla glared at her.

"I told him that it was your wand," Raven explained hastily. "So he'd bring it here. So I had to tell him you were a weather mage. He thinks Nuatta is the bird mage."

Penalla hissed. Awkwardly, she shooed off the other birds, trying to make it seem as if they were bothering her. Then she gestured to the boy. "Come here, lad," she commanded. He stepped a little closer. "I believe you have my wand?" she said in sugary tones.

"I was told it was yours," he replied, looking darkly at Raven.

"And so it is," Penalla said hastily. "Where is it? I need it to get rid of these pesky birds."

"In here," he said slowly, shifting the bundle off his back.

"Let me see it," Penalla said reasonably, "so I can make sure it is indeed mine. My silly apprentice here has been known to make mistakes."

The boy looked suspicious, but he untied the bundle and took out the wrapped wand. Penalla craned forward greedily as he unwound the linen to reveal the shining leaves.

"Yes!" she said. "That's it!" She took a step forward, reaching. "Give it to me!"

The boy hesitated. Raven tensed, ready to fling herself at him and peck out his eyes to get the wand for her mistress. Just then a hot gust of wind swirled around the bend in the stream, formed itself into a dervish of dust and feathers, and snatched the wand from the boy's hand. He cried out and leaped after it, but the clumsy oaf tripped and sprawled on the ground. The wind carried the wand out of sight around the bend and died away as quickly as it had come.

For a moment, the little valley was completely silent. Then the wind blew back from downstream, only this time it was cold and hard. And around the bend in the midst of the wind, carrying the wand in her clenched fist, came Nuatta.

Seven

arver, still sprawled on his belly, stared up at the mage who had just come around the bend. She was obviously powerful, obviously angry, and obviously the real owner of the wand. He wondered if this was the meaning of Zarah's vision: Mistress and Mage in the same angry person. If so, he had missed the warning. His heart shrank as she glanced his way, but she dismissed him in a moment and turned her angry regard to the other mage.

Carver quailed at the equally angry expression of Raven's mistress. Their faces marked the two women plainly as sisters: haughty, sharp-eyed, and hard. But no one, despite Raven's lie, would ever mistake one for the other. Nuatta was tall, whip thin, and crowned with a cloud of silver gray hair. Penalla was small and fine boned, with sleek brown hair, like a wren with the face of an eagle. There was a cloud crowning her head, too, but not hair. It was a real cloud, small and self-contained, that dripped on her constantly. Raven, still crouched on her shoulder, looked miserable. Carver knew at once that Raven had lied from the beginning. Nuatta was the weather mage, Penalla the bird mage. Who had been trying to steal her sister's wand.

What a dolt I am, he thought. Penalla's wand was obviously that feather. The birds, the house in the tree, the piled guano that gave the whole valley the smell of a hen yard—he should have known immediately. Carefully, he pushed himself to his knees, ready to jump up and run the moment either of them noticed him. But they were too intent on their hatred of each other.

"So, sister," Penalla hissed, "you've come to undo your little prank, I hope." She gestured at the tiny cloud with her long feather.

"Why should I undo it now?" Nuatta replied coldly to her sister's query. "I might have in a day or two—I'd hoped you'd learn your lesson by then, little sister—but after this tiresome trick . . ." She raised her wand slightly, and the clouds roiled above them. Carver glanced up nervously and pulled the cloak tightly about his shoulders.

"Kah! What did you expect?" Penalla shrilled. "That I would just sit still like a silly goose and let your nasty little cloud rain on me every day?"

"And what did *you* expect?" Nuatta snapped back. "That I would be so weak without my wand, the cloud would die? Or did you imagine you could dissolve the cloud yourself? You, use my wand?" She laughed acidly. "You, work the weather, my little pigeon herder? What a thought!"

Penalla puffed up in rage. "Pigeon herder is it?" she cried. "I'll give you pigeons!"

She slashed her wand above her head, and instantly a cloud of pigeons and doves rose from the great muttering flock on the tree and swooped toward Nuatta. Nuatta raised her own wand, and a gust of wind blew the birds back toward the tree, but pigeons are fast flyers, and a few beat their way through to dive at Nuatta's head and splatter her with droppings. Carver, squinting against the dust and feathers caught up in the wind, scrambled to the meager shelter of a bush by the steep wall of the valley. Penalla cackled at her pigeons' good aim. Nuatta, caught off-guard, lowered the wand and stared in dismay at the ruin of her clothes. The failing wind freed the other pigeons and they joined the attack, covering her in white stains from head to foot.

Enraged, Nuatta advanced on her sister, brandishing her wand. The little cloud above Penalla grew, darkened, and began to pour. But Nuatta didn't stop there. With a sharp flick of her wand, she turned the rain to stinging sleet, and then, as the cloud grew tall and flat above like an anvil, she turned the sleet to bruising hail.

Astounded, Carver saw a faint blink of lightning in the depth of the cloud, followed by a tiny rumble of thunder.

With a cry of pain, Penalla ran this way and that, hands over her head in a vain attempt to protect herself. She waved her own wand then, and half her flock came flying down to form a living shield. The other half tore through the cloud itself, shredding it by sheer force of numbers. And Raven, flying clear of the mass, labored high into the air, then turned and stooped like a hawk on Nuatta, stabbing at the mage's eyes with her powerful dark beak. Shrieking in rage, Nuatta beat at Raven with her bare fist. A lucky blow sent Raven spinning sideways. Carver winced and half rose to go help her. But the sting of cold rain stopped him. Swirling the silver branch, Nuatta created a tight whirl of wind that grew and grew to the beginnings of a tornado. It cut and twisted across the valley, sucking dirt, guano, and birds into its belly and throwing them out at the top. Carver threw himself flat and clung desperately to his bush as the wind pulled at his clothes and lifted him from the ground. Then it swirled back toward Penalla. Her birds threw themselves at the twister, trying to shred it as they had the cloud—even Raven, who was sucked into it with an outraged croak and whirled madly around with the rest.

At that, Penalla's rage grew to blindness. She sent a call to all her feathered minions, and they came, the big and the little, the meek and the fierce, wrens flocking with hawks and eagles, to strike directly at the weather mage. Nuatta battled back, sending her twister right and left across the valley, pelting them with rain and hail, battering them with gusts of wind that blew hot and cold from every direction. The ground turned to a muddy pit. Water sluiced down the sides of the valley. Branches cracked and broke and fell from the great tree. The roof of Penalla's home blew off, then the walls, to crash into the stream. And the stream swelled and raced in its bed, surging around the bend with a rumble that joined the pounding rain and blasting winds. The hawks and owls and even the eagles were thrown around like leaves and sucked into the twister, then shot high into the air. Nuatta, standing in a pocket of calm, washed clean of bird droppings, threw back her head and laughed.

But Penalla wasn't finished. Eyes flashing, she raised her wand a last time and shouted words that were almost blown away in the storm. In a moment, her hair had turned to feathers and her arms had stretched, her hands turned out, fingers fused, nose lengthened, chest swelled, tearing her robe. Her feet arched, talons jabbed from her toes, and she became a giant eagle herself, an eagle whose wings spanned a dozen yards. She clashed her cruel beak, as long as a man's arm and sharp as a dagger. Shaking off the remnants of her clothing, she raised one scaled foot and reached toward Nuatta with talons as cruel as meat hooks. Screeching a great cry that drowned out the roar of wind, rain, and stream, she launched herself into the sky and drove toward her sister with powerful strokes that made their own wind.

Nuatta ducked as Penalla flew over. A single talon caught in her hair and pulled her down on her back in the mud before tearing free with a trailing clot of hair and bloody scalp. Carver, watching numbly from his useless shelter, cried out. But Nuatta was a match for her sister in the blind need for revenge. Rising to her knees, she watched Penalla swoop ponderously up and around, turning for another attack. Taking her wand in both hands, Nuatta held it up and shouted, not magic, but ugly defiance. Then she slashed the wand downward. And from the dark and rain-choked clouds that completely shadowed Penalla's flooding valley came a blast of lightning, sharp and hissing and full of hate. Penalla dodged, but too late. The bolt struck her shoulder. Blue-yellow light encrusted her body. Feathers stood up straight and flew off in a dark cloud whipped by the wind. The bird shape hung for a moment in the tortured air. Then its great wings folded in hard angles, and Penalla plunged into the stream.

Nuatta stood frozen, wand raised. Penalla, still in bird form, stunned or unconscious or dead, turned twice in an eddy, then started to move downstream, slowly at first as the water slipped and washed on her swollen bulk, then faster and faster as she approached the bend.

Nuatta let her arm fall. The rain eased, the twister slowed, spilling birds and debris as it diminished. And Nuatta started to run downstream, calling her sister's name. Raven appeared from out of the clouds, tattered and soaked, with gaps in her wings where feathers had been torn away. Croaking despair, she raced after her mistress. They both disappeared around the bend. Nuatta followed, and Carver, weak-kneed from all that had occurred, leaped to his feet and pelted after them all till he came to the pool above the waterfall. The roar of the falls was deafening. The swollen stream surged willfully to the brink, then plunged fiercely over the edge. Penalla was already halfway to the lip, and Raven hovered above, beak locked on the tip of one eagle wing, trying desperately to pull her mistress toward the side of the pool.

Nuatta was standing on the bank, wand clutched in her hands. She tucked it into her belt and leaned forward, as if to jump in. Carver cried out to stop her. Whether she heard or not he couldn't tell, for just then the whole bank of earth beneath her gave way, undermined by the powerful flood from her rain. With a shocked cry, she fell into the water and was swept down in the dirty flow. Carver swore and ran along the bank. He tripped over a fallen branch, turned back to lever it free of the overgrown weeds, then raced again for the edge of the cliff, thinking perhaps he could snag Penalla with it, or hold it out for Nuatta. His heart was pounding; his breath came in gasps. His mind still reeled.

Nuatta splashed frantically and foundered, then came up again and struck out for Penalla. But then more birds came and, seeing Nuatta reach for their mistress, attacked her viciously. Raven let go and shrieked at them, but they ignored her, diving and pecking at Nuatta, who struck back and sank, came up gasping, only to be pecked and harassed again. Raven flew into the birds, trying to drive them off, then flew back to Penalla and tried again to drag her out of the current. But the stream still held her in its frantic rush to the falls. Carver reached the hard edge of stone at water's edge. Panting, he held out the branch. But the two mages, marked by the swooping, jeering birds, swirled back into the center of the stream, just out of his reach.

Nuatta finally reached Penalla and put an arm around the great eagle head, trying to hold it out of the water. She kicked toward shore, but Carver could see she was exhausted, and they went nowhere but down, toward the surging, plunging lip of the falls. Raven still pulled at the wingtip. The other birds still swooped and pecked. Carver yelled at them, shaking the branch, but it did no good. Suddenly, Nuatta stopped kicking and held her free hand aloft. The silver branch shone in the air. She waved it and tried to speak against the waves that splashed constantly into her mouth. A wind began to form, blowing upstream. It grew stronger, forcing the birds away, pushing at the water, wrestling with the elemental grip of gravity. Carver reached out, straining, trying to hook them with the tip of the branch. For a moment, the two mages stopped, lodged against the stone lip of the falls, supported by Nuatta's desperate wind. Raven pulled. Carver reached. But then everything gave way in a new surge of water. First Penalla, then Nuatta plunged over the edge. Raven flew after them with a cry that pierced the roar of water and drove through Carver's heart.

The wind stopped so suddenly that Carver almost toppled over the edge himself. He flailed wildly for a handhold and dropped the branch. It fell, twisting in the water's grip, to disappear in the mist and crushing splash at the bottom. He sat heavily on the rock, exhausted, his emotions surging like the current. Drained, numb, he stared down into the mist as the cliff fell into shadow. Finally, he saw something small and black flying laboriously up the cliff face. It was Raven.

She landed beside him and almost collapsed, so tired she was. She lifted her head to face him, and only then did he notice what she held in her beak. It was the silver branch, Nuatta's wand.

Raven held it out, and Carver took it reluctantly, vividly reminded of its power to destroy.

"It was all I could find," Raven said. "She never came to the surface. Neither of them did." Despite the bird voice and face, Carver understood her anguish. He felt tears start in his eyes and wiped them away quickly, feeling foolish and also angry.

Then he realized. "You're still a bird," he said.

Raven nodded, and Carver knew at once that, if birds could cry, there would be a flood of tears in those sharp black eyes.

Eight

arver helped Raven search for two days, but they never found the sisters' bodies, or any sign of them. Even the walls of Penalla's house had broken up and washed away without a trace. Back in the valley, a few birds returned to the great tree, but Raven sent them away.

"They're sitting ducks up there," she said. "Without Penalla, the hawks will go after the sparrows the minute my back is turned."

"You can control them?" Carver asked in surprise. Raven nodded forlornly. "Then why don't you stay here and be their mistress?"

Raven croaked at him in frustration. "I don't have that kind of power, Monkey Boy! I don't know enough. Look at me! I can't even turn myself back into a human."

"Why didn't the spell break when Penalla . . . went over the falls?" He didn't want to say *died*; Raven was still too broken up.

"Spells don't work that way. Once they're done, they're done. They can only be undone by someone who knows how to undo them." She let out a very human moan. "I'm done for."

"She didn't teach you how to change back and forth?"

"Only forth. I watched her, but I've never been able to change myself back. Not without her help."

"There must be someone who knows how to break the spell," Carver insisted. "Come with me downriver—we'll find another bird mage."

"That's no good. There aren't any."

"How do you know?"

"Penalla told me!" Raven snapped. "She said she was the only one, and that I was the only person she'd ever found with any kind of bird talent. I was the only apprentice she ever had."

From what he'd seen of Penalla, Carver wondered if that wasn't by choice of the other potential apprentices. He certainly wouldn't have wanted her for a mistress.

"There are four other rivers," he said. "There must be a bird mage somewhere who needs an apprentice."

She gave him an angry glare. "No," she insisted, and flew off to sulk in the woods.

Frustrated, Carver pulled out his block of wood and his knife and began to work on the carving he had started his first night on the road. He turned the piece over in his hands, studying the crude shape he had roughed out. It was a bird, because Raven had been on his mind when he'd started it. Now, with the disaster of the past days haunting his memory, he began to rework it. Time slipped by without his noticing. He paused to whet his knife now and again, but only when the sun dropped so low that shadow lay deep in the valley did he blink and look up to find the world still moving around him. The top of the great tree was still lit. The stream still flowed. And he was very thirsty.

"That's good," Raven croaked beside him, and he jumped in surprise. He hadn't heard her return, had no idea how long she'd been perched on the stone watching him.

"Thanks," he said, embarrassed. "I don't know why I chose her. I hope . . ."

What he held now was Penalla's last transformation, a proud and angry eagle. Her head was lifted, vicious beak poised to strike, one talon reaching out as she glared at the world.

"It's right," Raven muttered. "She would have liked it." She turned her head aside.

Carver studied the furious image he had created. "Why did they hate each other so much?"

"How should I know?" Raven snapped. "My mistress said her sister started it a long time ago, but she never said how. It was constant: First one would do something, then the other, to get even.

But then Nuatta sent that blasted cloud. It stayed over my mistress all the time, drizzling and raining. It made *all* of us miserable! Stealing that blasted wand was the only way to get rid of it. She deserved it, too! If only you hadn't grabbed it, Penalla would have been able to destroy it before Nuatta got here."

"Don't you blame me," Carver retorted. "I didn't grab it; you dropped it on me!"

"Oh, so now it's my fault, Monkey Boy?"

"Well, it's certainly not mine!" Carver shook the carving under Raven's beak. "If you have to blame someone, blame your mistress and her stupid sister. They're the ones who killed each other. Blazing mages! You'd think a couple of grown women would know better than to play around with their power like that."

Raven croaked derisively. "You think you'll be any better, Monkey Boy?"

"I'm not a mage."

"You want to be one," Raven jeered.

"No, I don't!"

"Then what are you doing with that wand? Why are you looking for a weather mage? Why did you ask me all those questions about being 'prenticed to a mage?"

Carver stopped short, his anger fading as quickly as it had risen. "I told you—I promised. And because, well, I guess because it seemed as if I could do it. I seemed to have more talent for it than painting, at least."

"Painting?" Raven croaked. "What's that got to do with anything?"

Carver sighed. "I'm supposed to be a brilliant painter, because my father was. Only I'm not. Anyone can paint better than me. Even you could."

"Thanks for the compliment," Raven muttered. "What about that?" She pointed her beak at the carving. "Isn't your name Carver?"

He looked at the eagle and felt some of his pride return. "Not really," he admitted, "but it's what I want it to be. After all," he went on with sudden insight, "you didn't start out as a raven. I mean, you're not really a raven even now. Your name isn't Bird or Mage, it's . . . it's whatever it is." He stopped and looked at her curiously. "What *is* your name?" he asked.

She clacked her beak sharply. "I like Raven," she said.

"And I like Carver," he declared. "Wait—does that mean you want to stay a raven?"

"Of course not!" she snapped. "Do you want to *be* a carving?"

Carver laughed, then caught himself. "I'm sorry," he said. "I see now. Why don't you come with me downriver? I still have to find a weather mage, and maybe he or she can teach you enough about magic so you can undo Penalla's spell yourself. Maybe all you need is more practice." He stared excitedly into Raven's black eyes. "Will you come with me?"

"What about the carving?" Raven said.

"Carving?" Carver sat back. "What do you mean?"

"If you 'prentice yourself to a mage, how are you going to be a carver?"

Carver stared at her, then at the carved eagle in his hand. He thought of the carvings he had seen in Lowing. There was a carver there; maybe he needed an apprentice. His heart raced at the thought.

Swallowing hard, he shook his head. "I . . . I can't," he said. "Not yet at least. I promised."

"Dolt," Raven muttered. They sat uncomfortably for a moment. "Well," she croaked finally. "I suppose this means you're going to keep that blasted wand."

Carver glanced at his pack, where the wand lay once again wrapped in its linen sheath. "I guess I have to keep it for now. Besides, you can't just leave something like that lying around."

"We could burn it," Raven croaked savagely.

"No," he said unhappily. "I promised."

"Kah!" She clacked her beak. "You have to be a weather mage

because you made a stupid promise! I don't know why I'm going with you."

"You'll come?" Carver exclaimed, sitting up again. "You'll come with me?"

"Until I get a better plan," Raven said begrudgingly. "I can't flutter around here forever."

"We'll leave first thing in the morning!" Carver told her, and he almost reached out to pet her sleek head. The glint in her sharp eyes stopped him just in time.

They made good time the next day and reached Lowing by midafternoon. The ferryman greeted them warmly and, when Carver said that he was heading downriver, pointed out a flatboat tied to the quay below the fulling mill.

"Maybe the bird can talk you aboard as a passenger," he said.

Laughing at his own joke, he took them over and introduced them to the boatman, and before he knew it, Carver was helping to wrestle the last of the heavy bales of felt and raw wool into the tight corners below deck, while Raven perched on the roof of the narrow cabin and obligingly croaked insults at the boatman and his sons.

They left the next morning at first light, the two sons and Carver poling the laden boat out into the current while the boatman handled the long tiller from his stand on the cabin roof. Carver's spirits soared as they left the town behind; it felt as if he was moving in the right direction again.

He tired of poling quickly enough. The boat was a good nine arms long and maybe half as wide, blunt at both ends and flat on the bottom. It was hard work pushing it through the water, even downstream. There was a cleated walkway along either side of the boat, and each boy had a long pole. Starting at the bow, one on each side, they set their poles on the river bottom, braced them against their shoulders, and walked back to the stern, pushing the boat along. Then they lifted the poles and hurried to the bow to do it again, and again, all day. Carver ached for the whole first week.

Luckily, the boat handled best with one poler on either side. The boatman switched the boys one at a time, so they all had a chance to rest. Carver spent his rest time massaging his sore muscles and thanking his luck that they weren't poling upstream.

They moored wherever they were when darkness fell, usually to a pair of trees along the riverbank, sometimes with another boat for company. The boatman and his boys slept in the small cabin at the stern, but Carver slept well on a nest in the wool in the hold. All in all, he thought it was a much better way to travel than walking, except that so much of it *was* walking.

Carver also used his break time to carve. He finished the eagle, then carved the top of his pole into a head with flowing hair and a girl's face, very much like his cousin Dulci. Then the boys each offered to take his turn poling in exchange for a carving. Carver happily agreed. Unfortunately, he was quick at carving and missed only three days of poling.

Raven had quickly gotten bored and spent most of each day flying out over the rolling countryside. She told Carver she was hunting, but once or twice he glimpsed her with other birds and hoped she was practicing her skills as a mage. He tried to ask her questions about magic that might help her remember how the transformation spell went, but he had to be careful not to talk to her too much in front of the others. She was supposed to be magicked, not a mage. People got nervous around mages. Having watched Penalla and Nuatta kill each other, Carver fully understood why.

The river broadened as they journeyed, each side stream adding to its flow. Then the land steepened to either side, and the river narrowed and began to run faster. The boys exchanged their poles for long sweeps. The boat swept around a tight bend, hugging the inner curve to avoid the roiling water in the center of the river, then shot between two rocks that jutted out of the surging water like a pair of jagged teeth. The boys strained, and the boatman heaved the tiller against the eddies that tried to turn the boat sideways to the swift current. The younger boy's sweep caught the top of a wave and skittered across the surface of the water as he went stumbling along the deck. The boatman swore at him, and Raven added a few jeering taunts from the top of the mast:

"Nice work, you jug-eared oaf! Stick that oar where it belongs! Stick it and heave!"

Somehow, the boatman managed to steer them right across the river to hug the next tight bend, dodging rocks and deep roils that hid even larger rocks just below the surface. Carver gripped the low rail. Spray dashed his face as they cut through the edge of a great swirling hole in the water. He wiped it away frantically. He didn't want to miss any of this, not the speed or the noise or the smell or even the wet. He glimpsed another boat, being towed slowly upriver by a horse on a path along the opposite bank. Then they were through the gorge and once more on broader water. The boys pulled hard to bring the boat to the right-hand shore, where Carver could see the wharves and warehouses of a sizeable town—Upperfall. Beyond it, the world seemed to end in a sharp lip over which the whole wide river disappeared.

They had come to the bottom of the upper reach. Carver had started at its very top, where the river fell from the forests of the high reach. He had traveled farther than anyone he knew. He looked around excitedly as the boatman's sons pulled the boat to the quays of this town at the edge of his world. They would unload here, then hire a horse and driver to tow them back upstream past the gorge. Carver would keep going.

First he offered to help unload, but the boatman kindly refused.

"You've paid your way with pole and knife, young Carver," he said.

So Carver set out along the quay with Raven on his shoulder, following a line of laden ox carts. The boatman's praise, said in the same breath as his new name, brightened his step.

Raven nipped his ear. "Settle down, Monkey Boy. If your head swells much bigger, it'll knock me right off your scrawny shoulder."

"It would serve you right, featherbrain," Carver retorted lightly. "All that good food has made you fat."

"Good?" Raven croaked. "Good for them they had a monkey to eat up the slop."

Teasing and laughing, they made their way past boats and warehouses till they came to where all the carts and barrows and porters had formed a long line of traffic. It inched slowly toward a massive gantry that stuck up over the tops of the carts. Carver's pulse quickened as the sky grew larger and larger before him. Then he was at the edge and his heart stopped for a moment.

He stood at a light railing of wood above a drop so high, his mind couldn't grasp it. Off to his left, revealed by the natural curve of the land, the river plunged in endless sheets. The noise and motion drew his eyes down and down to the great pool below, which seemed tiny from where he stood. The river left the pool to continue its journey, threading across a broad, flat plain marked by fields and pastures, towns and feeder streams, copses of wood and small holdings joined by a fine web of brown roadways and green canals that finally disappeared with the river into the haze of distance.

Suddenly, the world was a much bigger place than Carver had ever imagined. Or been told. Why had no one said it was this vast, this beautiful? Surely others from Wanting had gone down to the middle reach. Every apprentice spent a journey year working for other masters and mistresses. They couldn't all find places on the upper reach. At the very least, some of them must have come this far. But no one—not even Cousin Dora or Uncle Piper—had ever described this view. Carver wanted to rush back to Wanting and tell everyone what they had missed.

Looking down, he could just make out boats on the big pool that bordered the town at the base of the fall. Plumes of dark smoke rose here and there, and the sun glinted on tiny rooftops. He could see cloud shadows moving slowly across the great expanse of land. He could see dark specks moving through the air, specks that must be birds, flying below him instead of above, and he understood a little of why Raven had wanted so much to be able to fly.

It was Raven who finally distracted him from the scene, nipping his ear and calling him names that made the people in the line behind them laugh. Blushing, Carver tore himself from the railing and joined a line of porters that paralleled the line of carts and barrows and moved at a steady pace toward the gantry that hung out over the edge. It was fitted with huge pulleys, from which lines and lines of taut ropes stretched down toward the distant base of the cliff. Peering over the edge, he saw that the ropes connected to a pair of broad platforms that were moving slowly up and down the cliff face. The dropping platform held a mound of cargo of some sort and a knot of people; the rising platform was almost empty.

In just a few minutes, the rising platform reached the level of the gantry. Immediately, a team of porters unloaded the small cargo. The few passengers simply shouldered their own bags and went off. Then carts and barrows moved forward and the porters began to carry on a huge mound of crates, bales, kegs, and other cargo.

Carver turned to a cartman who was waiting his turn to unload onto the platform. "Is this how people get up and down?" he asked.

The man gave him a slow glance and shrugged. "If they can pay," he said.

"What if you can't pay?"

The carter pointed to the line of porters. One by one, the laden men went through a break in the railing, stepped over the edge, and walked out of view. Carver went over and saw them strung out like busy ants on a narrow trail that wound down and down along the cliff face, until it doubled back and disappeared below an overhang. He gulped and went back to the cartman.

"What's it like, that trail?" he asked nervously.

The carter shrugged again. "Wouldn't know," he said. "I've never been down." He snuffed loudly and spat on the roadway under his cart. "This reach is good enough for me."

Carver went back to the edge and watched the endless line of porters. "Well," he said at last. "Here we go."

"Meet you at the bottom," Raven replied, and she lifted off his shoulder and soared away from the cliff.

"Hey!" he cried, and faintly heard her croaking reply:

"Have a nice walk, Monkey Boy."

He watched forlornly as she swooped and spiraled in the drafts of air beside the great waterfall. Then he sighed, shouldered his bundle higher, and stepped into the line.

It took half a day to reach the bottom. The porters knew the trail and moved at a steady pace that seemed breakneck to Carver. He was forced to match them, hugging the inner wall and staring intently at the ground to make sure he didn't miss his footing or bump into any of the few porters who chose to walk back up. He hardly had time to look at the view.

At the bottom, the path leveled out and curved away from the cliff toward the town, which lined the far side of the pool where the river made its exit. Finally, it ended at the wharves. Carver looked around for Raven but didn't spot her. Legs aching, he sat on a barrel in the shade beside one of the warehouses. There was food cooking somewhere nearby, and he was wondering what he could barter to get some, when a sudden blast of sound made him jump up, heart beating. Coming toward the quay was a wide, flat boat with a thick plume of dark smoke billowing from its cabin. Hidden in the smoke, something was shrieking and whistling like a thousand frightened pigs. The shrieking stopped, but the smoke kept pouring out, and the boat moved toward him with a speed that was frightening. There was another shriek, and the water behind the boat began to churn and splash like a captive waterfall.

As he watched in complete amazement, Carver was startled by

another sudden sound from behind: a deep, sharp bang, like choked thunder, followed instantly by an angry, frightened croak. Spinning, he saw Raven struggling to fly, talons clasped on a skinned rabbit. A shouting fat man chased after her, brandishing a metal staff.

Nine

arver ran after the fat man, shouting, "Stop! Leave her alone!" He grabbed at the man's arm and just managed to snag a fold of cloth.

It was enough to spoil the fellow's aim. He swung his heavy staff but missed Raven by a hand's breath. Squawking angrily, she dropped the rabbit and soared up to the peak of the nearest roof. She paced back and forth there, croaking what Carver knew were choice curses. The fat man hurled back a few of his own. He looked down at the rabbit carcass lying in the dirt, glared back up at Raven, then spun on Carver.

"What do you mean grabbing my arm, boy?" he demanded.

His face was bright red. His breath stank, too, and Carver stepped back with a grimace. The man apparently took it for fear, because he puffed up like Zarah's rooster and looked down his bulbous nose at Carver.

"You like that ugly bird, do you?" he said nastily. "Well, we'll see how you like it when I've put a hole in it."

And with that, he turned, planted the fat end of his staff on the ground, and began a ritual that left Carver baffled. First, he took a cow horn that was slung over his shoulder, pulled a plug from the end with his teeth, and poured something into the staff. Carver realized the staff was a hollow iron tube. It had a carved wooden base that extended partway up the tube, and various metal bits stuck on here and there. Done with the cow horn, the man pulled something out of a leather case on his belt and dropped it down the tube. Then he pulled a wad of fleece out of another case and shoved that in, too, ramming it all as far down as he could with a

74

slender shaft that he pulled from the wooden base. All the while, he kept glancing maliciously up at Raven.

Finally, ramming the slender shaft back into the base, he lifted the staff, set the base against his shoulder, and pointed it toward Raven. It dawned on Carver that the thing was some sort of wand.

"Look out, Raven!" he cried.

Raven was already moving. She hurled one last taunt and dropped out of sight on the other side of the roof peak. Carver grabbed the fat man's arm just as the wand went bang again. This close, it was deafening.

The man turned on him, landing a heavy cuff that made his ears ring even more. Carver stumbled back and held up his hands to ward off the next blow, but a curt command stopped the fat man with his arm raised and his mouth half open in a curse.

A pair of tall men strode over. They wore dark red tunics with the Baron's bull head and knives emblazoned on them, and both carried long cudgels. They gazed at the fat man with complete authority. Carver stepped back in awe. He'd never seen two baronsmen together at once, and was very glad they weren't glaring at him.

"It's against the Baron's law to use firearms within the city limits," one of them said officiously to the fat man. "You've done so twice."

"I had reason," the fat man blustered, pointing down at the rabbit carcass. "A blasted crow tried to steal one of my rabbits."

"Your name?" the baronsman demanded, completely unmoved by the fat man's manner.

"Julius Hunter," he replied. "And how'm I supposed to make a living if I can't protect my bag from thieving crows? I have customers here depending on me." He puffed up some more and indicated two strings of dressed rabbits and fowl hung over the end of a barrel by the side of the nearby warehouse. "I provide fresh game to the best taverns in this burgh."

"Then get to them and sell your game before it stops being so fresh," the baronsman ordered. "And keep that gun unloaded. If we hear it again, you'll pay the fine."

The fat man blustered some more, but it was all show. He picked up the rabbit carcass, dusted it off, and tied it back onto his bag. Then, with a final muttered curse at Carver, he shouldered both bag and staff and disappeared down a side street.

"Follow your master, boy," the baronsman said.

"He's not my master," Carver stammered. "I've never seen him before."

"Then who is your master? What are you doing here?" Both men glared at him. Carver's mouth went dry and his mind blank.

"He's with us," another voice said.

Carver turned and gaped in surprise. Standing on the wharf was a short lad so smudged with soot that Carver thought for an instant his color was due solely to charcoal dust. But the gray in the boy's skin was too dark and even. And his hair was not only night black, it shone like polished iron. Carver had never seen anyone like him.

The baronsmen seemed quite used to such apparitions. "Who is 'us'?" the leader demanded.

"We're on the *Water Sprite*," the boy replied, pointing back over his shoulder at a boat tied to the wharf. "We just came up from Cutter's Landing." Almost absently, he wiped the soot from a small patch sewn on the breast of his tunic. It was the Baron's bull. The boy flashed a bright, innocent smile.

"Well enough," the baronsman said, his manner greatly improved. But he added to Carver, "Get about your business, and stay out of the way of your betters, boy."

"Yes, sir," Carver replied quickly. "I'll be very careful."

They strode off, and Carver turned back to his odd savior. The boy grinned at him.

"Thank you," Carver said, trying not to stare.

The boy shrugged. "You gotta be careful on this reach of the river. There've been a lot of runaways lately. The baronsmen, they catch you, they'll put you right on the farm."

"The farm?"

"The work farm." He chuckled at Carver's confusion. "Where're you from that you don't know about the work farms?"

"From the upper reach," Carver said.

The boy's eyes widened. "Hey, you *are* a runaway, aren't you?"

"No, I'm not!" Carver protested. "I'm . . . I'm on a journey."

The boy made a scornful hoot. "You're no journeyman. You're not old enough."

"No," Carver admitted, "but I'm still on a journey."

"What kind of journey? Where to?"

Before Carver could think up a good way to explain, Raven landed on his shoulder with a great flapping of wings.

"Mages save us," she croaked, "Monkey Boy's found a friend."

"That's good!" the boy said. "He talks just like a parrot!"

"He's a she," Carver said, grinning at Raven.

"Is she yours?"

"Sort of," Carver replied.

Raven nipped his ear viciously. "I don't belong to anybody," she snapped. "Least of all you, Monkey Boy."

The boy laughed. "That's good," he said again. "How'd you train her to know what we said?"

"She's got a talent for insults," Carver said, rubbing his ear. "But mostly it's just dumb luck. And I really wish she would leave my ear alone," he added, with a sideways glare at Raven.

She ignored him. "Where're you from, Grime Ball?" she asked the boy.

The boy laughed again. "You're one to talk, featherhead. Come on," he added to Carver, "I'll show you *Sprite*. Old Bozer's gone off to drink."

The *Water Sprite* turned out to be the same strange boat that had startled Carver with its shrill whistle and black smoke. Now it lay quietly alongside the wharf. It was built much like the flatboat

Carver had just left above the falls, but the middle area, where the hatch would have been, was taken up by a mass of machinery that left Carver mystified. There was a barrel-shaped apparatus, tubes of brass running here and there, various iron rods, and an iron teeter-totter with side arms that hung down into the hull and somehow connected below the deck to a sort of water wheel fastened to the stern. The boy called it a steam engine. Beside it in a large bin was a great mound of shiny black stone that the boy called coal.

"Bozer, he's the boatman, but I'm the fireboy," he said proudly. "He steers the boat, but I keep her running. Fireboy, that's me."

He led them on board and started naming the parts of the apparatus. Carver could feel the heat still radiating from the barrel thing—the boiler. That name he remembered, but the other words were too new piled on top of all the other strangeness he had encountered that day. It was near evening, and he was tired and hungry. Raven was muttering about finding something to eat.

Fireboy laughed. "That's good," he said. "You get her to do the asking. Well, you can sure stay for dinner. You can stay the night, if you please. Bozer's not back yet, so he won't be back till late, maybe not till morning. And by then he won't notice you're on board. He won't notice anything at all till he works it off."

"Is he a bad master?" Carver asked.

"Bozer's not my master," Fireboy said, leading the way into the cabin, which was at the bow instead of the stern. "He's just the boatman. The Baron Cutter holds my bond—and Bozer's, too. He's a bondservant, same as me. He just tries to act like some kinda master."

"A bondservant?" Carver asked. "What's that?"

Fireboy looked at him wide-eyed. "Blazes, you really are from upriver, aren't you? Never seen a steamboat, never met a bondservant. I bet you never saw any grayfolk before, either."

Carver admitted he hadn't. "Or one of those fire wands. That's strange magic."

"Firearms," Raven corrected. "They're not magic. Blasted things ought to be banned everywhere, not just in the towns. Along with the fat-headed, chicken-witted hunters who use them." Muttering, she hopped from his shoulder to the cabin table.

"How do you know about all this?" he asked her.

"I told you, Monkey Boy, I've seen every reach of this river."

"Are there monkeys here too?"

Fireboy and Raven laughed together. "Only in cages," Raven said. "Now shut up and let Fireboy here fire up some dinner. I'm starving."

Fireboy laughed again and began laying kindling and some of the black rocks, the coal, in a small firebox. Then he amazed Carver one more time by pulling out a strange tool and striking it sharply against his palm. Sparks flashed, producing a small, steady flame in a wick sticking from the end. Fireboy held the flame to the kindling till it caught, then blew out the little flame.

"Close your mouth, Monkey Boy," Raven croaked. "It's just a sparker."

Fireboy chuckled. Carver blushed.

"She's not just a trained bird, is she?" Fireboy said, closing the firebox door.

"Actually," Carver admitted, "she's not even a bird. She was apprenticed to a mage who turned her into a bird, but then the mage died and now she's stuck."

"Stuck with a bunch of lip-faced dolts," Raven croaked. "Why don't you just close your eyes and pretend I'm not here while you talk about me? And you keep cooking, Soot Brain."

"Who's stuck with who, I wonder?" Fireboy said, grinning. He put a pot on the stove and began adding meat and meal. "You got any plans to get unmagicked, Lady Bird?"

Raven glared at him. "You tell him, Monkey Boy," she croaked. "It's your idea."

"We're looking for a mage who can help Raven work out the changing spell," Carver explained. "Her mistress said there weren't any other bird mages on the river, but we're hoping there's some-one who can help. Maybe every mage knows about changing spells and could give us the general idea. Have you heard of any mages on this reach? Maybe a weather mage?"

"Why a weather mage?"

Carver didn't want to talk about the wand or his promise. The memory of the mage battle was still too vivid. "It's a long story, but a weather mage would help most."

Fireboy shook his head. "The Baron's got a water witch and a crop master. And the horse speaker, of course. There's the fal-coner—he knows a lot about birds, but he's got no magic, just trains the babies. There's midwives around, and an herb witch in every town. And there's a diviner I know of, claims to be a farseer—all kinds of cheats claim to be seers. But I sure don't know of any real mages on this reach, and I've been all the way down to First Falls."

"I told you," Raven muttered to Carver. "We're wasting our time."

"It's better than flapping around the upper reach living on mice and bugs," Carver insisted. "There's got to be someone! We'll just keep looking, even if we have to go up all five of the great rivers."

"You might want to go down to Dunsgow," Fireboy said. "There's a powerful mage there can do just about anything—fire, weather, divination, you name it. Maybe he's a bird mage too."

"That's impossible!" Raven croaked.

"Is not," Fireboy replied.

"Have you seen him?" Raven demanded.

"Me? Course not. The Baron doesn't take me with him when he goes down to Dunsgow. Me and *Sprite* run this reach top to bot-tom, but we don't go down the falls."

"Then how do you know he's not just a story made up by low-landers to keep us upriver dolts in line?"

"Because the servants who do go down with the Baron, they saw him. They told me. It's just about the only thing they talk about, the Duke's great mage."

"Lots of people told me, too," Raven retorted, "but my mistress said it's a pile of guano. She said no mage can do all the things that that one's supposed to be able to."

"Did *she* ever see him?"

"Of course not!"

"Then how did she know?"

"Because she's a mage, you wingless dolt!" Raven ruffed up her neck feathers and squawked insultingly at him. "Who are you going to believe—a bunch of cheese-eating muck worms or a mage?"

"But if it is true," Carver put in, "even if only part of it's true, he could be just the mage we're looking for. Come on, Raven, it's surely worth taking a look. What else do they say about him?" he asked Fireboy.

"Well," the boy replied, "some say he's the Duke's brother, the power behind the Duke, how the Duke got to be in charge in the first place. Some others say it's more than that; they say it's the mage running the Duke, not the other way around. And some say he's the Duke himself. But everybody knows he's real."

"There you are," Carver said to Raven. "A mage who can do more than one kind of magic. We have to go see if it's true; we can't pass up the chance."

"Right, right," Raven muttered.

Carver's heart quickened at the thought of going all the way downriver, to Dunsgow. Maybe they would find a weather mage. Maybe this was the mage Zarah had foreseen. Or maybe not. Maybe there weren't any more weather mages, and he would be relieved of his promise.

Then his mood darkened. Dunsgow was at the very mouth of the river. His parents had left him to go that way. Somewhere between here and there, they had decided not to come back.

Ten

The boatman didn't return until the first glimpse of dawn. Reeling and belching, he stumbled aboard and began ordering Fireboy around in the cabin. But his shouting lapsed into loud snores in midsentence, and Carver fell back to sleep by the firebox and slept until the sun was truly up. Then Fireboy brought out some seared meat and onions for breakfast. While Carver tried to get used to the funny little tongs that people on this reach used for eating, Fireboy stirred up the ashes and clinkers in the firebox and enlisted Carver's aid in shoveling coal. The coal burned hotter than wood, once you got the knack of arranging it.

Fireboy checked various tubes and levers, pumped water from the lake into the boiler, turned this handle, swabbed grease onto that bearing . . . it was a complicated ritual that Carver was sure was half magic, though Raven laughed scornfully when he suggested it.

"He's a greasy mechanical," she squawked. "No more a mage than your auntie."

"One of my aunties is a seer," Carver pointed out dryly.

"And her nephew has about as much sense as her stupid rooster," she retorted, and flew to the top of the stubby mast to preen. She reminded Carver more of a cat than a bird sometimes.

Fireboy kept him at the shovel, showing how to shape the pile of coal to get the best spread of heat below the boiler. Meanwhile, he went about the boat, pulling thick ropes from various places below deck. When the fire was going well, the two of them went to work attaching the *Water Sprite* to their tow, an old scow loaded with goods bound for the Baron's estate downriver. Though Fireboy called it a tow, it was tied at their bow, tight against a great mat of woven-rope fenders. Fireboy carefully lashed the two hulls together, all the while tending the fire and happily showing Carver what to do.

The whole process took a good two hours, but finally Fireboy announced, "Tow's ready, steam's up; time to cut loose." Then, to Carver's surprise, he undid the lines and ran back to the engine to twist some valves. The big wheel at the stern began to turn and splash, and Fireboy scrambled up a ladder to the cabin top to steer them away from the wharf.

"What about the boatman?" Carver called over the racket.

"Bozer? Still sleeping it off!" Fireboy yelled with a giant smile, and he yanked joyfully on a line that ran from the steering post to the cargo mast and down to the boiler. At once, a shrieking whistle blasted the whole waterfront. Streaming a plume of dark smoke, the *Water Sprite* nosed into the river, pushing the tow and a big wake before her.

Carver ran to the side to watch as they just cleared the stern of the boat tied ahead of them. Then he ran back to watch the big wheel shove at the water. At a shout from Fireboy, he ran to the firebox to lay more coal. Fireboy himself hurried down to set a valve, then clambered back up to the wheel. The crossbeam pumped up and down, cranks turned, and the stern wheel churned as they picked up speed and claimed the center of the stream. Carver's heart raced.

For half the day, they steamed downriver on their own. Carver quickly picked up the basics of fire tending, but there was a lot more to running the engine than that. Fireboy came down constantly to check everything himself. One time, he turned a valve that let a long plume of steam escape.

"You got to watch the pressure," he said. "We get too much, and *blooey!*"

"How do you know how much is enough?" Carver asked.

"You just get the feel for it," Fireboy replied. "No more coal now till I tell you." He flashed Carver a smile and hurried back to the cabin top.

The river wound through slow bends and tight oxbows, and steering was just as complicated as tending the engine. Fireboy brought Carver up to the cabin top for a while and tried to show him how to read the ripples; how the mud and sand built up on the insides of the curves; how fallen trees and floating logs could wreck the boat in a moment. They had to be spotted way ahead of the laden tow, which stuck out in front by a score of long arms and made turning a slow process. Raven laughed from her perch on the masthead as Carver fumbled at the wheel and set the bow veering heavily back and forth until Fireboy straightened him out. Carver was surprised; he had thought that boatmen had a simple, even dull, life.

It got harder when Bozer woke up. The boatman slammed out of the cabin and stumped over to the rail to relieve himself, then went to the bucket by the cabin door and splashed water on his face. Dripping, he squinted around meanly at the passing riverbank.

"Fireboy!" he bellowed. He turned toward the engine, saw Carver with the shovel, and came stumping toward him, only to stop, wipe his eyes, and look again. Sooty as Carver had become, he was obviously not Fireboy.

"What kind of failed curse are you?" Bozer grunted. "Where in blazes is my fireboy?"

"Up on the cabin, sir," Carver replied, as politely as he would to any master. "I'm just helping out."

"Helping? A scrawny git like you? That I'd like to see."

And with that for an introduction, he turned his back and stumped forward to haul his bulk up the cabin ladder and confront Fireboy.

"What do you think you're doing, boy?" he demanded in a nasty tone that carried clearly to Carver by the engine. "Where on this stinking stretch of sewer are we?"

Carver couldn't make out Fireboy's reply, but apparently it didn't satisfy Bozer. The boatman raised his hand threateningly. Fireboy dodged down the ladder.

"Get back to your stinking grease!" Bozer yelled after him. "And tell that worthless git you let on board to bring me up some breakfast or I'll throw you both off at the next sandbar!"

"That Bozer, he's a charmer," Fireboy said, taking the shovel. His usual grin was stiff.

"Is he always like that?" Carver asked.

"Only when he's awake," Fireboy replied. "And he's worst after a drink. After just one trip, I swore I'd never touch wine or ale in my life."

"Where's my breakfast?" Bozer bellowed from the cabin top.

"There's more stew on the stove," Fireboy said, "and take him up a mug of ale from the cask under his bunk."

"More ale?" Carver said.

"Don't worry, I keep it real watery," Fireboy said. "It's mostly just so it smells right."

Carver got the stew and watery ale and carried them carefully up the ladder to Bozer, who eyed him blearily. The boatman smelled of sour wine and old sweat. He was squat and big bottomed, with rank hair and a coarse chinful of black stubble that sprouted into fur at the neck of his jerkin and fuzzed his burly forearms. He downed the ale in one continuous swallow, belched, and spooned a glob of stew into his mouth.

"I hope you aren't expecting a free ride, boy," he grunted around the stew. "Nobody gets a free ride from me, least of all a scrawny runt of a runaway who ought to be thrown onto the farms with the rest of 'em."

"No, sir," Carver said. "I'm no runaway, and I'm ready to work for my passage."

Bozer looked him up and down scornfully and swallowed another mouthful of stew. "Doing what?" he demanded. It seemed his basic speaking voice was either a bellow or a grunt.

"I can help Fireboy—"

"Don't need another coal heaper! What else can you do?"

"I can carve."

Bozer snorted, then gulped the last of the stew and squinted into the empty bowl. "Can you cook?"

Carver hesitated. "I—"

"Doesn't matter. It's bound to be better than the swill that blasted Fireboy serves up." He shoved the empty mug and bowl at Carver. "You'll cook. And you'll clean up. And you'll help shovel coal, too."

"Yes, sir."

"Now go make lunch!" Bozer raised his hand threateningly, just as he had at Fireboy. Carver dodged like Fireboy and escaped down the ladder.

"And boy!" Bozer bellowed, leaning over and glaring down at him. "Don't you dare water my ale, you hear?"

"Yes, sir!"

Carver went into the cabin and started looking through the cupboards to see what food there was. He decided more stew would be the safest thing and put some meat and cabbage in the pot with a little water and some barley. Carver had never used coal before that morning, but it was easy enough to stoke up the embers in the little firebox. Soon the pot was bubbling away.

The *Sprite* steamed on through a countryside that seemed to be one giant farm straddling the tree-lined river. Carver tended his stew from a chair set in the doorway, where there was a breeze. Everything inside was sooty, and the place stank of oil and Bozer. Carver itched for activity, for something to carve, but there was no firewood. Then he noticed Bozer's ale keg. Pulling it over between his knees, he took out his knife and studied the untapped end. There was already a maker's mark painted on it—rather poorly, Carver thought. It showed a crude portrait of a plump young woman holding a tankard of ale. Letters around the rim read *Grimson Brewer—Underfall.* Shaking his head, he began to carve.

The next thing he knew, there was a strong smell of burning in the cabin. Carver jumped up, dumping the keg out onto the deck, and rushed to the stove. Smoke was billowing from the pot. He grabbed the closest container at hand and poured in liquid. Too late, he realized he'd grabbed Bozer's mug of ale. Frantically, he stuck the ladle into the beery steam to stir up the mess on the bottom of the pot.

"What in the blazing mages are you doing!" Bozer bellowed, stomping into the cabin with the wayward keg cradled to his chest.

"Just finishing your meal," Carver stammered. "Um, I was just about to pour your ale and the keg slipped out of my hands."

"You be careful with this!" Bozer snapped. "This is the best ale brewed in the middle reach. And it's got the prettiest bottom, too," he added, with a leer and a pat on the end of the keg. Suddenly, he felt the grooves that Carver had made in the wood. With a thick scowl he turned the keg and stared at the picture, now carved in relief on the bottom of the keg. "What in . . ."

Carver quailed. "I'm sorry," he said. "I didn't realize it was special to you."

Bozer glared. "You did this?" he demanded. "You carved here? Right on my little lady?"

"Yes, sir," Carver said dejectedly.

"I ought to throw you off on the next mud bank!" Bozer raved. "You're supposed to be cooking!"

"Yes, sir," Carver agreed. "I was just starting to serve."

Bozer sniffed the beery steam and grunted. He took another look at the keg and grunted again. His glare softened. "You made her rounder," he growled.

"I can fix it," Carver offered hurriedly.

"Don't you touch her! And where's my food?"

Carver grabbed a bowl and was just starting to ladle out some of the black mess when Fireboy cried out. The river was bending left, sending the *Sprite* right toward the bank. With an oath, Bozer threw the keg into Carver's arms and grabbed for the ladder. Bowl, ladle, and stew went everywhere. The boat lurched as Bozer reached the wheel and swung it hard over. Carver staggered against the table and ran outside, clutching the precious keg. Raven, swooping overhead, laughed and mimicked Bozer's curses. With painful slowness, the front end of the tow swung away from the bank, but now the stern was swinging in. Bozer, still cursing, fought to straighten their course. Raven laughed some more.

Finally, the boat and tow were back in midchannel. Bozer gave himself a shake, like a big dog lumbering out of cold water. He glared down at Carver.

"See what you did with your blasted carving!" he bellowed. "Now, don't make me come down there again, or I'll give you a taste of my fist!" He shook it threateningly.

Carver didn't need a second warning. He ran into the cabin, grabbed the ladle and bowl, and quickly spooned out more stew, then raced up the ladder. Bozer grabbed the bowl from him, then eyed the ladle with a glare.

"How am I supposed to eat with that?" he demanded.

"Get him a shovel," Raven cawed from the masthead. "That ought to be big enough!"

Bozer spun, squinting up. "What sort of blasted curse is that stinking crow?" he grunted.

"Go sit on a stick, Fur Brain!" Raven retorted. "I'm no crow and you're no boatman!"

Bozer snatched the ladle from Carver's hand and flung it with all his might at Raven. "Get off my boat, you great croaking git!" he bellowed.

The ladle clipped Raven's tail, and she flapped off the mast with an angry squawk. Muttering a colorful description of Bozer's conception, she flew across the river and disappeared behind a row of trees.

"Stupid bird," Bozer grunted. "Where on the five rivers . . . ?" He turned to squint at Carver. "Is it yours?" he demanded.

"Um, I think I'm more hers," Carver said, backing quickly toward the ladder. Just then, a flock of ducks rose from the water by the far bank and headed right toward them. Carver dropped to the deck and ducked into the cabin just as they soared overhead, pelting Bozer with droppings.

Eleven

ozer cursed a lot, but after he'd had his bowl of beery stew and made Carver clean the duck droppings off the cabin top, he settled down to an occasional mutter. He eyed every duck and goose with great suspicion and winced whenever a shadow passed overhead. Fireboy watched him with glee.

"That's good," he said. "It's about time that Bozer got some back. Usually he just gets to give it out. When he makes a fist, you want to move fast."

They tied up that evening at a small town with busy wharves. Bozer left as soon as he had eaten, ordering them to stay on board and out of trouble. As soon as he was out of sight, Raven soared in from the other side of the river and landed on the rail.

"Where's Sweat Ball off to?" she croaked.

"The nearest alehouse," Fireboy replied. "He'll be gone till midnight probably. He doesn't stay out so late when we're on the way home."

"Where's that?" Carver asked.

"Cutter's Landing," Fireboy said.

"The Baron's estate," Raven explained, clacking her beak in disgust.

"Have you been there?" Carver asked.

"Seven years," she said harshly.

"What do you mean?" asked Fireboy.

"I lived there," Raven replied.

"As a bird?"

"Of course not, Hen Wit! My mother was a house servant; I lived with her."

"You're a runaway," Fireboy said slowly. "That explains a lot."

She ruffled her feathers. "What's that supposed to mean?"

He laughed. "Nothing bad. Just explains how you got so sharp tongued. Or were you always like that?"

"Seven years in bond to Cutter is what did it," Raven snapped. "You'd feel the same if you weren't such a steam brain."

For the first time, Fireboy showed a temper. "I can't say running away did much for you, Bird Face."

"Calm down," Carver said, reaching out toward them both. "What are you arguing about, anyway?"

"No argument," Raven croaked. "Shovel Head here belongs to Baron Cutter. I don't. It's that simple."

"I don't belong to nobody," Fireboy stated. "Baron Cutter holds my bond, that's all. I *work* for him. When I pay off my bond—"

"*If,*" Raven put in.

"When!" Fireboy retorted.

Raven clacked her beak. "Do you know anybody who's ever paid off their bond?"

"Sure! Lots of them!"

"Name one."

"A boy in First Falls told me two months ago he'd met a man from another river, Baron Stoner's man he'd been."

"Did you see him?" Raven croaked. "Did you talk to him? No, you didn't. You just heard about him from somebody who says he met him but probably just heard about him from somebody else. Name me one person you've actually met, one person from this river, from Baron Cutter, who's paid off his bond."

Fireboy clenched his jaw but said nothing.

"You can't, because it never happens. Nobody pays their way out of the monkey cage!"

"Stop!" Carver shouted. They both looked at him in surprise. "What," he demanded, "is a bond? Will you please tell me?"

"It's what you owe your master," Fireboy muttered.

"It's the price for your freedom," Raven said. "It's what the

Baron paid to buy you. And feed you and train you to be his servant. And you stay his servant till you pay it off. Which is never!" she added, with another angry look at Fireboy.

"But what about all the work you do?" Carver asked. "Doesn't that count for anything?"

"That buys your clothes and food and bed," Raven said. "Anything left over you can use to pay down your bond, but there's never anything left over. Steam Brain here probably doesn't even get paid yet because he's still learning. By the Baron's rules, he doesn't deserve any pay."

"I get paid," said Fireboy sulkily. "Baron gives me three demislugs every trip."

"What's a demislug?" Carver asked.

"The Duke's new money," Fireboy said.

"What's three of them worth in old money?" Raven croaked.

"I don't know," Fireboy admitted. "A deed, I guess."

"More like half that, I bet," Raven muttered.

"What's your bond?" Carver asked.

Fireboy shrugged. "Fifty talents."

"Fifty talents?" Carver exclaimed. "How many trips do you make?"

"Ten or twelve a year."

Carver was astounded. That was only twelve deeds a year at most. There were one hundred deeds in a skill, and twenty skills in a talent. "Blazing mages. That'll take forever to pay off!"

"Exactly!" Raven crowed.

"I'll get a lot more when I'm boatman," Fireboy said.

"How much more?" Raven demanded. "And how much will you be able to save once you have to start paying for your own food and clothes? How much does Bozer save?"

"That sot?" Fireboy snorted. "I'm not like him; I can save. I *will* save. I'll pay off my bond and get my own boat." He was almost crying when he said it.

Carver suddenly felt great sympathy for him. He could understand feeling trapped.

"How long will it take us to get there, to Cutter's Landing?" he asked, to change the subject.

Fireboy swallowed hard. "Five days," he said, not looking at them.

"Is your family there?"

"My father is. My mother . . . the Baron sold her bond to Miner a while ago. She's a house servant there."

"Sold her . . . ?" Carver began, then realized how much it cost Fireboy to say it. He stumbled to a halt.

"Families don't mean much when you're a bondservant," Raven said harshly.

"How about your mother?" Carver asked quickly, trying to forestall another argument. "Is she still there?"

Raven was silent for a moment, then replied, "I guess so. She wouldn't come with me."

She said it so flatly, neither boy knew how to respond.

Instead, Fireboy turned to Carver. "How about your family? Where are they?"

Now it was Carver's turn to hesitate. Then he shrugged and told Fireboy his parents' story, as much as he knew of it. "So they went downriver," he finished.

Fireboy regarded him thoughtfully. "Is that why you left?" he asked. "To find them?"

"No," Carver said, frowning. "And I plan to go back." He told about the wand, the mayor, and the runes; of meeting Raven and the fight between the sister mages. Raven put in a detail now and then.

"So there's a couple of reasons," Carver finished. "I have to learn how to use the wand; the whole village needs me to. And there's Raven—she needs to find a mage who can help her be human again and finish her training."

Fireboy shook his head. "That is some story! You're a mage?"

"That's what everyone expects," Carver said. "That or a painter."

"But your name's Carver."

"Not back there."

"You changed it yourself?" Fireboy said. "Now, that's something. Well, I guess I did, too. Now I'm Fireboy. That's what I want to be and that's what I am. Even if I am in bond." He shot Raven a sullen look. "You stay on board and keep cooking like you do, and we'll get you down to Cutter's Landing. From there, you should be able to hop a boat down to First Falls. *Sprite* might even head that way after we unload."

"That'd be great fun," Raven croaked. "Another trip with Sweat Ball."

"You can fly when you want, raven girl," Fireboy said. "Carver here has got to float or walk, and floating's a lot easier."

The journey quickly settled into routine. Bozer came back drunk and snored into the morning. Carver cooked breakfast while Fireboy built the fire. After eating, they got the *Sprite* under way. When Bozer woke up, Fireboy took over the shovel, Carver went in to cook, and Raven flew out of sight. Each evening, they tied up in a town and Bozer headed for the tavern. Then Raven came back on board and they ate and talked. Carver found a particularly large and fine piece of coal in the pile. It was more brittle than wood but had a subtle grain and bright sheen. He found he could work it with a scraper and the heavy cooking knife from the cabin. He kept it hidden, though, not sure if it was good enough to show the others.

The last night, Bozer came back earlier than usual and not nearly so drunk.

"Be careful tomorrow," Fireboy warned. "He's got to sober himself up before we reach the landing."

The next morning, Bozer forced himself out of bed before they'd finished breakfast. He even tried to wash himself with a bucketful of water from the river. Seeing him standing hairy, naked, and dripping on the deck, Carver didn't know whether to laugh or gag.

"Now, that's a monkey!" Raven squawked, then flew off quickly, chuckling to herself.

Bozer glared at her and, when Carver brought him some bannock, sniffed it suspiciously.

"Did you put ale in this?" he demanded.

"Yes, sir," Carver said. "To make it rise. I always do."

Bozer pitched it overboard. "Make me another!" he barked. "And no ale in it!"

"But the alcohol cooks off," Carver tried to explain.

Bozer would have none of it. "No ale! No ale again, not in anything, do you hear?" He raised his fist, and Carver dodged back into the cabin.

It went like that all day. Bozer never spoke below a bellow, and he raised his fist almost every time he spoke. Twice, he cuffed Fireboy on the ear without warning or reason. Fireboy lost his smile. Raven herself flew over then and let Bozer have it from behind, but it was Carver who paid the price. Bozer made him clean up the mess—and gave him a hard kick while he was bent over scrubbing.

Finally, they reached Cutter's Landing, a stand of buildings marked by a substantial wharf. Across the plowed fields that lined the river, Carver could make out a walled estate surrounded by orchards. Bozer sounded two blasts on the whistle and angled the tow in. Fireboy twisted his valves to let off steam. The wharf loomed closer. Two other steamboats were already tied there longwise, and Bozer seemed to be aiming for the space between them. To Carver it looked like an awfully tight fit. Bozer nosed the *Sprite* in and bellowed for reverse.

Fireboy threw a lever. The engine groaned as the big wheel churned and backed. The *Sprite* jerked and started to swing sideways into the empty slot. It looked as if Bozer had timed it perfectly and they would slide right in, like a knife into a sheath. But the space proved too tight. With a crunch that rattled Carver's teeth, the *Sprite*'s paddle wheel swung against the boat behind them. The tow veered in sharply, slamming against the wharf, then smashed into the leading boat. With a great splintering of wood, paddle blades split off it and dropped into the water.

Men on the wharf were shouting and running to the other boats. Fireboy was blowing off a tornado of steam and hanging on to a massive lever, trying to stop the slowly churning wheel. Carver ran back and threw his weight on the brake.

"Don't let go!" Fireboy shouted, then ran to the side, grabbed a mooring rope, and leaped across the widening gap to throw a hitch over one of the pilings. He jumped back on board and raced forward to grab another line and throw it to one of the men on the wharf. Together, they ran on forward to fasten the tow. Up on the cabin top, Bozer stood by the wheel post, watching everything with a look of dull surprise.

The paddle wheel finally stopped, and Carver let up on the brake lever. Fireboy came back to join him and gave him a sick look. They went aft to check the damage. Luckily, the wheel was mostly intact. Two of the long paddles had lost their outer corners, but that was it. All the spokes, ribs, and attachments seemed solid.

They went back to the engine and saw Bozer had finally come down from the cabin top. He stood on the deck, shoulders slumped, facing a tall, blocky grayfolk man with grizzled hair and a hard, angry face.

"You've been drinking again, Bozer." His tone said instantly he was the master here on Cutter's wharves.

"Haven't," Bozer grunted. "I'm as sober as a post."

"Then how do you explain this?" The wharfmaster gestured roughly at the damage.

"I'm sober," Bozer repeated stubbornly, and Carver thought maybe that did explain it.

"Fifty Kovacs," the master said. "I'm charging your bond fifty Kovacs."

Bozer sputtered with outrage. "That's . . . that's three talents!" he exclaimed.

"It's five, oaf."

"You can't do that!" Bozer bellowed. "I'll go to the Baron!"

"Go," the master agreed, never raising his voice. "I'm sure he'll enjoy hearing about this."

Bozer's mouth opened and closed without a sound. Then he turned and pointed toward Fireboy. "It was his fault!" he shouted. "He didn't reverse when I told him! He didn't blow steam when he should have!"

The wharfmaster turned his hard eyes on Fireboy. "Five Kovacs on the boy, then," he said. "And five more on you for training him so poorly. And be grateful I don't just charge you outright for the repairs. Both of you."

He gave them a cold glare and turned to go. Then he noticed Carver.

"Who's that?" he said.

Bozer glared at Carver and Fireboy. His narrow eyes glinted. "Some little git the fireboy snuck on board back at Underfall," he said meanly. He stalked over and grabbed Carver's arm, dragging him painfully across the deck to shove him at the wharfmaster. "Another runaway, I guessed. I kept him on board so you could take him to the farm."

"I'm no runaway!" Carver exclaimed.

"Who's your master, then, boy?" the man demanded coldly. "Where are you from?"

"I'm from Wanting," Carver said, "at the top of the upper reach. My master is William Painter there, my uncle."

"What are you doing here then?"

"I'm on a journey for the mayor and the baronsman," Carver explained. "To Dunsgow, to find a weather mage."

"A weather mage? In Dunsgow?" The big man's voice was skeptical. "What for?"

"To learn how to be one," Carver said.

Bozer laughed and winked at the master. "A nice tale, eh?"

The master ignored him, but his gaze didn't soften.

"What's your name?" he demanded.

"Carver, sir."

"And your uncle is a painter?"

Carver opened his mouth, then realized how stupid it all sounded. "Yes, sir," he said weakly.

The wharfmaster gave a grunt of disbelief. "Not good enough, boy," he said.

"It's true!" Fireboy called, and he ran over to stand by Carver.

"Hold!" the master barked, glaring at Fireboy. "You're this close to the farm yourself." He held his fingers a hair's breadth apart, and Fireboy fell still. Before Carver could say anything else, Bozer cuffed them both so hard they almost fell.

"They've been like that all trip," he told the master, "thick as thieves. I had to sit up and watch them every town to make sure they'd still be there in the morning."

The master made no reply. He took Carver's arm and pulled him to the rail, handing him over to one of the other men, who hauled him onto the wharf and quickly tied his wrists.

"Take him to the manor," the wharfmaster ordered. "The Baron will want to see him. He might be better use here than on the farm."

The man pulled Carver across the wharf by the rope and heaved him into a wagon. Then he climbed onto the driver's bench and started the horses toward the distant buildings. Carver crouched in the back, staring helplessly at the receding *Water Sprite*. The other men had gone over to the tow. Left alone, Bozer knocked Fireboy to the deck and started hitting him again and again.

Twelve

R aven perched on top of the highest warehouse and watched the wagon drive toward the manor. She'd gotten a great laugh out of Bozer's disastrous attempt at a landing, but now she was angry and—she had to admit—worried. She knew the wharfmaster; he was hardheaded and cold as an iron shackle. As soon as Bozer said "runaway," she knew Carver was headed for the farm.

"Chicken-witted dolt!" she groused. "Duck brain! He should have realized this would happen. Steam Head should have warned him!"

But Carver was from upriver and Fireboy was just a greasy mechanical. She was the one who should have known. Now she had to get him free.

"Dolt!" she croaked.

Fireboy wasn't going to be any help. Bozer was done beating him for now, but stood over him shouting pointless orders as he tried to shut down the fire and see to the engine. Raven lifted from the rooftop and winged slowly toward the estate.

The manor was surrounded by fields already showing new grain. Within its old, high wall, the familiar many-winged house and adjoining stable were surrounded by green lawn and flowering gardens that made the slate walls and roof seem drab and unfriendly. Several people were at work in the stable yard. A fire burned under the baking ovens out back, tended by kitchen boys and scullions. She recognized old Liddy Cook by her white hat and squat legs. The wagon drove through the back gates and pulled up by the summer kitchen. The driver called to one of the scullions, who disappeared inside. Then he got down and pulled Carver out by the rope. Cook and the others stared curiously. Carver stared back with a dazed look. Raven settled into the branches of a fruit tree at the edge of the kitchen garden to spy.

In a few minutes the Baron himself came out. Raven felt her hackles rise and barely suppressed the urge to hiss. The stinkard wasn't big or impressive or ugly; in fact, he had a roundish face, wispy gray hair, and a pleasant little smile that he used a lot. But she knew what a disguise it was. He listened to the driver, all the while smiling at Carver. Just as Carver tried to speak, the driver noticed the knife on his belt. With a hard jerk on the rope, he snatched it away. Carver gave a cry and grabbed for it, but the driver hit him hard on the side of the head, then threatened him with his own knife.

The Baron shook his head. "We've no use for him here," he said in a cold drawl that turned his smile ugly. "Look at his face—a born troublemaker. Destined to hang. Lock him up till we can spare someone to take him to the farm."

To Raven's disgust, Carver stood there gulping like a fish while the Baron disappeared back into the house. The driver, accompanied by the Baron's fat red-faced steward, gave another jerk on the rope and pulled Carver to a cell at the far end of the garden. It was a tiny stone shed built against the wall and covered prettily with ivy. Flowers lined the walkway that led to it. But the door was heavy oak, with massive hinges and a huge lock. There wasn't even a window, just a narrow gap at the bottom of the door through which a plate could be passed. Raven shivered as the driver shoved Carver in and slammed the door. The steward turned the lock with a big, complicated key. As they walked away, Carver began pounding on the inside of the door. Raven clacked her beak. The muck head was bruising his hands for nothing.

Raven sat in the tree for a long time after Carver had given up pounding. She didn't dare fly down to talk to him; the gardeners were too near. The best she could do was fly overhead, make a few loud croaks, and hope the dolt would realize it was her. Frustrated, she flew back to the river.

Fireboy was at his sacred engine, working on some bit with a huge wrench. Sweat Ball was nowhere in sight, but there were other men on the wharf. The tow had been untied from the *Sprite* and was being unloaded into a line of wagons. Two more men were on the damaged boat in front, taking apart the smashed paddle wheel. The hatchet-faced wharfmaster was moving about, keeping a stern eye on everyone.

Raven swooped in low over the *Sprite*'s railing and landed behind the engine, hidden from view of the wharf. She hopped up to Fireboy and tapped him on the back with her beak.

He yelped and dropped his wrench with a great clatter.

"Quiet, you steam-brained oaf!" she hissed. "Pretend I'm not here!"

Sucking scraped knuckles, he glanced furtively at the men on the wharf.

"Blazing mages!" she snapped. "Don't look so blasted guilty! Pick up your stupid tool and act like you're working." Fireboy fumbled for the wrench and fitted it onto a big bolt. "Where's the stink ball?"

"Bozer?" Fireboy muttered. "In the lodge. Wharfmaster sent him away."

"What did he do this time?"

Fireboy grimaced. "Started drinking, then came out to hit me some more. Wharfmaster told him to stand off or he'd be working the fields the rest of his life." Fireboy smiled vengefully. "That'd be worth getting hit for."

Raven clacked her beak. "You think so? Your head's more full of soot than I thought."

Fireboy glared at her, but his face quickly sank. "You're right, birdie," he admitted. "Nothing's worth getting beat like that." He hunched his shoulders, as if feeling Bozer's blows. "What happened with Carver?" he asked abruptly, barely hiding the catch in his voice.

Raven told him. "We have to get him out somehow," she finished. "They'll beat him on the farm a lot worse than Sweat Ball beats you."

"He doesn't belong there anyway," Fireboy said. "He's no runaway."

"No one belongs there," Raven said flatly. "Have you got something that'll cut hinges or smash the lock?"

Fireboy nodded slowly. "I guess I do."

"Right. Finish what you're doing. Meet me back here at dusk with your tools."

"I'll be here," Fireboy said. "I don't ever leave *Sprite* if I can help it." He patted an ugly, oily gear affectionately, then cast a worried look around. "I got a lot to do here, now that Bozer's smashed her up. Lucky she's a solid lady."

Raven made a gagging sound. "Right, Boat Brain. Just be ready."

She came back at twilight. There was no sign of the moon yet, which was fine in some ways, bad in others. Her night vision was terrible, but the darkness would also hide them from human eyes. Luckily, she had found a local owl. Luckier still, she'd been able to calm him before he attacked her. He was a very reluctant ally.

Fireboy wasn't waiting for her on the boat. Instead, she found him slouched in the shadows of one of the warehouses. He quickly wiped his eyes as she landed, but she saw the tracks smeared on his cheeks.

"What happened?" she asked. "A few more friendly strokes from Slime Ball?"

He shook his head.

"Well, it's done now, and we've got a job to do."

"He threw me off," Fireboy said, choking back more tears.

"Off? You mean off your boat? Who, Bozer?"

Fireboy shook his head miserably. "Baron's steward did," he said. "For letting Carver on."

"Stinkard!" Raven hissed. "For how long?"

"I don't know. Till they could trust me, he said." He wiped his eyes again.

Raven cursed the steward, the Baron, and Bozer all together, though it didn't make her feel much better. "Do you still want to help Carver?" she asked finally. "It'll be risky."

Fireboy nodded. "I brought him here," he said. "I'll get him out."

"Have you got everything we'll need?"

"I think so," he replied, lifting a small bag to his shoulder.

She eyed it skeptically; it seemed tiny. "Well, hold still." She flew to his other shoulder.

"Ouch!" He winced as her claws squeezed his tunic.

"Sorry," she said, loosening her grip. "I don't sharpen them; they just get that way."

"It's not that," he grumbled. "I got bruises."

"Oh. Sorry." Silently, she cursed Bozer again.

At her direction, Fireboy started up the road toward the estate, staying in the shadows by the warehouses. There were lights and voices in the lodge, but no one was outside. The stars brightened by dozens until the sky glittered, but it wasn't much to see by. Raven shut her eyes and reached out to the owl. With a surge of relief, she found him.

Stay near, she ordered, though his will was so strong, it felt more like a request. *Watch for humans. Warn us.*

When she opened her eyes, she could just make out his dark shadow flying silently ahead.

Fireboy followed the line of trees along the road and the lights that beckoned from the distant manor. Raven didn't see the owl again as the gloaming turned to night, but she could feel him. He hooted once, and Fireboy jumped.

"Don't worry," Raven muttered, "he's with me."

As they neared the walls of the estate, a dog started to bark. Raven told Fireboy to cut across the field to the right and come up from the back. Instead he went left.

"This way we're downwind of the dogs," he whispered.

"Good plan," Raven said grudgingly. She always forgot about smell when she was a raven.

Walking the wide loop across the fields seemed to take forever. The owl stayed ahead, dutifully watching for people, but he didn't warn them about pitfalls. Fireboy stumbled through drainage ditches and rows of seedlings. Once he ran into a thick bush. Raven croaked indignantly as a branch whipped across her face.

"Watch out, oaf!" she croaked.

"Watch out yourself, birdbrain," he retorted. "I'm the one doing all the walking."

Finally, they came near the back gate. The owl hooted ominously.

"Blast!" Raven muttered. "Get in the shadow by the wall. Somebody's coming."

Fireboy stooped and ran the last stretch to the wall, then crouched his way along, hugging the ivy and stone. Just as they reached the gate, two men came out. Fireboy pressed against the wall, almost knocking Raven off. She dug into his shoulder and he stifled a cry of pain. The men stopped. One of them lifted a dark lantern. The other struck a sparker, but it didn't catch. He struck again, and again.

"Forget it," the other grunted. "It's not far. You can see the lights."

"I don't care," sparker man said. "It's dark. I feel like the shadows are watching me."

The one with the lantern gave a curse and started walking. The other cursed back and hurried after. They disappeared into the darkness toward the field houses.

Raven didn't breathe again until the sound of their footsteps had died away. Then Fireboy made a strangled moan and grabbed at her talons. She loosened them quickly.

"Sorry," she hissed. He growled dully in reply.

Carefully, he slid up to the gateway and peered around the corner. Raven craned to see past his head. There were still a few scullions in the summer kitchen, but the garden was dark and empty. Fireboy scooted quickly across the opening and into the shadow of the far wall. Raven strained her ears. There was no sound that they'd been noticed. She reached out to the owl. Nothing. She reached again; still nothing. He was gone. Probably distracted by a blasted mouse, she thought. Those dumb raptors were all stomach and pride.

She pointed her wing, and Fireboy continued to creep along the wall. Luckily, they were moving away from the stables and kennels. There were a few lamps burning in the main house, but most of the windows were dark; the servants' quarters showed a bit more life in the pallid guttering of cheap tallow candles. Faint voices carried across the night. Finally, the shed loomed before them, a dark block jutting from the darker wall.

Fireboy pressed against the thick door. "Carver?" he whispered. "Are you in there?"

"Where else is he going to be?" Raven muttered. "Carver! Wake up, Chicken Wits. Wake—"

"Raven! Fireboy! Is that you?" Carver's voice seemed to bellow through the door.

"Quiet, dolt!" Raven hissed. "You'll have us all in there!" She paused, but there was no outcry from the kitchen. "Now listen," she ordered. "Fireboy is going to cut off the hinges."

"No, I'm not," Fireboy said.

"He's going to smash the lock."

"No, I'm not."

"He's going to do something!" Raven snapped. "Be ready to run."

Fireboy put down his sack and rummaged inside, then pulled out a couple of small tools that Raven could barely see in the darkness. Brandishing them like a pair of daggers, he advanced on the door.

"What in blazes are you doing?" Raven demanded.

"Opening the door," he replied quietly.

"With those?" she demanded. "How? Splinter by splinter?"

"I'm a greasy mechanical," he said, applying the tools to the lock, "remember?"

Fireboy shoved, pried, twisted, and the lock gave a loud *clunk*. With a poke and a twist he eased another *clunk* out of it. Then, with a final twist and a satisfied grunt, he turned the handle and pulled the door open. Carver stumbled out into his arms.

"Slow down," Raven hissed. Then, grudgingly, "Nice work, Fireboy."

"Thank you," Carver whispered fervently. "Both of you." He held out his tied wrists. "I couldn't get loose! They took my knife!"

"We'll get you another one," Raven said hurriedly, struck by the despair in his voice.

"Hold still," Fireboy said. He dropped his tools into his bag and pulled out his own knife. A moment's sawing and Carver's hands were free. Carver rubbed his wrists, wincing, and thanked them again.

"Right, right," Raven snapped, hopping onto Carver's shoulder. "Let's get you out of here."

They crept back to the gateway and dashed across the opening. It was just as dark outside the wall as in, but Raven could feel the sky open around them. She drew in a deep breath. They hurried down the roadway till it forked. Fireboy went right, toward the river, but Raven stopped Carver.

Fireboy came back. "What's the matter?" he asked.

"That just goes back to the landing," Raven said. "Carver and I have to be a long way away by dawn."

"What about me?" Fireboy said.

"You go back and pretend you've been asleep all night."

"You're heading downriver, right? To Dunsgow?"

"Yes."

"Well, you won't get far on land," Fireboy said. "Baron'll have Hunter out with dogs and riders out as soon as they see you're gone."

"What are we supposed to do?" Raven snapped. "Swim?"

"We'll take *Sprite.*"

Raven and Carver both stared at him.

"You can't take the *Sprite,*" Carver said. "They'll never let you on a boat again."

"They tried that already," Fireboy muttered. "Now come on." He headed down the road.

"Steam-brained dolt," Raven muttered.

"What's going on?" Carver asked.

"Steward threw him off the water," she explained. "He's not a fireboy anymore. Better follow him, Monkey Boy. He looks determined to steal that blasted boat. Besides, he's right about the horses and dogs."

They hurried down the road to the landing, then crept past the dark lodging.

"We'll untie the ropes," Carver said.

"Not yet!" Fireboy hissed. "I've got to get steam up."

"How long is that going to take?" Raven demanded.

"Not long. About an hour."

"An hour?" Raven croaked.

"I can do it in less," Fireboy snapped. "Just stay out of my way." He hurried on board the *Water Sprite,* Carver at his heels.

Grumbling, Raven flew to the masthead and kept her eye on the lodging. She winced as the firebox door clanked open, then winced again as Fireboy shredded tinder and snapped kindling. The strike of the sparker seemed like an explosion, the rattle of coal an avalanche. But no one stirred on shore. The minutes stretched. Carver shuttled anxiously between the firebox and the railing. His footsteps sounded like drumbeats on the deck. Then the boiler started to tick and gurgle, louder than the chirping crickets. The night seemed to ring with boat sounds.

Raven flew down to Fireboy. "Can't you be more quiet?" she demanded.

"Not if you want steam."

She flew back to the masthead and tried to stay calm as the

ticks and gurgles grew. But the lodging stayed dark, and she started to relax a little.

Then there was a loud belch from beyond a warehouse. Raven heard stumbling footsteps that deepened as the feet lurched from the cartway to the wooden wharf. Carver ducked below the railing. Raven dropped to the deck to warn Fireboy. He froze, shovel in midswing. The footsteps came nearer. They heard muttering, punctuated by another loud belch.

"Bozer," Fireboy mouthed.

The boatman staggered onto the deck. ". . . throw me off my own boat," he muttered. "Fat-headed scut. That's what he is, scut. Thinks he runs the whole river." He stumbled into the side of the cabin, felt his way to the door, and lurched inside, still mumbling. There was a clank, a muffled curse, another belch. Then silence. Then a loud snore.

Fireboy relaxed and emptied the shovel into the firebox. "He's done for the night." He smiled grimly. "Then he can take a swim."

"How much longer?" Raven demanded.

"Another quarter hour."

Just then there was a loud cough from the cabin. Bozer burst from the door, groped for the rail, and heaved the contents of his stomach into the river. He coughed and heaved again. His retching shattered the night. A light sparked on in the lodging. A window banged open.

"Time's up!" Raven croaked.

"Carver, get the stern!" Fireboy shouted, running forward.

Bozer stopped retching and pushed himself off the rail. He turned to stare blearily at the running boys. Raven launched herself at him, talons aimed at his face. He threw up his hands and tumbled over the rail with a shriek, hitting the water with a satisfying splash. Raven turned and swooped to the bow. There was an angry call from the lodging.

"Hurry!" she croaked.

Fireboy freed his rope and pushed the bow away from the wharf.

He ran back to the engine and opened a valve, then scrambled up to the cabin top. Slowly, the water wheel began to churn. There was another shout from the lodge. The wheel churned harder. The bow swung out farther. The door of the lodge slammed open.

Raven flew at the figure running toward them and hit his head hard with her talons. He swore and tripped heavily, rolling in the dirt. It was the wharfmaster. Turning, she labored for altitude. But more men were coming from the lodge. The sound of barking hounds rose from the estate. Cursing, she swooped back to the *Sprite*.

Carver was still trying to untie the stern line, but the wheel was churning too hard and he couldn't get enough slack to slip the knot.

"They're almost here!" Raven croaked.

Carver strained at the knot, but it refused to let go. Then Fireboy ran up with an ax and cut the rope with one solid whack. They all lurched as the *Sprite* surged away.

Fireboy dropped the ax and sprinted toward the cabin. "Tend the fire!" he shouted back.

Carver ran for the engine. Raven flew back to the masthead. The *Sprite* just grazed the tow, then headed directly across the river. Fireboy reached the wheel and spun it. The current made the boat sway and heel. Behind them, a man sprinted along the wharf and made a flying leap for the *Sprite*. His hands caught the railing. He hung there, feet thrashing in the water as he tried to pull himself up. Raven swooped to the rail. It was the wharfmaster again, his gray face clenched in a furious snarl. She pecked hard, first one hand, then the other. He splashed into the river with a curse. Raven flew to the cabin top.

"Good work," she told Fireboy. "How soon before they can follow us?"

"Too soon. We're not near hot enough to keep up this speed." He looked at the dark sky. The moon glow was higher but still easterly. "How much longer before sunrise?" he asked.

"I don't know," Raven admitted.

Fireboy grimaced and hurried down the ladder; Raven flew

after. He turned a valve on the engine, and it slowed its labored pace.

"Hey!" Raven croaked.

"We've got to build up more steam," Fireboy said. He took the shovel and adjusted the bed of coals in the firebox, then handed the shovel back to Carver. "You're doing fine," he said. "Just don't smother it. I'd better go steer."

Raven watched him climb purposefully back to the cabin top. She watched Carver spread another small scoop of coal onto the fire. Feeling suddenly useless, she flew back to the masthead. They steamed on slowly for at least an hour, the wheel splashing monotonously. The air grew damp and chill. The clouds thickened, and the moonlight grew even more indistinct. Both banks were completely lost in the darkness, and Raven wondered how Fireboy could steer. Another hour crept by while Fireboy carefully tended the fire, slowly but steadily building up their speed. Then Raven heard something new. Only a difference in rhythm made it stand out from the sound of the splashing wheel. She cocked her head, hoping she was wrong. But it was there all right: another paddle wheel, still a distance behind but getting closer.

She flew to the cabin top. "Full speed ahead, Soot Brain. We're being followed."

Fireboy stared back through the darkness. "I don't hear anything," he said.

"It's there. I've got ears like a hawk, remember?"

"Blast," he muttered. "How'd they get steam up so fast?" He scurried down the ladder, twisted a couple of valves. The engine picked up, the wheel churned heavily, and the *Sprite* surged ahead, pushing a white line of froth at her bow. "You'd better hope the sun don't rise this morning," Fireboy said.

"Why not?"

"Once they can see us, they can shoot at us."

Thirteen

awn did come, slowly and gray. Gray clouds hung just above the plume of black smoke churning from the *Sprite*'s stack. Gray mist swirled along the water. The river was iron-plate gray. Carver even felt gray, inside and out. He was exhausted, sore, grimy with coal dust and ashes. He longed to stop shoveling, to dip his head in a bucket of water, rinse off his hands, curl up in a corner to sleep.

Only he couldn't. The pursuing boat was a white blotch in the gray behind them, topped by a line of black smoke that scratched at the gray ceiling. They had pulled ahead at first; far enough that they saw it only on long, straight reaches of river. But now it kept pace with them. If they slowed at all, they'd be caught.

Shortly after dawn, Fireboy came down to relieve Carver. "You go steer now it's light," he said, taking the shovel from Carver's aching hands. "My eyes are so tired from staring at nothing, shoveling will seem like a nap."

Carver hauled himself wearily up to the cabin top and took the wheel. The river stretched ahead of him, wide and gray, a broad curving swath under the clouds. Looking back at the pursuers, he could just make out a few tiny figures on the cabin top and at the bow.

"I've counted eight of the muck-eating stinkards," Raven said. She hunched on the cabin rail, looking thoroughly disgruntled. "There're probably more back at the engine. Working in shifts so they won't get tired."

"Do they have fire wands?" Carver asked, taking another look back.

"Arms, dolt," she grouched. "Fire*arms*. And yes, they have them." She looked up at the clouds and fluffed out her feathers grumpily, shedding a fine layer of mist. "With any luck, it's too damp to use them."

Carver had an idea. "Would rain help?" he asked.

Raven gave him a sour look. "Forget it, Fur Brain. All we need now is a good bolt of lightning right down the smokestack."

Carver's spirits sank even deeper. "Sorry."

"Blazing mages, it's not your fault!" Raven snapped. "You can't help it if you haven't had any training." Suddenly, she spread her wings. "I'm going for a closer look." She launched herself off the railing.

"Wait!" Carver yelled. "What about the fire wands?"

"Arms!" she croaked. "Can't you get anything right?"

She flapped toward the bank and disappeared behind the trees. Carver caught glimpses of her as she flew upriver. Down by the engine, Fireboy stopped shoveling and watched too. He looked at Carver with a big questioning shrug. Carver could only shake his head and shrug back. He hoped she would be careful but knew her too well to expect it.

Now they were approaching a bend to the left. The river was so wide, there was plenty of room to maneuver, but Carver remembered that sandbars usually formed on the insides of bends. He stayed well toward the right bank. Suddenly, Fireboy came scrambling up to the cabin top and swung the wheel to the left.

"You got to cut the corner as close as you can, Carver," he said. "These boats are alike as two peas. The one that goes the shortest way is going to win."

"Sorry," Carver said. "Maybe you should keep steering."

"No, we got to take turns or we're going to wear out. Then they'll catch us for sure."

Carver thought they didn't have much chance anyway, but he kept it to himself. The other boat was just slipping out of sight behind the curve of the bank. There was no sign of Raven. He felt his stomach twist.

"Just watch the water closely," Fireboy said, stepping away from the wheel. "If there's a bar, you'll see ripples, maybe branches sticking up, maybe even see the bottom. Go as close as you can, all right?"

"All right," Carver said.

Then both of them froze at the crack of a shot. They looked back upriver, but the other boat was still hidden by the bend. The plume of black smoke reached above the trees, marking its progress. They searched the tree line. There was still no sign of Raven.

Suddenly, the *Sprite* gave a slight jolt, and something bumped along her bottom. Carver and Fireboy both spun around, grabbed the wheel, and swung it right, away from the nearing bank. Something clattered under the paddles. The *Sprite* seemed to skip a beat, then churned back up to speed.

"Must've been a small floater," Fireboy said, wiping his face.

"Sorry," Carver said again. "I should have been watching."

Fireboy nodded distractedly. They both looked upriver. It was still empty.

"Blast," Carver muttered. "Where is she?"

"Maybe she . . ." Fireboy didn't finish the sentence. They stared in silence, each with one hand clenched on the wheel.

Suddenly, there was a loud croak from right above. Carver jerked his head up so fast, he hurt his neck. Raven came soaring down and landed heavily on the railing.

"You're slowing down!" she snapped. "One of you dolts get down and shovel!"

"Where have you been?" Fireboy demanded.

"What happened?" Carver asked at the same time.

"The cowpile missed," Raven said. "And I didn't stay around to give them another chance. Now, get down there and shovel coal!"

"Blazing mages!" Fireboy said. Shaking his head, he scrambled down the ladder and ran back to the firebox.

Carver turned his attention to steering, but he couldn't help frowning at Raven. "That was a stupid thing to try," he said.

"Well, now we know their blasted powder's dry."

"You could have been killed."

"Kah! Not likely. I can see when the piss pots start to pull the trigger."

"All eight of them? All at once?"

"They don't all have firearms, Monkey Boy. Besides, there's twelve of them."

"That's great news," Carver said. "They won't even work up a sweat."

Raven clacked her beak.

The race went on throughout the morning, and they began to lose ground. Carver steered as close to the inside banks as he dared, but the pilot on the other boat was better. Finally, on a long straightaway, Carver went down and took the shovel from Fireboy.

"You'd better steer," he said. "I'll stick to shoveling."

Fireboy looked at him closely. "You sure?"

"It's getting too easy to see their faces," Carver said, digging the shovel deep into the mound of coal.

"Oh." Fireboy hesitated, then went forward. He was back in a minute with some bread, a small apple, and a mug of water. "Make sure you eat," he said. Then he hurried up the ladder.

Carver felt too tired to eat, but he also felt weak. He threw another shovelful of coal into the firebox, then reluctantly bit into the apple. The next thing he knew, he was licking the last of the bread off his fingers and wishing there were more. He drank a last gulp of water and went back to shoveling. He had more energy, but now he felt starved.

Fireboy did a better job of keeping their lead, but still the other boat gained. They churned around bends, hugging the bank. Several times they bounced over mud banks or scraped against the reaching branches of fallen trees. Twice they plowed through small towns, sending a huge wake splashing up against the wharves and the boats. The second time, Fireboy had to swerve to avoid a ferry in midstream and almost swamped it. Carver could see the frightened faces of the passengers as they barreled past. He hoped the ferry would be well away when the chasing boat charged through.

By evening, Carver was dazed with fatigue. His arms were heavy and stiff as water-soaked rugs. His stomach ached. Still he shoveled. He had a bigger worry now than sore arms or hunger: The pile of coal was getting low. Then he heard the crack of a firearm.

He ducked instinctively. Nothing happened, so he stood up straight, reasoning that he was shielded by the wheel and the mass of the engine. He ducked again at the sound of a second shot. He looked up and saw Fireboy crouched on the cabin top, staring back toward their pursuers. When he noticed Carver staring at him, Fireboy stood and shouted down.

"We're still out of range. They're just worried it's getting dark."

But the next crack was followed by a woody *chunk* in one of the paddles. The *Sprite* gave no sign she'd noticed, but Fireboy winced and ran down to look at the wheel more closely.

"Lucky shot," he told Carver as he ran back by. "They can't hurt her that far away."

As it got darker, the shots became more frequent. There were more *chunk*s, and Carver added broken paddle blades to his list of worries. He prayed for nightfall, but the long gray twilight stretched on. Fireboy crouched in front of the wheel and steered over his shoulder. Raven hunched beside him. Then a splinter hummed past Carver's head. A shot hit the side of the cabin. Another struck the railing and ricocheted through the side cabin window in a shower of glass. They needed night fast, but it just wasn't coming.

Carver threw down the shovel and ran into the cabin. He fumbled around blindly in the gloom, feeling on the shelves and the bunks for his bundle. He finally found it wedged far under Fireboy's bunk. Dragging it out, he rushed back on deck just as another shot clanged on something in the engine and screamed away. His stomach churned.

"Shovel!" Fireboy yelled down. "They're gaining!"

Carver didn't answer. He yanked open his bundle and groped inside. The wand was there at the top, wrapped in its linen. He pulled it out, shook off the cloth, and clasped the smooth branch in his shaking hand. He stared at it a moment. He hadn't held or even looked at it since Nuatta's death. He felt a moment of fear and uncertainty. Then the familiar tingling sparked in his palm. Energy seemed to pulse up his arm. His heart strengthened.

Raven dropped to the deck beside him. "What the blazes are you doing?" she squawked.

"Making it darker," Carver said.

He held the wand high and stared up into the mass of cloud hanging so low above them. This was different from the first time he had used the wand. Here was raw material, a great slab of soaked cloud ready to pour down. He just had to make the right hole.

"Don't be a—" Raven began, but there was another crack, another *chunk.* "All right," she said. "Blast the dungherds if you can."

"Just hope for rain," Carver said.

He blanked out Raven and concentrated on the wand. He tried to envision rain, great sheets of pouring rain. He tried to envision the clouds massing, surging, tearing open like a sheet of rotten fabric. He stabbed the wand upward and slashed across the sky. A shock trembled his arm. The clouds swirled and bunched. A canyon opened above him. He could see clear sky.

"No!" he shouted, and he swung the wand again, teasing the edges closed, willing the clouds to thicken. The tingling grew on his arm. He recognized the feeling, knew what would come if he couldn't control it. He gritted his teeth, took the wand in both hands, and swirled it round and round, drawing the clouds lower. A line of drops showered onto him. He pushed them aft with the wand, over the splashing paddles and into the growing darkness astern. He swirled the wand again, cutting out another line of shower, sending it back toward the pursuing boat. The air grew thick with damp. Water dripped from every surface. But still it didn't rain.

Exhausted, Carver dropped his arms. Black gloom almost blinded him.

"I'm sorry," he said. It seemed all he said today was *sorry*.

"What for?" Raven said.

"I couldn't do it. I couldn't make it rain."

"That's all right. Fog is fine."

Carver looked up. Soft gray walls enclosed the *Sprite* in a strangely quiet world. The clouds had settled on the surface of the river. And it was getting darker every second. There were no more shots.

Relief flooded Carver's body. He almost collapsed on the deck. But Fireboy came hurrying through the gloom. He grabbed the shovel and began heaping coal into the firebox.

"We can't keep going all night," he said between shovelfuls. "Not enough coal. Can't see to steer anyway. That's all right," he added quickly, seeing Carver's look of dismay. "They can't either. But I got an idea. We're gonna jump off. Swim to shore. Sneak away overland."

"They can track us on horseback," Raven said.

"We'll give them something else to think about," Fireboy said, carefully shaping his fire. "Quick now; Carver, you get up top. Keep us in the channel. Can you do it?"

"I'll try."

"Raven, you go help. Be ready to jump when I yell."

"What about you?"

"I'm going to prepare a surprise."

He flashed a strained grin and kept shoveling.

Standing at the wheel with the fog streaming past his face as the *Sprite* rushed on in darkness was as bad as getting shot at. Carver strained his eyes and ears, trying to tell where the channel ran. He started at every shadow, every swirl in the fog. Raven hopped up to his shoulder and added her eyes to his.

"Watch out! Right! Go right!"

"I am! Shut up!"

Then Fireboy hurried back up the ladder. He gave the wheel a slight turn to the left, then set it straight again.

"Come on!" he whispered. "Time to jump!"

They tumbled to the deck. Carver grabbed his bundle. Fireboy pushed him to the rail.

"Swim as quietly as you can," he said, still whispering. "Keep the current hard on your right side and stay close so we don't get separated. All right? Go!"

Together they dropped over the side and kicked furiously to get wide of the paddle wheel. Even so, the wake slapped Carver hard. He swallowed a big chunk of river and gagged. Fireboy grabbed his arm and pulled him along. Raven flew ahead and came back, ahead and back, keeping pace with them silently.

The *Sprite* churned quickly out of sight. Her splashing progress, muffled by the fog, quickly grew dim. But very soon, Carver heard the splashing of the other boat. He and Fireboy slowed, trying to stay as quiet as possible as it passed by them more than halfway across the river. They pushed on, helped briefly by its wake. Then Carver's hands hit mud and he was pulling himself and his sodden bundle awkwardly through the shallows. Clinging together in the dark, he and Fireboy slogged out of the water and stumbled up a steep, brushy bank.

Just as they reached the top, the *Water Sprite* blew up.

Fourteen

Carver jumped at the sound, a sharp, hideous boom that ended in a long, fading wail even the fog couldn't muffle.

"What was that?" he asked, grabbing Fireboy's arm.

"*Sprite*'s whistle."

"She blew up?" He stared at the red glow across the river and far downstream. "Mages save us, we got off just in time!"

"I blew her up," Fireboy said.

Carver looked at him sharply. Fireboy's face was turned away.

"They'll be looking for us down there," he went on in a low voice. "Looking for our bodies in the water. They won't look over here for a while. Come on."

He pulled away and stumbled between the trees that lined the bank. Carver took another look at the fire. Raven settled on his shoulder.

"Get moving, Monkey Boy," she said. "He bought us a little time. Don't waste it."

"But why?" Carver wondered.

"If they'd caught us, he'd have lost the boat anyway. Assuming they didn't kill us first."

Carver shook his head sadly and plodded after Fireboy.

There was a narrow field beyond the trees, and beyond that a road. Fireboy turned onto the road and began walking downstream without a word.

"Wait a minute," Carver said. "We'll walk right into them."

"If you want to get to Dunsgow, we got to go downstream," Fireboy said.

"I think maybe we want to go sideways first. How far are we from First Falls?"

"A couple days on the river. Walking? I don't know."

"All the rivers come together at First Falls, right?"

"Yes, at the lake above the falls."

"Then it can't be that far across the hills here to the next river, right?"

Fireboy stared at him as if he was crazy. "Go across the mountains?" he said. "Nobody goes across the mountains."

"Why not?" Carver asked.

"It's the high reach," he said. "People don't go there."

"So it's the last place they'll look. What do you think, Raven?"

She clacked her beak. "Not a bad idea, for a monkey. Lead on."

"All right?" Carver asked Fireboy.

He shrugged. "I just know the river. You're the boss on land."

Carver led them off the road and across the field on the other side. As they got farther from the river, the fog lifted, and they were able to make good time. Then it started to rain. Raven cursed.

Carver sighed. If only it had come when he'd ordered it. "At least it'll wash out our scent," he said, trying to sound cheerful. The others didn't reply.

They plodded onward through deepening gloom. Mud clung to their boots. Raven seemed to grow heavy with water, and Carver's shoulder, already aching from the long bout of shoveling, began to burn with pain. He asked her to change sides. Fireboy offered to carry her instead.

"You're both so tired, you're about to fall down," Raven said. "We need to find someplace to rest awhile."

"Not yet," Carver said. "We've got to get across these fields."

Finally, they stumbled against a low stone wall dividing the muddy fields from a dripping copse of trees. Carver and Fireboy helped each other clamber over the wall and in among the straight trunks. Carver sank down in the vee between two gnarled roots, hunched his back against the trunk, and was asleep almost instantly.

He awoke in dim light, sore, cramped, and still blindingly tired.

Fireboy lay beside him, head slumped on Carver's shoulder. Carver shifted slightly, but Fireboy didn't make a sound, and Carver slipped back into sleep.

When he woke again, it was much brighter. Fireboy had slid down and was lying with his head pillowed on a root. The rain had stopped.

"Raven?" Carver whispered, looking up into the trees.

"I'm here," she said from somewhere among the leaves.

"See anything?"

"I took a look a few minutes ago. No sign of the stinkards on our trail."

"How about the hills? How far are they?"

"Close enough. I could fly there in an hour." She clacked her beak. "Another night's hike for you mud huggers."

Carver's stomach growled at him. "Any sign of food?" he asked, without much hope.

"Here," she said.

Leaves rustled, and a well-pecked loaf of bread fell into Carver's lap. It smelled wonderful. Saliva filled his mouth. He tore off a chunk and stuffed it in.

"Where did you get that?" Fireboy was up on one elbow, staring at the loaf as if it were a five-course feast conjured by a food mage. Carver passed it over, and Fireboy bit off a huge mouthful.

"There's a farmhouse back toward the river," Raven said, dropping into view on the lowest branch. "Someone left the kitchen door open while they went out to the privy."

Carver gulped down his bite half chewed. "They didn't see you, did they?"

"Don't worry, chicken heart, I made use of a handy collection of crows."

Carver did worry, all through the day. Fireboy and Raven dozed on and off, but he was too sore and anxious. In late afternoon, they made their way to the far side of the copse and saw the hills rising beyond the last fields. The clouds had lifted, and the hills looked reasonably small, particularly compared with the mountains that had bordered the reach above his hometown. He felt confident they could cross into the other valley. By daybreak, they were climbing the first steep rise. Raven flew ahead, looking for a place to hide. She found a thick stand of pines with a soft bed of brown needles completely hidden from the outside. It was also thick with mosquitoes, but Carver pulled out his damp cloak and gave his spare shirt to Fireboy. Swathed against the whining swarms, they managed to sleep for a while.

They headed out that afternoon in broad daylight, after Raven had scouted the area and declared it safe. They hiked steadily until darkness. The evening was chilly, and they risked a small fire, then continued at dawn after a meager breakfast of flower shoots and tree buds that Raven said were safe to eat but that tasted like peppered grass and bitter pitch. A day later, they scrambled up the last rocky ledge to the height of land.

"Which river is that?" Carver asked, looking ahead.

"The River Down," Fireboy said, looking back at the River Slow, just visible between two slanting ridges. He turned to follow Carver's gaze. "I've never been this high before in my life."

"Nice, isn't it?" Raven said.

After two more days, they came off the hills into leagues of grapevines staked neatly in long rows that ran toward the distant line of the River Down. Following the rows along the rolling downs, they came out on a bluff above the blue swirling water. This river was much more narrow and winding than the River Slow. Its banks were steep and ledgy, the water deep and strong. Raven flew downstream to scout.

"Now, if we just had *Sprite* . . . ," Fireboy said. He stopped with a catch in his throat and sat forlornly on the rough grass at the edge of the bluff.

Carver sat beside him. "You saved our lives back there," he said. "You and the *Sprite*."

Fireboy shrugged.

"Come with us to Dunsgow," Carver said. "I'll bet you can find a boat to work on there."

"There'll never be another like *Sprite*," Fireboy said. He stared at the river, blinking hard.

Carver opened his bundle and dug inside. At the very bottom he found the lump of carved coal he had put there just before they'd arrived at Cutter's Landing. He held it out to Fireboy.

"Here," he said. "I made this for you. It isn't quite done yet. I was going to give it to you when . . . whenever we said goodbye back there. But that didn't happen, so . . ." He trailed off. "It's a thank-you," he said finally.

It was the *Water Sprite*, as near as Carver could make her with coal and a heavy kitchen knife. The smooth black surfaces flashed like dark mirrors. Fireboy frowned. He reached up and took it almost reluctantly. He held it stiffly and turned it around, looked at the bottom and both sides; the blunt bow; the paddle wheel at the stern; the tiny firebox and boiler.

"It's not really finished," Carver said again, feeling foolish. He wondered what had made him think a simple model could ever replace the real thing.

"She was beautiful," Fireboy said.

"She was."

"The best on the river."

"Because she was your boat."

Fireboy looked up at Carver. For the first time in days, he smiled. "I guess I can find a boat I can work on in Dunsgow," he said, "but I'll never forget her."

He cradled the model in his hands while they waited for Raven. When she finally returned, triumphantly carrying not only half a loaf of bread but the better end of a sausage as well, he set the model gently on the grass. After they'd demolished the food, he carefully wiped his hands before picking it up again. He held it out to Carver.

"I don't have any good way to carry it," he said. "You'd better keep it in your bundle. Besides, I imagine you're going to want to finish it."

"I will," Carver promised. Then he frowned "As soon as I can get a knife."

Immediately, Fireboy pulled something out of his pouch and pushed it into Carver's hand. "Take mine," he said. "I don't need it half as much as you do."

Carver looked dumbly at the object in his hand. It appeared to be a knife handle, but there was no blade, just a ridge of steel set in a groove along its length. "The blade's missing," he said.

"It's a folder," Fireboy explained. "Boy, you really are from up-river." He took it and snapped the blade out, then folded it back in. "See? So you can keep it in your pouch."

Carver took it again and pulled it open. The blade snapped into place with a satisfying click. It was smaller than his old knife but fit his palm well. He checked the edge with his thumb; it was good steel. He tried to say thank you, but his throat was clogged by a huge lump. He could only smile. Fireboy grinned back.

Raven clacked her beak. "It doesn't take much to excite you two monkeys, does it?"

They headed downriver along the bluffs and soon came to a road that meandered through the vineyards. In the evening, they made camp in a wooded ravine cut by a sparkling stream. Raven went foraging and returned with more bread and a lump of cheese.

"Crows are easy when there's food involved," she said.

"The local flock is going to get a bad reputation," Carver remarked, mouth full.

"Everybody hates crows anyway," Fireboy said. "Even other birds."

"They're not so bad," Raven said. "Sometimes they can be a lot of fun."

"I suppose so," Fireboy said. "If you like gangs of greedy cowards who don't know when to shut up."

"You mean like people?"

"Aren't crows just little ravens?"

"Aren't people just big monkeys?"

They continued downriver, through more vineyards, around villages, across rocky pastures filled with goats. The countryside stayed ragged and rolling, the river quick and winding. There was always some hollow or copse to hide in at night, and Raven kept them supplied with a variety of stolen food. Occasionally, they hid from wagons, some carrying great jugs of oil and barrels of olives, others with cask after cask of wine. Finally, Raven returned from a scouting flight to say that she'd seen the big lake where the five rivers came together above First Falls.

"That's not the lake yet," Fireboy said. "It's the Stoney-Slow. The Stoney River and the Slow come together just upstream. Then the Down comes in here, at Downrun, then the Hurry, then the Wynde. That's where the lake starts."

"Well, it's big enough to be a lake already," Raven said. "We'll be there in a couple of days."

She and Fireboy both looked at Carver expectantly.

"We'll be able to get a boat there, right?" he said. "We'll offer to work our way down to First Falls. Then we'll hike down the cliff and find another boat to Dunsgow."

Fireboy grimaced. "I don't think it's going to be that easy."

Late the next day they came to a sudden drop, where the river tumbled through a series of violent cataracts. There was a low dam at the top, diverting water into a canal that descended in nine deep locks to the town of Downrun at the river mouth. From the top of the towpath, they could see the wide Stoney-Slow. Lines of boats waited at both ends of the canal: flatboats, steamboats, skiffs, and tows. At the bottom, wagons, donkeys, and people filled the streets of Downrun and bustled up the alleys and steps that climbed the hillsides.

Raven flew off, soaring high, where she could keep them in sight but not be obvious herself. Carver and Fireboy made their way down to the town, blending into the thickening crowd. There were crafters in rough clothing, porters with bundles on their heads, well-to-do merchants in bright cloaks, beggars limping on crutches, vendors with pushcarts and huge baskets. There were grayfolk, too, like Fireboy, and some with olive-colored faces and others with ivory skin and bright red hair—it was more fuss and people and strangeness than Carver had ever seen before.

There were shops that sold a tantalizing array of foods. The smells made Carver's stomach churn. He was tempted to swipe a piece of fruit or bread, but decided it was too risky after he saw a sharp-eyed shopkeeper land a solid blow on the back of a hapless beggar who'd wandered too close to his wares. Then Fireboy bumped into him, apparently by accident, leaving a warm pastry in his palm. Carver shook his head but swallowed his guilt with the food.

The sun dropped farther, till the streets were barred with lines of shadow and light. The crowd thickened again as laborers began to make their way home up the sides of the valley. The vendors did a brisk business, hawking their foodstuffs in ringing cries. An old blind man led by a ragged child confronted Carver and begged for a few spare coins. The people spoke with a musical accent that made Carver realize how very far he was from home.

Finally, they came to a district of warehouses and taverns built right out onto the wharves along the river. Carver stared hopefully at the mass of watercraft there, wondering if they could arrange a passage before night fell. He made his way over to Fireboy to ask what would be the most likely boat to approach.

"Nothing with Cutter's bull on it," Fireboy said. "Or any emblem. Something plain."

"How about that one?" Carver asked, pointing out a smallish flatboat marked only by peeling paint and worn wood.

"Too shabby," Fireboy said. "Probably only works the Down."

They went on, discussing and rejecting various boats, till they came to the mouth of the river. Carver stared in awe at the great rolling expanse of the Stoney-Slow. The Down swirled into it, blending blue into the iron-gray current. He peered downstream, trying to spot the entrance of the Hurry River on the opposite bank, and stumbled right into Fireboy.

"Sorry," he said, but Fireboy grabbed his arm and started pulling him around the corner.

"What—?" Carver began. Fireboy hissed for silence and pointed up the wharf.

One of Baron Cutter's steamboats was moored there, and standing on the deck was Bozer.

Fifteen

Carver followed Fireboy into the shelter of a doorway around the corner.

"Do you think he saw us?"

"I don't think so." They were both whispering, despite the building and the wide wharf between them and Bozer.

"Do you think he's searching for us?"

"Bozer?" Fireboy curled his lip. "They wouldn't trust Bozer with that. He's just steering the boat. But probably for a bunch of baronsmen."

They both peered up and down the street, and Carver scanned the strip of sky overhead.

"Blast!" he said. "I wonder where Raven is. We could use a scout now."

They hurried up the street and took the next alley leading away from the wharf. The crowd had thinned as the day waned, so they kept to back passageways, heading into the steep neighborhoods on the hillsides. Twice they saw baronsmen in the distance.

"Those are Baron Vintner's men," Fireboy said. "This is her valley."

They still kept their distance. They were peering around a corner to check for uniforms when Raven landed on a signboard right over their heads. Both of them jumped.

"Don't do that!" Fireboy whispered. "You nearly scared the pants off me."

"That would be an ugly sight," she croaked. "What are you two skulking around for?"

"We almost ran into Bozer down on the wharf," Carver said.

"Bozer?"

"That's right," Fireboy said. "Where were you? You're supposed to be keeping watch."

"I got mobbed by pair of falcons nesting in the cliff," Raven snapped. "I'm lucky I've still got eyes, let alone tail feathers."

"Well, we're lucky we're not on the way to the farm!"

"Calm down!" Carver said. "We're still in one piece and we aren't caught yet. Now, let's find a place to hide tonight."

Muttering under her breath, Raven made a low flight through the deepening twilight while Carver and Fireboy continued up the alleyways. They finally found a niche under an arched stairway where the buildings perched like mud-swallow nests on the steep hillside. Fireboy produced a battered meat pie from under his tunic for dinner. They wolfed it down, then huddled on Carver's cloak and tried to come up with a plan.

"Disguises," Raven said. "You need some kind of disguises."

"Like what?"

"You could smudge your face gray and get some different clothes. Get a hat to cover your hair. They're looking for a white boy and a gray boy—you could both be grayfolk instead."

"There's a lot more white boys walking around loose. Two gray boys would stand out," Fireboy said.

"We can paint Carver gray with soot, Steam Brain. How are we going to paint you white?"

"What about you?" Carver said. "You can't just paint your face and throw on a cloak."

"I'm a bird. I'm not stuck on the ground with you two."

"No, but you're big and black and very obvious. If they see a lone raven soaring around up there, they're going to look for us down here."

"Maybe you could hide under Carver's cloak," Fireboy said.

Raven clacked her beak. "Nobody's stuffing me under anything, Muck Worm."

"Right," Fireboy said. "We'll just paint you brown and pretend you're a duck."

"And you can shave your head and pretend you're a horse turd."

"Hush!" Carver said. "We're tired. We'll think of something in the morning."

But Carver fretted most of the night. He lay there replaying the day's events in his mind, still amazed at the size of the town and the crowds. Then the memory of the beggars gave him an idea. At first light, he woke Raven and Fireboy to tell them.

"I'll dress up like a blind man, and Fireboy can be my guide."

"That might work, I guess," Fireboy said.

"We'll need old, ragged clothes," Carver went on, "and Fireboy will need a hat. I'll cover my eyes with a rag."

"What about Raven?" Fireboy said. "Is she just going to ride on your shoulder?"

"Sort of," Carver said. "I'm going to be a hunchback."

"Hunchback?" Raven said. "More like hunch brain! I told you last night I wasn't getting stuffed under some dirty cloak."

"You won't be wrapped up," he explained, remembering how she had panicked at their first meeting. "We'll get a basket and tie it to my shoulders. You'll have room under there. And," he added quickly, "you'll be my voice."

"What?" Raven and Fireboy both said together.

"You'll be my voice. I'll keep my head down in my cowl, and you'll do the talking for me."

"Why in the five rivers would I do that?" Raven demanded.

"Because you think fast. You've got a quicker tongue than me."

"That part's right, at least," Fireboy said.

Carver could see that Raven was pleased by the compliment. "It's just till we get down the falls," he said. "And whenever we're out of sight, you can put your head out."

"Of all the stupid . . . ," Raven muttered.

"Please," Carver said. "We'll never be able to do it without you."

130

"Oh, all right, Monkey Boy," she said. "But the minute I say 'out,' you let me out, or I'll rip your fat ears off."

"Absolutely."

They set right to work finding old clothes before the town woke up. They were on the edge of the poor district that clung to the side of the valley, and Raven quickly found a line hung with clothes three stories up across an alley. While Fireboy kept watch, she plucked them off and dropped them into Carver's waiting arms. Carver, with a twinge of regret, left Aunt Singer's good cloak and his spare shirt behind in exchange.

Finding a usable basket took longer. Beggars had scoured the alleys behind the shops, taking every discarded item that wasn't complete trash. And Raven insisted on a clean basket. Finally, after three rejects and leagues of alleyways, they found a good one outside the back door to an apothecary. Carver suspected it had just been set there by someone who expected to reclaim it momentarily, but he stifled his sense of guilt and raced off after Fireboy, basket clutched to his chest.

In another alley down by the wharves, they put the pieces of their disguise together.

"What a minute," Fireboy said, holding up the garment Raven had nabbed for him. "This isn't a tunic, it's a dress!"

"If I can squeeze under that basket, you can wear a dress," Raven said. "Besides, sweetie, there's a pretty cap to go with it."

"I can't wear this!"

"Yes, you can," Carver said, wincing at the wretched clothes he would have to wear himself. "They're looking for two boys, not a girl leading a blind hunchback."

Grumbling, Fireboy put on the dress and cap. They might have just been washed, but they were stained and threadbare. Carver tore a strip from the tattered hem of his cloak and made a bandage to wrap around his eyes. Then he took out the knife and cut Fireboy's old tunic into strips to tie the basket onto his back.

"Blazing mages!" Raven croaked. "I can't fit under that."

"If I can wear this dress . . . ," Fireboy said.

"Go eat muck," Raven replied. But she let him put her under the basket and kept quiet as he pulled the cloak over Carver's shoulders and adjusted it. They found that she could peek out from under the cowl if Carver hunched up his shoulders enough.

"Can you breathe?" Carver asked.

"Barely," she muttered.

"You'll have to speak louder than that," Fireboy said.

"How's this, Monkey Breath?" Raven snapped.

"Ouch!" Carver said. "My ears!"

They practiced talking for a little while, with Fireboy coaching Carver on how to hold his head and move his mouth.

"I guess it'll work," he said finally. "Let's go."

But Raven needed a breath of fresh air first. From the way she was clutching his tunic under the basket, Carver knew she was fighting to stay calm. He didn't rush her, and finally she ducked back under by herself. He pulled the bandage over his eyes and held out his hand. Fireboy slung Carver's bundle over his shoulder and led the way onto the wharf.

Carver could see a little bit through the rough fabric of the bandage, but it was awful not being able to talk. Fireboy would lead them to a boat and call out in a reedy voice, asking if they could ride down to First Falls. Then Raven would say a few words for Carver. The first few times, it went so badly the boatmen chased them off for the frauds they were. Eventually, they worked out a routine, so each knew what to say and when it should be said. On the twelfth try, it worked. The boatman was a softspoken man with a son and daughter as crew, heading to First Falls with a load of olives and oil for Dunsgow.

Soon the boat was moving out of the Down and into the Stoney-Slow. The swift current took them rapidly downstream, boatman and son working long sweeps while the daughter steered. By midday they had passed the confluence with the Hurry. Then they passed the Wynde, and the hills dropped away, revealing the lake in its giant bowl, four leagues across at least, and four times that long. The boatman and his son put down their sweeps and hoisted a long spar to the masthead, unrolling a broad triangular sail. It caught the favoring wind and sped them along in a ruffle of wake. There were sails all over the lake, and plumes of smoke from a dozen steamboats. At the far end, bright in the afternoon sun, was the sharp edge of the reach.

They arrived at First Falls at twilight. The town sprawled a great way along a thin lip of rock on the right bank of the lake at the very edge of the falls. And the falls stretched in a long, long jagged line marked by a perpetual rising mist shot through with rainbows. Carver, who had been amazed at Upperfall, was amazed again. The world never stopped growing.

They landed at a set of wharves some distance from the edge. With a quick thank-you, Fireboy led Carver off into the darkening streets. Keeping a close eye out for baronsmen, they found a hiding place in a rundown district. They slept with rats and cats again, but at least the ground was flat. The next morning, Raven and Fireboy filched some food—Carver didn't ask where—and they set off for the falls.

"What is it like?" Carver asked, as Fireboy led them toward the constant roar.

"Big," Fireboy replied. "Very big."

Big it was, mind-stopping big. Carver peered from under his bandage at the immeasurable sheet of water that spilled out of the lake and fell in a solid, pulsing wall toward the lower reach, far below. It wasn't as high as the Middle Fall, but it was so much broader, stretching a league or more. The town vibrated constantly. Everything was damp with a fine mist that lifted back up the cliff face. And the noise filled Carver's chest.

They made their way along the walled edge. There was no path they could hike down; everything was lowered by steam-powered gantries that puffed gouts of black smoke into the misty air. The platform under every gantry held mounds of crates, barrels, bales, baskets, jugs, logs, coal, ore, stone—every imaginable container and product. A few passengers accompanied the goods. Among them walked baronsmen in the five colors of the rivers. And there were other uniforms too: the gold braid of Duke Kovac's guarda. They watched the loading and unloading with bored faces.

Carver squinted through his bandage at the crowd milling before the nearest gantry. "How do we get down?" he whispered.

"I don't know," Fireboy replied.

Raven had been peering out from behind Carver's neck. "Go up to that beefy lout there," she said, indicating one of the Duke's men. "Let me do the talking."

Fireboy grimaced and shambled forward.

"Excuse me, lord," Raven said in a wheezy voice. "Are you from below?"

The man smiled condescendingly. "I am, old fool."

Carver smiled vaguely past the man's shoulder, then let his head droop, nodding.

"I thought as much," Raven said. "I told the girl to find a man who looked above the rest, a man of matter. Tell me, lord, do you know the great mage?"

"I know of him," the man replied.

"I knew it!" Raven said. "I could feel you were that elevated. Is it true, then? Is it true he can cure the lame and . . . and the blind?"

Her voice shook with hope. Stifling a smile, Carver reached out imploringly.

The man watched Carver's hand, careful that it didn't get too close. "So I've heard," he said with a mean smile. "I've never witnessed it myself, but I know some who have."

"It is true!" Raven said, and Carver gripped Fireboy's shoulder in feigned joy. "We have not come all this way in vain. Tell me," she implored, "where do we go to get down? Point the way for my girl. She is my eyes."

"That's easy enough, old fool," the man said. "Just hand me the fare and you can walk straight ahead onto the platform."

"The fare?" Raven asked. "What fare?"

"The fare to ride down."

"I . . . I see," Raven croaked.

"I'm sure you do see," the guarda said, sneering. "Now, move along before I have you hauled off to the lockhouse!"

Fireboy hurried away, Carver stumbling along behind.

"Now what?" Carver asked, when they had put some of the crowd between themselves and the guarda.

Fireboy squared his shoulders. "There's more than one lift," he said. "Come on."

He led Carver farther along the cliff, while Raven muttered crossly under the cloak.

"Quiet!" Fireboy whispered. He studied the crowd in front of the next gantry. Three merchants were arguing with the guarda, while a team of porters shifted a good-sized stack of barrels onto the platform. Four men came up, each straining at one corner of a huge crate.

"Right?" he said.

"Right," Carver agreed.

Together, they scooted forward, putting the crate between themselves and the guarda. In a moment, they were on the platform, crouched among the barrels. A minute later, the merchants came on with a few other passengers, and the lift began to descend. Carver and Fireboy shared a huge grin.

Raven groused under the basket until Carver hunched his shoulders so she could see out. They all fell silent at the view. The river flowed away from the broad pool at the base of the falls, cutting through a flat and surprisingly short reach. It had just enough length to sweep slightly right and back left again before it branched into a narrow, many-fingered delta. Beyond that lay the sea. Carver gaped at the expanse of water that stretched on and on to the distant curve of the horizon. It made the lake above them seem as insignificant as a puddle.

As they dropped lower, he noticed a grimy cloud hovering at

the very mouth of the river. There lay Dunsgow, a broken, sprawling jumble of gray buildings that spanned several channels of the delta. A winding wall enclosed most of it, but here and there buildings broke loose, like dirt spilling from a cracked basket. Jutting above the sprawl were dozens of tall chimneys, each one spewing smoke and steam into the yellow-gray cloud. And the river, which flowed blue-brown up to the city's wharves and canals, came out gray, staining the sea for leagues beyond the shoreline.

The platform came down by a canal that led around the bottom pool of the falls and into the quieter water downstream. A Duke's man waved them off into a melee of passengers converging from all the lifts, and they simply kept to the center as it flowed past the cargo boats and onto a small passenger steamer bound for the city. Fireboy almost gave them away by stopping suddenly to stare at the small engine sitting in a central well, but Carver pushed him onward to the opposite rail.

"Did you see that tiny engine?" Fireboy said; then he stiffened.

"What?" Carver demanded, heart racing.

"There's no wheel! This boat doesn't have a paddle wheel!"

"So?" Raven croaked.

"So how does it go?" Fireboy went to the stern and peered down into the water. He came back mystified. "I can't see how it goes!"

By whatever magic, it went. The boatman let blast a shrill whistle that joined the deeper wails of cargo steamboats as they jockeyed down the canal toward the river. Carver squinted anxiously through his bandage. Raven was growing restless under the basket, whispering curses at the slow progress of the boat. She seemed to weigh as much as a small pig, and Carver's shoulders ached from the prolonged hunching. A young woman dressed like a laborer came near and pretended to study the shoreline, but she seemed to be studying them more, from the corner of her eye. Carver's anxiety grew.

The passage down to Dunsgow took them through worn farmland marred by frequent diggings. Both banks were ragged and overgrown. In places, debris spilled over the banks and into the shallows, to form untidy jetties of slag, rubble, broken brick, and rusted iron. The bent wheel on an overturned, half-drowned cart spun slowly in the current. As they approached the city, the sunlight yellowed, filtered by the dirty cloud spewing from the multitude of chimneys. An acrid, burned odor overpowered the earthy smell of the river. Carver wished he could sit down. The edge of the basket cut more and more into his back.

They went past the first spike of wharves and factories, then turned into one of several small canals that branched off toward the nearing mass of buildings. Carver lifted the bandage and stared in amazement at the grimy wall looming ahead of them. It was made of closely fitted stone, stained and pitted by years in the city's rank air. The top was capped by a massive chain, with dark links as big around as his body. It stretched to the right as far as he could see; to the left, a knot of men worked at a portable forge set up on the wall top. In the din of iron on iron, they beat another massive link onto the chain. For some reason, the sight made his stomach churn. He felt exhausted.

Then the boat tucked under a shadowed archway in the wall. Carver cringed at the sudden chill. It seemed to squeeze his heart, and for a moment, he thought he was going to throw up. Raven squawked in alarm. The weight on his back grew so suddenly that he staggered forward, almost dropping to his knees. The basket strained against its straps, twisting his arms painfully. It splintered loudly. Something large and heavy slid down his back and hit the deck with a dull thump, thrashing under his cloak. Carver pulled away in panic, yanking at the cloak to free himself. It tore loose, and he fell back against the rail. He wrenched the bandage from his eyes.

At the same moment the boat glided out of the shadow of the wall into a shaft of dirty light. Carver gasped. Huddled against the wall of the deckhouse was a dark, naked girl. She was thin, sharp featured, and as gray as Fireboy. But instead of hair, the top of her head was covered with sleek black feathers. She glared at him with bright, familiar eyes. He stared in dumb surprise. She clacked her teeth angrily.

"Raven?" he stammered.

Sixteen

W ho do you think, Muck Brain?" Raven glared at the startled, staring passengers and crossed her arms over her chest.

Suddenly, a woman snatched Carver's cloak off his back. "Blazing mages, give her some clothes!" she exclaimed, stepping quickly to Raven and wrapping her up.

Raven pulled away. She was grateful for the cloak but didn't like being shoved about.

"What happened?" Fireboy asked.

"Raven changed herself," Carver said. "Somehow."

"I didn't change myself," Raven snapped. "It just happened! You think I'd do something like that right out in front of everybody?" She glared at the woman who had helped her. "Who are you?" Raven demanded.

"I'm Digger," the woman said. "Who are you?"

Raven didn't answer.

Carver butted in. "That's Raven. And I'm Carver. Thank you for helping."

The woman shrugged, and Raven realized she wasn't as old as she looked, maybe only a year or two older than she and Carver were. She was tall and leggy, with narrow gray eyes that seemed worn. Her skin was pale under a layer of grime. The bit of hair that stuck out from under her cap was white as undyed linen.

She looked at Fireboy, who drew himself up to his full height. "I'm Fireboy," he said, emphasizing the "boy."

One side of her mouth lifted wryly. "I wondered. The dress had me fooled at first." She turned back to Raven. "You're a mage, aren't you?" She spoke in a whisper.

Raven glared back, still suspicious. "Yes."

"An apprentice," Carver said, butting in again. "An apprentice bird mage."

"Shh! A bird mage? That's new. Paskovek never said there were bird mages."

"Maybe I'm the only one left," Raven retorted.

The girl shrugged again. "Maybe." She glanced around warily at the other passengers. Heads quickly looked away. "You'd better put up your cowl. Cover those feathers."

"Feathers?" Raven reached up and felt what should have been her hair. Instead, there were feathers, smooth and cool under her palm. She liked that. "Why should I cover them? I'm not ashamed of what I am."

"The Duke hunts down mages. There's only one allowed on this reach: Krimm."

"Is that the great mage?" Carver asked.

"The Duke's brother?" Fireboy added.

Digger grinned her half grin, but her gray eyes were cold. "That's him."

Carver almost gushed with excitement. "We came here to find him," he told Digger. Raven clicked her teeth and gave him a warning glare. "We, um . . . we have questions for him," he finished.

Digger snorted. "Not much chance you'll get to ask them. Particularly if the Duke's guarda spot those feathers."

Still frowning, Raven pulled up the cowl and covered her head. "All right, Spider Legs. Now what?"

"We'd better get off. Too many people saw you grow out of your friend's back."

Digger scanned the canal ahead of them. It was crowded with a steady traffic of slim wherries, interspersed with steam launches like the one they were on, spewing grimy smoke into the reeking gap above the water. Raven's nose burned. After so long without a sense of smell, the stench of coal smoke, filthy water, garbage, sewage, and—most of all—crowded people almost made her gag.

The canal was lined with gray-faced stone buildings, four, five, and six stories high, built straight up from the surface of the water. An occasional shadowed alleyway led inward from the water's edge. A bridge loomed just ahead, and Raven could see carts and wagons above the railing, and a stream of pedestrians crossing back and forth. A low stone wharf ran along the wall under the bridge, with steps leading up to the street. The boat angled toward it.

"Come on," Digger said. She grabbed Raven's hand and pulled her toward the railing.

Raven snatched her hand back.

"Come on, Raven," Carver said. "People are staring."

Raven clicked her teeth, but she went. Before the boat even started to slow, Digger stepped up onto the railing and jumped across the gap to the wharf. Carver and Fireboy were right on her heels. Raven went last. The hop onto the railing, the leap to the wharf, the run up the steps—it felt good to pump legs and swing arms after being trapped so long in a bird's body.

The stairs led them up to the busy street. Digger slipped into the traffic without stopping. Carver and Fireboy dodged after her. Raven had no choice but to follow. The dense crowd made Down-run seem like a country village. Raven ducked around fat merchants and scruffy errand girls, clerks and porters. Digger's long legs carried her quickly through the press. Raven had to hug the old cloak tight to her sides to keep it from flapping open. Her bare feet slapped on the gritty cobbles. After a few blocks, she found herself wishing she could fly again.

Digger never slowed. Her narrow eyes moved constantly, choosing the right gap, avoiding collisions, yet never meeting the eyes of the people coming at her. No one looked directly at anyone else. Carts and carriages, pulled by everything from dogs to horses, took up the centers of the streets. Pedestrians swirled along the edges. Darting among them all were strange contraptions on two wheels, one in front and one in back of a single rider who seemed to run in place between them, making the thing go by some arrangement of belts and pulleys that Raven couldn't figure out.

One of them came careening out of an alleyway and nearly ran over Fireboy before bumping into an old man who had been slowly working his way down the very edge of the street, using the buildings for support. He fell with a feeble cry, and the wheeled thing fell on him. The rider scrambled up with a curse, adjusted a leather satchel that hung on his back, snatched up his contraption, and wheeled off without a backward glance. Digger paused long enough to help the old man get up. No one else even seemed to notice.

"What was that?" Fireboy asked as they hurried off.

"Some blasted courier," Digger said.

"I meant what was he riding?"

"Oh, that. It's a pedaler. You really are from upriver, aren't you?"

Fireboy flushed. "How's it work?" he demanded, hurrying to keep up.

"You sit on it and pedal," she said.

"That's a big help," Raven muttered to Carver.

"I guess she's not a mechanical," he said.

"We don't know what she is, we don't even know who she is, and here we are following her all over this blasted city like a flock of dumb ducks." Raven stopped dead in the street. Several people had to stumble to the side to avoid bumping into her.

"Hey, Spider Legs!" she shouted.

Digger glanced back. Raven stood there, glaring. Digger turned and glared back. Raven thought she was being mocked. She stepped closer and Digger immediately started to move on.

"Wait a minute!" Raven snapped. "Where are you taking us?"

Digger came back in a couple of quick strides. Her gray eyes were cold. "Never stand still in this city," she said. "You'll get noticed."

"Where are you taking us?" Raven repeated.

"Walk with me and I'll tell you."

Digger turned and continued up the street, but she slowed her pace. Raven hesitated, then caught up. Carver and Fireboy fell in behind.

"I'm taking you to Paskovek," Digger said. She spoke quietly. Her eyes never stopped scanning the crowd.

"Who's he?"

"A mage. The last one in the city. Besides blasted Krimm," she added.

"What kind of mage?" Raven asked.

"A truth sayer."

"A seer?"

"Seer, sayer." Digger shrugged. "Both, I guess. He can tell the truth about you." She glanced directly at Raven, one side of her mouth lifted in her cold grin.

Raven glared. "I already know the truth about me. Where does this Paskovek live?"

"You'll see when we get there."

"Tell me now."

"Have you ever been in Dunsgow before?"

"No."

Digger grinned again. "Then you still won't know if I tell you." Before Raven could protest, Digger took her arm and steered her out of the crowd into yet another alley. "Anyway, we're here."

The alley was blocked by an arched iron gate set in a gray stone wall. The gate was shut tight with a chain and bolt, but Digger twisted the bolt, and the gate swung just wide enough for them to squeeze through.

"I see why you got so skinny," Raven muttered.

"Food isn't cheap," Digger replied.

The alley continued around a corner and ended at another busy canal. Digger led them through a low, narrow doorway in the left-hand wall and down worn steps into a dank hallway lit only by a small barred shaft. There was a heavy wooden door in the shadows at the far end. Digger knocked twice, then once.

A thin slit opened at the top of the door. "Say," a low voice demanded.

"Digger."

The door swung open slightly, and Digger slipped through. Raven hesitated. Carver and Fireboy crowded against her. Feeling caged, she forced herself to go in.

They were in a long room lined with stone walls. Two arched and barred windows set high in one wall provided gray light and deep shadow.

Everything in this blasted city is stone and arched and barred, Raven thought. She felt more caged than ever.

Digger was talking quietly with a man in dark clothes who sat at a blocky wooden desk under the near window. Another man, or maybe it was an old-looking boy, was barring the door behind them. A woman stood at a table under the other window, changing a silent baby. There might have been other people in the shadows at the end of the room, but Raven couldn't tell for sure. Her hearing, like her eyesight, was once more flat and human.

The man at the desk regarded her with obvious interest through sagging, deep-set eyes. Then he studied Carver and Fireboy in turn. The fingers of his left hand played constantly with a coarse black goatee that tipped his pointed chin. He beckoned them closer.

"I'm Paskovek Mage," he said. His fingers played in his goatee as he studied them even more closely.

"I'm Carver."

"I'm Fireboy."

"And you are Raven," Paskovek said when she stayed silent.

He stared under her hood, and she pulled it back defiantly.

He nodded slowly at her feather hair. "You'll want a good cap." His gaze fell to the tattered cloak. "You'll want a full set of clothes."

"She can have this," Fireboy said, flapping his dress disgustedly.

"First I want to know who you are, Goat Face, and why she brought us here," Raven demanded.

Paskovek lifted an eyebrow and twiddled his pointed beard. "Those are reasonable questions," he said. "To answer the second first: Digger brought you here because you are a mage—an apprentice, at least. And a bird mage?" He pointed at a spot below Raven's chin. She reached up and touched the small pendant hanging there, the black feather on its silver chain, the gift from her mistress.

"All right," she said, shrugging. "I'm an apprentice bird mage. So what?"

"So nothing. You are still a mage. You are also newcomers, from the middle reach." Paskovek glanced at Carver. "Perhaps even from the upper reach. You do not know the situation regarding mages here in Dunsgow."

"The Duke doesn't like mages," Raven said. "According to Spider Legs, at least."

Paskovek raised both eyebrows. "You can trust Digger," he said.

"Can I trust you?"

He smiled slightly. "You fly from trust like a bird from cats. But that's just as well here in Dunsgow." The smile faded. His eyes sank back under his brows. "Let me add to what Digger has told you; you can decide for yourselves whether or not to believe it. The Duke has arrested all the mages in Dunsgow, except a few who fled. And myself, hidden."

"Wait a minute—what about Krimm?"

"Krimm lives on an island several leagues beyond the river mouth. He seldom bothers with us mere humans. He leaves that to his brother, and the Duke has been very good at his work. He has taken away the mages. None have reappeared."

"So how did you manage to escape?"

Paskovek looked at his hands for a moment. They were as dirty as anyone else's. "I think I'm no longer worth the trouble," he said, looking back up with his slight smile. "My magic protected me at first; I was able to detect informers before they could detect me. However, I suspect that they have long since given up trying, or even caring. Because my magic doesn't work anymore, yet I remain undiscovered."

Carver looked dumbstruck. "Your magic doesn't work?"

"No magic does, in Dunsgow," Paskovek said, but he studied Raven's feather hair thoughtfully. "Although there appear to be lingering effects around newcomers. Which is why Kovac still hunts them down and ships them off for disposal."

"Why?" Raven demanded.

"Why which?" Paskovek asked back. "Why does he arrest mages? Because he and his brother desire power. Why does magic not work?" Paskovek shook his head sadly. "I don't know, but ever since Kovac became our Duke and Krimm his First Mage, magic has waned here. Only Krimm, on his island, has the power, and he works only for his brother. Elsewhere in Dunsgow—across the entire reach—hardly a dram of magic remains, and that is fading. Even now, my young mage, your hair is returning."

Raven's hand flew to her head. She felt a strange coarse texture, neither feather nor hair. She clutched at the feather pendant and reached for the magic she had worked so hard to learn, the power that let her change and fly. She found nothing. She squeezed the pendant till it cut her palm. She chanted the words and made the signs that would change her back to a raven. Paskovek watched her mutely, his eyes filled with pity. She stared at the light in the grimy windows and shouted the final syllables of her spell.

She touched her head again. And found hair, all hair. And smells. She could still smell the stench from the water and the people around her. She was completely human. She backed away from the table, backed all the way to the wall and felt the cold stones press into her back. She stared at the window, at the gray light. At the bars.

Seventeen

T he wand was dying. Its leaves curled inward, browning at the edges. Carver held it gently, afraid they would fall off if he moved too quickly. It felt dead in his hand already, like any old stick. He turned to show Raven and saw her huddled by the doorway. He went to her, holding out the branch. He could hardly speak.

"Look," he whispered.

She dropped her eyes from the window and stared at him with a sickly expression. She noticed the wand, and her look grew even more strained. Her right hand was clenched so tightly, her fingers had turned almost white.

"Are you all right?" he asked, forgetting the wand for the moment.

Her grip loosened slowly, like a knot coming unraveled. The little feather pendant fell against her chest. There was blood on it. She reached out and touched the wand, barely touched one leaf with shaking fingers. It broke off. They watched in horror as it drifted to the floor between them, landing with a faint, dry rustle.

"Blast!" she whispered. "Blast, blast, blast!"

Paskovek came from behind his desk. He stooped over them, thin and brooding, fingers stroking his beard.

"It's . . . it's dying," Carver told him, holding the wand stiffly, afraid to move it at all now.

"This is a wand?" Paskovek asked.

Carver nodded. "A weather wand. I brought it here to show a mage. To show Krimm. I have to learn how to use it." He stared at the withering branch. "What should I do?"

"I'd say you'd better put it in water. Digger, find some kind of vase, please. And you," he said, turning to Raven. "What about you?"

"What about me, Goat Beard? You can't put me in a vase." Her voice was thin and hoarse, her defiance faked.

"No," he said, "but you're stronger than that wand. First we'll get you some proper clothes. Then we'll think of something you can do to maintain that strength."

"I know what I can do," Raven croaked. "I can get off this blasted reach. Get back where I belong, upriver."

Paskovek shook his head. His deep eyes were sad. "No one is allowed up the lifts without a pass from the Duke," he said. "I'm afraid you can't leave. Not unless you can fly."

Carver winced at the pain in Raven's eyes.

"Right," she said, breathing hard. "We're stuck here. For now. Right. I'm . . . I'm going to go outside for a minute. I'm going out. . . ."

She turned and began fumbling blindly at the bar on the door. Carver stepped toward her, then froze as another leaf tumbled from the wand.

Paskovek laid a hand briefly on his shoulder, then went to Raven. "I'll go with you. We'll sit by the canal," he said, lifting the bar and pulling the door open so she could bolt through. He followed her quickly.

They were gone a long time. The light from the high windows grew even more gray and dingy, and the woman with the baby lit some lamps that were mounted on the wall. They gave off a strange, hissing light. Then the boy who had first opened the door helped her start making dinner in a side room that was both kitchen and pantry. Meanwhile, Digger found a bottle and some water for the wand, which now drooped on the window ledge.

She also found some clothes for them. They too were strange, made of a smoother cloth than the linen and wool of the upper reaches. Digger said it came from a land far down the seacoast. The trews—she called them breeches—were loose and full-length; the stockings hardly reached above the ankle. Instead of a tunic there was a short, sleeveless overshirt held shut with round toggles that went through slits in the front edge. Over that went a heavy thigh-length topshirt, also with toggles, but also with clever sewn-in pouches in which to carry things.

"That's better," Digger said, looking them up and down. "We can't have any of you wearing rags from upriver. You'd look like beggars."

"That's what we were trying to look like," Fireboy said. He kept playing with the toggles on his topshirt.

"The guarda hunt beggars, too," Digger said. "For the lock houses—the Duke's workhouse prisons. No one's allowed to beg in Dunsgow."

"What if you're blind or crippled?"

"You still work."

"Well, I guess that's better than begging." Fireboy settled his hands deep in his pouches with a satisfied smile.

Digger frowned. "It's not good work." The way she said it killed Fireboy's smile.

Carver listened with only half an ear. He couldn't keep his eyes away from the wand. No more leaves had fallen, but every time he looked, it seemed more withered. Something in his heart felt shriveled too. He had come all this way for the wand; now he had no idea what to do.

Paskovek and Raven finally came back in, both of them silent and brooding. Soon after, other people began to arrive. They came alone or in pairs, never more than three at once. The boy verified each one and barred the door after, even though he was obviously expecting more. As they arrived, they went to Paskovek, who sat at his desk and questioned them in his low voice about their day. Some gave him money. A few brought in various items that ranged from cheese and fruit to spoons and jewelry. The food went to the kitchen. The rest went into a box by Paskovek's desk. Digger kept a tally in a small ledger.

Soon there were more than a score of people, men and women, children and adults. They set up benches and a trestle table at the back of the long room, then chatted quietly or played cards. Two or three sat under the hissing lamps and read. They glanced from time to time at Carver, Fireboy, and Raven, but they kept their distance. Each time someone new came to the door, they grew quiet until they heard a familiar name. Carver wondered what sort of nest the three of them had stumbled into.

At some point everyone must have been accounted for, because the door boy left his post and went to the table. The cook now had three helpers, who brought out dishes and platters of food. Paskovek led the newcomers over and introduced them. There was a blur of names, spaces were made, and they were each given a spoon and tongs. Then everyone dug in.

There was just enough food to go around. Then a different crew cleaned up and the table was cleared away. It was deep twilight now, and more lights were lit. They hissed steadily in their brackets against the wall. Fireboy was fascinated, and Digger told him they burned something called coal gas. Pallets were laid out in alcoves and where the table had been. Some people went to bed immediately, others talked. A few left again. Everyone seemed to know what to do and where they fit in. Carver felt lonely and lost.

Paskovek, who had been conferring with Digger and several others, called the three of them over. They sat on stools facing him. Digger had outfitted Raven with a set of city clothes that bagged on her thin frame and left her ankles bare. She sat twisting the loose cloth as if she wanted to squeeze it out of existence.

"This is how we live," Paskovek told them, gesturing around the big room. "We pool our earnings and share them with people who aren't able to work, so they won't have to beg and risk the Duke's mines and lockhouses. You're welcome to stay here with us. You don't have to, but you are welcome. Know that if you do stay, you'll have to work."

"What kind of work?" Fireboy asked.

"That depends somewhat on what you can do," Paskovek replied, "but mostly on what we can get for you. Some of us have jobs we like. Most of us simply work."

"What does she do?" Raven asked, looking at Digger.

"She is our recruiter," Paskovek said. "She is also my quartermaster and lieutenant. Occasionally, she robs a rich merchant for us." He smiled slightly at that, a smile echoed by Digger's one-sided grin, but Carver could tell he was serious.

"You rob people?" he said.

"We do," Paskovek replied. "Every day and night some of the household go into the better parts of the city to relieve the wealthy of a small portion of their excess. That is how we feed the poor."

Carver stared at him. "I can't do that," he said finally. Fireboy nodded agreement.

"I didn't expect you to," Paskovek replied. "Not even you," he added to Raven. "But before you condemn us, look around. See what castoffs we're wearing. Remember what little we ate for dinner. Breakfast won't be any more substantial. Lunch will be a small bit of bread and cheese, if we have any on a particular day. We aren't getting fat, or rich, or even comfortable."

"What *are* you doing?" Raven demanded.

"That depends on whom you ask. Some of us are helping the poor, working purely from the heart. The rest aren't so sure. They like to think they're doing good, but they also hate the Duke and his Barons. They've escaped from his mines or lost family to his lockhouses, so they do it for hate. I'm here for both reasons, but mostly because I hate Krimm."

"Why Krimm?" Carver asked. "Why not the Duke?"

"Him too," Paskovek said, "but Krimm more. Once there were scores of mages in Dunsgow. Why were they all removed? Why does magic no longer work here? I sense . . . I believe he is at the root of it. Not the Duke. Krimm."

His stained fingers had knotted into fists on the desktop. Watching him, Carver remembered Aunt Zarah's vision. Here was a mage crossed by another great mage. But what did that have to do with the Blade or the Mother or the talking broom handle? He felt even more lost and confused.

Paskovek took a slow breath and untangled his fingers. After a moment, they went back to scratching his goatee.

"I don't expect you to hate anyone, at least not yet. And I don't expect you to steal." He glanced at Raven. "At least not yet. As I said, I do expect you to work if you stay here. Tell me what you've done before, apart from what your names tell me, and we'll see what we can find for you. I don't promise a perfect match."

They started work the very next morning, and Paskovek lived up to his nonpromise. Fireboy went to work on a canal boat, but it was a wherry, not a steamboat. With an oar and a pole, he and another boy and a boatman ferried people and wares around the city. Carver found himself in a workhouse that made paint. It was so different from Uncle Piper's studio that he could hardly believe it was the same task. Close to a hundred people worked in a huge shed of a building, mixing oil and pine spirits and pigment in room-sized vats that were stirred by mechanical paddles. In another shed, various rocks were heated over great fires, then crushed to powder between steam-powered rollers. Tub-sized scoops slung from moving chains carried the powders to the vat shed, and pipes led from the vats to a third building, where the mixed paints were decanted into buckets made of thin metal.

What made it horribly the same was the smell, a stench of paint fumes compounded by coal smoke and the swill of the nearby canal.

Carver worked in the canning shed, pounding lids on cans as they passed by him on a rotating platform. By evening, his hands were so stiff, he could hardly hold his spoon and tongs. At the end of the sixth day of work, he was given a few small coins in pay. They were gray and uninteresting, with the Duke's profile crudely stamped on one side and a letter D on the back. At the household, as they called it, he gave them to Paskovek and asked what the metal was.

"Iron," Paskovek said. "Kovac means *Smith* in the old tongue. Blacksmith. Names don't mean much in Dunsgow now, though the Duke's forebearers did work iron. As the city grew, they became important fabricants and ironmongers. They ran several workhouses and controlled the guild. Kovac was born to that." His frown lengthened. "The guilds named Kovac their chancellor, and the Barons accepted him on the council. Then he named himself Duke and abolished the guilds. He took over all the other ironmongers. Iron was too vital to leave to the whims of trade, he said. He fixed low prices for the Barons, so of course they approved. Then he started building his chain all around the city. A symbol of our strength and prosperity, he said. The Barons didn't care what he did with his extra iron, just so long as their prices stayed low. Then he brought out his iron money."

Paskovek lapsed into a brooding silence, and Carver was almost afraid to break in.

"Are all the coins iron?" he asked finally. "Even the talents and skills and deeds?"

Paskovek blinked and came back to the present. "I'm sorry," he said, attempting a smile. "You asked a simple question; I turned it into a lesson in politics. A bad habit of mine. Yes, the coins are all iron. For some reason, our iron-loving Duke hoards gold, silver, and even copper. There are no talents here, no skills or deeds. Only Kovacs. Slugs, people call them. Your share is two demislugs. Save it or spend it; you'll find it's worth very little, I'm afraid."

Carver stared at the two gray coins in his palm. Everything about this reach was strange.

He was tired after dinner but didn't feel like sleeping. His belly felt half empty and his brain overstuffed. He rubbed his hands and stretched his fingers to loosen them, then got his bundle from the corner where he slept and brought out his knife. He hadn't carved since before they'd reached Downrun; too much had happened. He'd always been too tired. Now he pulled out his second small block of pear wood, hoarded since the very start of this strange journey. He quelled the feeling of frustration and failure that threatened to choke him whenever he thought of the wand, still standing dry and shriveled in its bottle on the window ledge. He stared hard at the block of wood, trying to imagine what he would carve. Nothing came to him; his thoughts were heavy and slow. All he could see was a piece of wood.

He looked across the room at Paskovek and Digger, bent over their ledgers. He liked Digger. She could be curt at times, but she was never mean, and he realized now she had probably saved them from the Duke's workhouses. He stared at the wood again, trying to see Digger's face in the grain. He took a slice with his knife. His hand shook, and the blade scratched a jagged tear in the hard wood. Frowning, Carver stretched his fingers again. They felt thick and clumsy. He took a breath and tried another slice. The wood resisted; the knife balked. Again the blade went wrong, scoring the grain.

Carver leaned back against the wall and stared at his hands, the knife, the block of wood. He heard Raven make some sharp comment to Fireboy, clear and bitter over the quiet murmur of the rest. He forced himself to study the wood, to breathe slowly. He leaned forward again, held the knife firmly. It felt all right. He pressed the blade to the wood, hesitated, pressed harder. The edge slipped, then caught in a turn of grain, sliced outward, and cut deeply into his thumb.

He dropped the wood with a clatter and stared at the blood oozing from the end of his thumb, staining the blade of the knife. Then the pain started, and with it near panic. He threw down the knife and grabbed his thumb. It throbbed in his fist. He felt hot blood in his palm. He had never felt that before. Never cut himself. Never. He stared at his hand, numb with shock. Then he had another thought and looked up at the wand, wilted in its bottle. Gray. Dying. His panic grew. He tore his eyes away. Looked at nothing.

I can't do it anymore, he thought. I can't carve.

Eighteen

Raven leaned hard, cut between a wall and a slow wagon, hopped a step, and careened along High Bridge. The bridge arched in the middle, and she pedaled hard to maintain speed. A knot of pedestrians was tying up traffic at the top of the arch, but she squeezed past, scraping the railing with her right pedal. A man yelled something rude as she brushed his fat bottom with her knee, but she ignored him, accelerating down the opposite side of the arch, weaving around two more wagons, and flying off the end of the bridge into the crowds of the old Guild District.

She reached her destination—the counting house of an importer named Seaman—quickly chained her pedaler to the horse post out front, and hurried up the steps with her pouch banging on her back. The pouch gave her instant entry to almost any house or hall in the city. Couriers might be cursed on the streets, but they were vital to the machinations of the merchants and fabricants who made their profits on the crowds and the filthy canals. Raven strode past the guard at the doorway into the shadowed entry hall. A tall wooden bench blocked the way deeper into the building, where clerks sat at high desks, flicking beads on their counters and scratching in fat ledgers.

Panting a little in the stuffy heat, Raven pulled a tied bundle of papers from her pouch and handed it briskly to the bench clerk. As the woman inspected the knot and seal, Raven scanned the room, making note of the number of clerks and the people walking by the doorway that led upstairs to Seaman's private offices. The seal passed inspection, and the woman signed Raven's receipt pad. Smiling, Raven strode back outside. The seals always passed inspection, even the ones that Paskovek had opened on their way by.

Raven was one of only three couriers in the household. Others, like Fireboy, delivered people and goods along the canals. They brought Paskovek constant news of the city and the lower reach, from the falls to the harbor. The couriers brought more: letters, bills, and papers that detailed the activities of the merchants and moneylenders and even the Barons. He brooded over their meaning, seeking truth as he might have searched a person's face when he was still a mage. For Paskovek, it wasn't enough to rob the rich and feed the poor. He wanted change.

Raven didn't care one way or the other; she just wanted out of Dunsgow. She would be a courier for a while, until she found some document that would get her onto the lifts and up the cliff, away from the maggoty crowds and whatever it was that killed magic. There were times when she wanted so much to get out of her earthbound body and into clear air that she was willing to risk being a raven forever. Then she would pedal as fast as she could, feeling the wind. Pretending. But the ache in her legs and the stinging, filthy air at the back of her throat were a constant reminder of her situation. She took a drink of warm water from her flask, but nothing could wash the bitter taste from her mouth.

She got back to the household that evening late, as usual, to put off going inside. The rest were already eating, the table full, which gave her an excuse to take her plate over by the high windows. Raven looked up at Carver's wand. He still watered it every day, the dolt, as if that would somehow bring back its power. He'd been moody ever since they arrived. He didn't even do any carving anymore, just went out in the morning and came back at night stinking of paint. And watered the stupid wand. His thumb had been pretty ugly for a while after he'd cut it, but it was healed fine now—no excuse to mope around like a blasted mourning dove.

Fireboy finished eating and came over to plop down next to her.

"Hoy," he said. All the boatmen said that. It made her itch. "I got to go on a steam launch today. We took cargo off her." He gave a huge grin. "I got a real good look at the engine."

He went on to describe it in far more detail than Raven wanted. She watched Carver, who was on kitchen duty that night. He was wiping the table as though it were a silver mirror that needed polishing. Intent, that's what he was. Like he used to be when he was carving. Blocking out the rest of the world. When he was done, he came over, sat down beside Fireboy, and listened just as intently as Fireboy repeated the tale of the steam engine. As if he really were interested. Raven clicked her teeth in disgust. Fireboy and Carver looked at her.

"Kah!" she snapped, and went outside for the last few minutes before sleep.

The next day, the dispatcher sent her down to the harbor to pick up documents for another delivery to the Guild District. As she sped off the wharf and under the old wall with its ugly iron chain, Digger stepped from a side alley and flagged her down.

"The Barons are all here, and the Duke is coming out to meet them," Digger said. "Go by the Plaza."

Normally, Raven welcomed any diversion, but Digger's curtness always rubbed her wrong.

"That's out of my way," she protested. Which was true; the city had any number of plazas, but only one Plaza. It fronted the Duke's Hall at the opposite edge of the Old City from the Guild District.

"Paskovek wants you there," Digger said. She gave her half smile. "He thinks you still have bird sight."

"I can hear better than you too," Raven said.

Digger gave her a disgusted look. "Get close enough to hear, then."

"I will," Raven snapped, and she pedaled off before Digger could say anything more.

The streets in the Old City were hardly more than alleyways.

They followed a winding, broken route between old, low buildings that hung out over the roadway, even bridging it completely in places. It didn't take much traffic to clog things up, and everyone seemed to be heading toward the Plaza. Raven needed bell, voice, and quick reflexes to dodge through. Sharp elbows helped. She reached the Plaza just before it started to fill.

One or another of the Barons might come to Dunsgow each month, but seldom all at once. Whenever that happened, they met with the Duke. They were a sort of overcouncil, though as far as Raven could tell, what they did mostly was bow and scrape and agree to whatever the Duke decided was the law at that particular moment. A Baron might be jealous of the Duke's power, but there being five meant no one of them could get the upper hand. Besides, the Duke had Krimm. If he wanted to dry up one of the five rivers, he probably could.

Raven was curious to see the Duke. She had seen his steward, Scharl, a knobby, awkward-looking man who commanded the guarda and did the Duke's dirty work. He had the habit of appearing at unexpected times and places about the city, always with a squad of the biggest, meanest guarda. He wore an odd wire frame on his face, with thick lenses that made his eyes seem owlish, but everyone was afraid of him. Digger called him Snarl.

Scharl was in the Plaza already, with his usual squad of meanies. They stood just inside the ornate iron gate that separated the Plaza from the courtyard of the Duke's Hall. More guarda formed a semicircle out into the Plaza, to keep the gawkers from pressing too close. Raven hopped off her pedaler and pushed nearer to the gates. There were trees spotted around the Plaza, and she chained her pedaler to one, then scrambled up into the branches, cursing. Everything was so blasted difficult now. But her high roost gave her a good view of the courtyard. She could even hear two of Scharl's guarda talking over the constant mutter of the crowd. There's to you, Digger, she thought.

The muttering rose as a small party came out of the Hall and crossed the courtyard. It was Baron Stoner, with his steward and a fancy woman who was probably his wife. Baron Vintner came out next with her group. She looked drab next to Stoner's fancy woman, and she sipped constantly at a cup of something that one of her retainers kept filled. Then Miner and Miller came out together. They greeted the others in low, cool tones and acknowledged Scharl with curt nods. Then everyone waited. Stoner muttered something to his wife, too low for Raven to catch. She shook her head, looking very put upon. Vintner turned to Scharl and demanded to know what was keeping that blazing Cutter. Raven smiled.

Finally, there was a commotion at the canal that bordered the far side of the Plaza. A launch had pulled up at the quay, with Cutter's bull and blade flying over the deckhouse. Scharl sent a small group of guarda to clear a path through the crowd. Cutter strolled almost casually at the head of his party. His benevolent mask made him seem fatherly and wise. Raven wished she could fly over and stain his bright new cloak as he passed into the courtyard. The other Barons greeted him coolly. Cutter never lost his fatherly smile.

A short fanfare rang out. The crowd shifted, then began cheering. On a small ornate balcony centered over the entrance to the Duke's Hall stood a tall man with stooped shoulders. His large forehead was crowned with thick hair so blond it was almost white. His cheekbones were high, his nose sharp, his skin chalky. Most striking were his eyes: deep-set and dark, contrasting completely with the rest of his pale features. Except for those eyes, he seemed almost ghostly. They gleamed, unblinking, as if he were watching from a great height, like an eagle on soar. Raven shivered. The Duke raised his hand to the crowd, and the clapping settled into an even beat. It pulsed off the buildings that fronted the Plaza.

The Barons stepped forward, leaving their attendants behind, and formed a rough line facing the Duke. The clapping and cheering continued. Finally, the Duke raised his other hand to signal silence, and the crowd stilled. He studied them a moment longer, then looked down at the Barons. They bowed, more or less together. He nodded his head, spotting each one with his deep, unblinking gaze. He greeted them with a few simple words, and the shape of the balcony projected his voice into the Plaza. To Raven it sounded like the rest of his body looked—strained and flat. She wondered if the Duke was ill, if that was why he hid in his fancy cage.

The appearance was over in moments. The Barons bowed again, and the Duke waved once more to the crowd, then disappeared back into the Hall. The Barons followed Scharl through the main entrance. The crowd quieted and began drifting off.

Raven stayed in the tree. She wondered what was going on inside. The brief public show told her nothing, except that Cutter was still a puffed-up, maggot-eating vulture. She hated to go back to Paskovek with so little to report. Her eyes went to the empty balcony, and she recalled the Duke's bleached skin and stooped shoulders, his stark cheekbones. She wondered again if he was ill. After all, the man never came out of his ornate Hall. He controlled the reach without ever seeing it, using Scharl and the guarda as his eyes and fists. She looked at the tall metal gate. Did it keep the commoners out or the Duke locked in?

She shivered again. "Dolt," she muttered. "Blasted dolt."

Nineteen

Carver pushed his barrow toward the quay, and the farther he got from the fumes of the paint house, the better he felt. He'd been moved from the canning machine to delivery, and felt as if he'd been delivered himself.

The paint house was on the outermost island of Dunsgow and faced the wide main channel of the river. A breeze was blowing upstream from the sea, and Carver breathed deeply, forcing the reek of paint and coal smoke from his lungs. He gazed downriver, past the long edge of the city and the crowd of masts at the harbor, visible above the city wall. He could make out figures on a stretch of the wall that bordered the river. Black smoke rose from a makeshift smithy on the wall top as they forged another link in the great chain. They were just one of a dozen crews scattered along the wall, working from dawn to dusk every day on the Duke's crazy project. Beyond them, the sight of the broad, curving river refreshed his eyes as much as the air cleared his lungs.

A wherry came pulling upstream close to the quay, moving swiftly on the rising tide. As he raised his hand to hail it, Carver recognized the lead oarsman. "Hoy, Fireboy!"

Fireboy turned and waved.

The boat came alongside, and Fireboy helped load the barrow. Then they were off downstream and back up the next canal, where Fireboy and his mate exchanged their oars for poles. Their boatman cut through a side canal, barely wide enough for one boat, to reach a tiny wharf close to Carver's destination. He had barely waved goodbye to Fireboy before the next fare was climbing on.

Carver approached his first customer with anticipation. It was a furniture house, and maybe they would need a new helper. It wouldn't be carving, but it would have to be better than making paint. He pushed open the delivery door and peered inside.

A blast of noise hit his face; whining, rasping, tearing wood. Across a small space crowded with cans of pegs and glue was a workroom filled with machines and belts and turning wheels. In a haze of dust, people bent over metal benches where sticks of wood slid or spun or rotated under speeding blades. From somewhere in the back came the stench of coal smoke, capped by the clang of a firebox door. Some other machine began shrieking. A shower of coarse sawdust sprayed across the room.

To the side, a door filled with glass panes revealed ranks of identical chairs. Two small boys were painting them all the same shade of gray. Carver quickly unloaded his cans, took the receipt from the surly stock clerk, and hurried away. He didn't ask about jobs.

Outside, people brushed by him, their rushing footsteps a constant undercurrent in the pervasive grinding of the workhouses. Doors flew open; people hurried out or in, never noticing the old, carved ornamentation around the doorways. Carver stopped to look at as many carvings as he could find under the layers of paint and grime. As he got farther from the city center, the buildings got newer. Grimy brick replaced filthy stone and the carving disappeared; all the buildings were sharp cornered and plain. Carver felt as if his eyes, too, had been covered with grime, and no amount of tears would clean them.

Late in the long day, with leagues of water and cobbles behind him, he stumbled to a halt in front of his last delivery and stared in wonder at the half-timbered wall. He was in one of the twisting lanes that passed for streets in the old district. The buildings were small and hung out over the walkways. The cobbles were rutted with age and bounced his barrow annoyingly. It was dim, the storefronts faded and worn, the air musty. But here was carving he could not ignore.

The shop's wooden frame protruded from its plain stucco finish, like that of many buildings here. But everywhere wood showed on this wall, it was carved: around the door and upstairs windows, out to the jutting ends of the joists that supported the projecting second story, and still up to the eaves and rafter ends. There were vines and fruits and birds, animals of all kinds, the river and its boats, a village in minute detail. Carver studied it with awe.

Then he gasped. There, at the upper corner of the door frame, someone had patched a broken figure with carving that matched the old one almost exactly. And it was new, the bright, unpainted wood still free of grime. He wondered who in this drab, hurried place had found the time or desire to do that. Smiling, he hefted the last two buckets from his barrow and shouldered open the door.

Inside, the shop was small and surprisingly sparse. A coal stove faced the doorway from a raised hearth against the back wall. Along the left side, lit by a small, high window beside the stove, ran a bank of shelves crammed with carved objects. On the opposite wall, under another high window, stood a stout workbench. A rack of knives and chisels hung on the wall above it. A mallet and chisel rested on the bench in a nest of chips and shavings that spilled onto the floor. Carver looked from the bench to the shelves and back. It was like a scene from one of his dreams.

Someone coughed, and Carver tore his eyes from the bench. An old man was standing in a doorway under the high window by the shelves. He squinted curiously at Carver.

"Thank you," the old man said. "No one's looked that closely at my work in a very long time." Carver could only stammer in embarrassment. The old man waved it away. "What have you got for me?" he asked, stepping over to his bench to sit stiffly on a three-legged stool.

"I . . . I have the paint you ordered," Carver said. He lugged the two buckets over and set them down. Inside each were several small cans, in a variety of colors.

"Ah, yes," the old man said. Brushing his hands along his

apron, he took the bill of lading and compared it to the small cans in the buckets. Carver noticed that the man's fingers were stiff and bent, with knobbed joints and thick tendons. Several were wrapped with bandages. All of them showed scars and chilblains and chipped nails.

The old man noticed him staring and grunted. "Yes, it's stickly work, boy. When you fiddle with edges all day, you get cut now and again. At least I do." He looked at the list again. "I wish you people would make smaller cans," he grumbled as he turned back to his workbench. "Half will go dry before I need it." He reached under the bench and pulled out a small wooden box, breathing heavily. "If I live that long," he added.

He counted out some coins from the meager pile in the box; then, while he dug a pencil out of the chips on his workbench and signed the bill with a shaky hand, Carver went to the shelves. They were filled with figurines of the people and animals carved into the building's frame.

"These really are wonderful," Carver said, studying the faces in particular.

The old man came over and handed him the bill. "I'm glad you think so," he said. "Not many do these days. I've lived too long— gone out of style. Get by mostly by fixing things, chairs and doors. Still, a few come by who are willing to pay a little for a bit of carving to take home. Not everyone has forgotten how to see." He went back to his bench, lowered himself onto the stool, and picked up a knife and a block of wood. He turned the piece over, eyeing it critically, then began to slice off small, careful chips. "I keep at it. Even if no one buys the blasted stuff, you have to keep at it."

Carver watched his stiff, bandaged fingers as they deftly turned the piece and wielded the knife. A face began to grow from the wood. "Thank you," he said quietly, and let himself out.

Back in the street, Carver grabbed the handles of his barrow, then paused to take a last look at the new carving by the door. He trundled away slowly, barely seeing the street.

You have to keep at it. Despite the lack of interest, despite the cuts, the old carver kept carving. Through years of make-work, stiff with age, he kept at it. Even when no one cared.

Carver stopped dead in the street, overcome for a moment with a deep sense of shame. He had not kept at it. He had come all the way down the river, through floods and magics, locked up and let out, through fog and over land, in hiding and in disguise. And here, in reach of his goal, he had stopped. The wand had wilted to a stick on the windowsill. His knife lay rusting in his bundle back at the house, stained by a little blood he had not even bothered to wipe off. Two things he had come to do, and he had done neither. His hands clenched on the barrow shafts.

How did this happen? he wondered. *Why did I let it happen?*

He looked at the dingy storefronts and up at the grimy sky. The gray darkened as evening approached and the city closed in on itself even more. There was something about this place that smothered him, that narrowed his vision and made things seem hard and impossible. And it wasn't just him; everywhere he looked, people walked with their eyes fixed forward. Or sat behind dirty windows, bent over ledgers or machines or moving belts of endless selfsame wares. Even the rich, in their bright, padded clothing, seemed dull and weighted.

But how and why didn't matter, he realized; the important thing was that now he could see it.

He picked up his pace, hurrying through the dull evening crowd to be rid of his barrow and return to the household. Once there, he dug his knife from his bundle and snapped open the blade. He got out his whetstone and cadged some oil from the cook, then slowly and carefully cleaned the steel and sharpened the edge so fine it could split hairs. When Fireboy and Raven returned, he hardly noticed their greetings. He rushed through dinner, barely tasting his food. Then he took out the scratched and marred block of pear wood, drew in a deep breath, and began to carve.

Twenty

aylight was fading into Dunsgow's rusty gray gloaming as Carver traced his way along the narrow lanes to the old carver's shop. He stopped when he reached it and studied the intricately carved framing. The repair was painted now to match the rest, and the surface was already starting to dull under a fresh layer of grime. Soon it would be impossible to tell from the original. Carver felt the newly carved piece in his pocket. It wasn't painted—he would never paint his work—but in his mind's eye he could easily compare it to the old carver's work. His technique was different, more shaving than chipping, but the quality was good. Maybe not quite as good yet, but good enough to show.

It had taken him a week to finish the piece, a week of evenings spent hunched under the gaslights at the household till his eyes watered and Digger ordered him to sleep. A week of cramped hands and nicked fingers. A week of doubt, fatigue, and bleary mornings when he wondered how he had ever carved before. It felt as if he had to relearn everything from scratch, as if he'd never held a knife. But he kept at it. Every time his mind went dull and his heart ached with frustration, every time he added a new bandage to his fingers, he thought of the old carver and took off a few more shavings.

Carver flexed his tired hands and went through the door. The small shop was dim and silent. The workbench was bare. Even the floor was bare; not a single chip or shaving littered the stark wood surface. It felt hollow.

"Hello?" he called timidly. "Anyone here?"

There was a noise from the back room. An old woman came

through the doorway under the high window by the shelves. She was dressed all in black, and her lined face was too drawn to give any hint of greeting.

"Hello," Carver repeated. "Is the master here? I . . . I have something to show him."

She shook her head. "Do I know you?"

"No. I just . . . brought the paint last week." He pointed lamely at the shelf of paint cans.

"Paint?" The old woman's voice cracked with more than age. She glanced at the cans, then shook her head again. "Can't use it now," she said, and her face turned briefly to the bench. "He's gone. Just two days ago, you know." She swallowed and glanced at the ranks of carvings. But her eyes couldn't rest there either. They fixed on a point past Carver's right arm.

"Don't know why he ordered it anyway," she said. "No one's been in to buy anything for months. Years. Didn't stop him, though. He kept at it, the old goat. Couldn't stop. Would have been . . . the death of him."

She trailed off, then reached up to wipe at one eye with the tail of her sleeve. Carver stood numbly in the middle of the room. He couldn't speak; couldn't think of anything, and couldn't have said it anyway.

Finally, he managed to clear his throat. "I guess I'll go, then," he said. "I'm sorry."

"Thank you," she whispered, nodding and turning.

"He was a wonderful carver."

She shrugged and left the room.

Carver stood there a moment longer. Then he took out his own carving. It was a likeness of the old carver, small and detailed, holding a mallet and chisel. Carver set it on the bench and let himself out quietly. He took a last look at the carved framing and went slowly down the lane.

Deep in thought, he turned a corner, then another, not really watching where he went. Right now it didn't seem important. But finally he noticed the street in front of him. The last turning should have brought him to a bridge, but here was a wharf instead. He looked right and left, decided left seemed the right way to go. He went a few blocks and turned left again, certain the canal would be just another block or two ahead.

But the street ended at a tee and he was forced to turn again. He peered down each alley, looking for a glimpse of water. The dingy twilight deepened. A pair of roughly dressed men entered the street behind him. Carver walked faster, even though he had nothing to steal but a few demislugs. And his knife. He clutched it in his pocket, hand suddenly sweaty. There was an intersection ahead, more people, safety in the crowd. He rushed to the corner and heaved to a stop, breathless. The two men went by him without a glance. With a sigh of relief, he leaned against the wall by a doorway, trying to figure out where in the city he was. It was all unfamiliar. Some people went into the door beside him, and he heard the clatter of crockery from within. He glanced up at the sign over the door.

Uncle Piper smiled back at him.

"I nearly fell over," Carver told Raven and Fireboy as he led them along the dark streets toward the tavern. "For an instant, I thought it must be a vision. . . ." He shivered. "But there's no magic here in Dunsgow, and I'm not a seer."

"Your mother was," Fireboy pointed out. "You could have her talent."

Carver shook his head grimly. "I didn't get either of my parents' talents."

Then they turned the final corner and he pointed at the sign hanging above the tavern door. It was Uncle Piper, complete with his pipes. Despite faded paint and years of grime, his cheeks gleamed with the effort of playing. His eyes squinted slightly, focused inward on his music. Arching over his head in bold script was the name of the tavern: The Happy Piper.

"How do you know your father painted it?" Raven asked skeptically.

"All my life I've had his work shoved in my face," Carver said. He swallowed a hard lump in his throat. "No one else paints like that. Besides, who here would know my uncle?"

"So what's the old windbag doing hanging here?" Raven demanded.

Carver shrugged. "My father must have been here once."

"Did you ask?" Raven made a wry face. "Did you even go in?"

Carver shrugged, embarrassed.

She looked at him sharply. "You're afraid he's still here, aren't you? You're afraid to go in and find out by yourself."

"No," Carver replied. "It's just—"

She cut him off. "You probably should be afraid. He may be able to paint well, but the muck head deserted you once already, didn't he?"

"It's not that," Carver said, glaring at her. But it was, and he knew it. He didn't want to face his father alone. He was afraid, not of his father, but of himself, of what he might say or do.

But Raven was already opening the door. Carver followed her into the room, a wide hall with a low ceiling lit by bright gas lamps. Long tables took up most of the floor. A grate on the broad hearth radiated acrid heat to every corner. Despite that, a dozen or so people sat close to the grate, drinking and talking in low voices punctuated by an occasional laugh.

The taverner came over to greet them. He was balding and sweaty, with a dark fringe of damp hair and beard that circled his entire face.

"Come in," he bid them. "Close the door. Unless," he added, with a suspicious squint as he got a good look at them, "you've just come to beg. In that case, you can go right back out."

"We don't beg," Raven said, so sharply that the taverner started. "We have a question. If you can answer it properly, red face, we'll buy a cup of cider each."

"Right," he said, huffily. "Buy the cider first; then I'll answer your question."

"It's a simple enough question, sir," Carver said politely, stepping in front of Raven. "The man who painted your signboard, was that Thomas Painter?"

"Why, yes, it was," the man replied, his mood softening a little. "He did that mural, too." He waved a sweaty hand at the wall behind them.

Carver turned, and his breath caught in his throat. The entire wall was a scene from home. Uncle Piper stood in the common at Wanting, playing his pipes for the entire village. He looked so alive, you could almost see his fingers dance along the holes of the chanter. Aunt Singer was there beside him, beating a tambour, her mouth wide in a silent accompaniment. All the people he knew danced along around them, or sat at tables clapping. There was Silas Joynter and his wife, and Miller, and Baker. And there was the mayor, off to one side, making a speech that no one was listening to. And there was Aunt Zarah on the opposite side, complete with a trio of hens dancing around the hems of her colorful skirts.

Carver blinked away tears.

"Did it in less than a week to pay for room and board," the taverner was saying. "Not that it ever paid me back," he added sourly. "Then he and his wife—Anna Fowler she was—they went off and never came back. See, it's not even done."

He pointed at the background behind the mayor, where a building had been sketched but not painted. Carver gaped. It was the new town hall, something his father could never have seen.

"He was going to come back and finish it," the taverner said, "but he never did." He shrugged. "Probably came to a bad end."

"Where did they go?"

"I don't know. They kept kind of quiet about things." There was a note of frustration in his voice, as though he were still irked at not being able to pry out their secrets. "And that's two questions. You'll be wanting your cider now?"

"Yes," Carver said. "Thank you."

"And you'll be paying now?"

Raven scowled, but Carver pulled out his few coins. He paid the man, and they wound among the tables to the back corner for a wider view of the mural.

"Blazes," Fireboy said, "your father was a paint mage."

"So I've been told," Carver replied. "Not that anyone here seems to care."

But he found it hard to feel bitter about this mural; there were too many people in it he loved. Despite himself, he couldn't help feeling his father had loved them too. He wondered again why his father had ever wanted to leave, and for the first time wondered if it had been an easy choice. He studied the faces and suddenly noticed his grandmother Weaver, seated at a table behind Piper and Singer. She was singing along, and on the bench beside her were two children, younger versions of his cousins Dora and Dulci.

Then another face caught his eye, and a chill brushed the back of his neck. He went closer. There was a boy standing in a shadow behind Grandmother. A young man almost, with cropped brown hair and wide eyes that seemed to look right at you, wherever you were standing. He was holding something, and as Carver went closer, another shiver ran down his spine. It was a silver gray branch tipped with bright-green teardrop leaves.

"That's you," Fireboy remarked.

"And there's that blasted wand," Raven muttered.

Carver could only nod. He turned numbly and stumbled back to the table. They followed and sat close on either side. The taverner arrived with their cider.

"When was that painted?" Carver asked.

"Oh, that would be ten years ago," the man replied promptly. "It was just before Kovac made himself Duke and took over the council."

Ten years ago. They had come right here, then left again after painting this one mural and signboard at a cramped tavern on a back street in an insignificant district of the city. Yet he had stumbled onto it. It was almost as though they had expected him. He studied the painting long and hard, but if there was some kind of message there, he couldn't see it.

He took a sip of his cider and looked at his friends.

"I was thinking," he began.

"That's always helpful," Raven said.

"Well, I haven't been doing much of it lately. But I realize now that we've forgotten what we came here for. It's like the city cast some kind of spell on us, a curse that washed out all our plans. We settled in so easily . . . too easily." He shook his head in frustration. "It's hard even to talk about it. But we need to get out of here. We need to move on, to finish."

Raven smiled for the first time in weeks. "I like those thoughts, Monkey Boy."

He smiled back. "I thought you would. But I didn't want to talk about it at the household, where Paskovek and Digger could hear."

Fireboy frowned. "You think they'd stop you from leaving?"

"I don't know. They're so caught up in hating the Duke and the mage. They make everybody there a part of their plotting. I don't know what they'd do if someone tried to leave."

Raven was looking at Fireboy suspiciously. "You said 'you,' Steam Brain. You said, 'stop *you* from leaving.' Don't tell me you like it here."

Fireboy hesitated almost guiltily. "I guess I don't," he said finally. "The air and the water stink, not clean and wet, like upriver. And it feels like we never stop working. But there are some wonderful things here, things I like. Those little steamboats. Propellers. Pedalers. If we had those upriver . . ." He stopped and a strange expression came over his face. He looked down at his clothes, held out the sides of his topshirt. "How come we don't have things like this upriver? Topshirts and toggles. Coal-gas lights. Propellers and small engines and all that."

"Tongs for eating," Carver added. "We don't have those on the upper reach. Or any kind of steamboat. Or firearms. Or counting houses."

"You can keep your stinking counting houses," Raven said.

"But why don't we have them?" Fireboy demanded. "People go up and down the falls all the time. The porters do, at least. The Barons do. The buyers. How come they never brought this stuff up with them? They never even talk about it. I rode back with Cutter from trips to Dunsgow, and he never said anything about pedalers. He never wore a topshirt. Why not?"

Carver shook his head slowly. "I don't know. Maybe this spell I'm feeling covers more than Dunsgow. Maybe it spreads up and down all the rivers, all the reaches, wiping new ideas from people's minds."

"Only it's like smoke," Fireboy agreed. "It gets thinner the farther you get from the engine." He looked at Raven. "Do spells work like that?"

"Some of them do." She shrugged. "I have to be close to a bird before I can charm it. But somebody thought up those steamboats and pedalers. Some cheese brain even thought up the counting houses. Not everybody's stopped thinking. Besides, a spell like that would be powerful magic, and magic doesn't work in Dunsgow, let alone stretch for hundreds of leagues up waterfalls and mountains. Even the great mage couldn't do that, and he's stuck here, too."

"No he's not," Fireboy said. "He lives on his island, leagues away. I've seen the Duke's boat go off to visit."

"Does anybody else go?" Carver asked.

"Scharl does, with some of the guarda. I've seen them go with the Duke."

Carver looked at Raven and Fireboy. "We need to go there," he said. "That's what we meant to do." He turned to the mural, seeking himself in the shadows. "We need to finish what we started."

"How do you plan to do that?" Raven said. "Ask Scharl for a ride?"

"Why not?" Carver replied.

"Sure, why not?" Raven echoed. "Next time I see him, I'll just—"

At that moment, the door slammed open and two of the Duke's guarda shouldered into the room. They stood at either side of the door, hands on their firearms, coldly surveying the startled guests. The taverner came from the back room in a red-faced rush. Sweat ran down his forehead in streams.

An officer came in, followed by two more guarda carrying the signboard of the Happy Piper, taken from its chains above the entry. Last came a tall, knobby man with thick lenses over his eyes. Carver and Fireboy both looked at Raven in amazement. It was Scharl.

"What'd you do, conjure him?" Fireboy whispered.

Scharl stepped toward the taverner. The man cringed but managed to croak out a good evening.

"Is this your signboard?" Scharl demanded.

The taverner swallowed and said yes.

"Do you have any others like it?"

Everyone in the room looked at the mural. Scharl turned and saw it.

"Ah," he said. He stepped back and let his eyes sweep along the full length of it. "Very good," he rasped. "Yes. Very good."

He stepped right up to the wall and examined the surface closely.

"Plaster on lathe," he told the officer. "You'll want sharp saws, very fine toothed. Probably hacksaws. Bind all the way around it with strips of fabric and hide glue. But mind you stay clear of the people."

The officer hurried outside. In moments, he was back with a squad of men bearing tools. Under Scharl's direction, they began to cut away the entire face of the wall holding the mural.

"My Lord Steward!" the taverner exclaimed. "That's my wall!" He stepped forward imploringly, scrubbing his face with the skirt of his damp apron.

Scharl glanced at him, then nodded to the officer. The man went to the taverner and began counting out a pile of slugs. The taverner took the coins greedily, his mural finally paid for.

It didn't take long for the team of guarda to cut the wall free. It was bigger than the doorway, but they simply cut a notch through the top of the doorjamb right up to the ceiling. Then they braced the back with slats of wood, padded the front with blankets, and carefully hauled it away, along with the signboard. The taverner stared after them, then shrugged and carried his money into the back room. The other guests immediately began a hum of close conversation, wondering at the events.

"Come on," Carver said, and he hurried to the door.

Raven and Fireboy jumped up and followed him. They stared down the dark street at the disappearing troop of guarda with their odd spoils. Carver started to follow them.

They kept to the shadows at the edge of the street, dodging the occasional stripes of light from uncurtained windows. They tried to keep quiet, but the squad of guarda was making enough noise hauling the piece of wall to cover any footfalls half a block behind.

"They're heading toward the docks," Raven said after the third turning.

The squad marched past darkened warehouses onto the wharves along the river. The water glinted darkly as it slipped by the walls and pilings. A light glowed ahead, and Carver slowed. As they crept nearer, the light resolved into a lantern on the stern of a steamboat.

"That's the Duke's boat," Fireboy whispered.

They ducked behind a stack of boxes and peered around. The squad was loading the sign and mural onto the boat. There was no sign of the Duke, just the boatman and a uniformed fireboy at the engine. Scharl and three or four of the guarda stayed on board; the officer led the rest back onto the wharf. Then the boat gave a clank and a wheeze and quietly pulled away.

"They're going downriver!" Fireboy exclaimed. "Out to sea!"

"Out to Krimm's island," Carver said.

"You think?"

"I'm sure of it."

Twenty-one

W e'll need a boat," Carver said.

"I'll find one," Fireboy replied.

"Not a boatman. Just the boat."

"I know that."

"And it's just to borrow," Carver insisted. "We'll try not to blow this one up."

"We'll let Krimm do it this time," Raven muttered.

They were crossing the central canal now, still several blocks from the household. They spoke in hushed voices, but their words seemed to echo in the dark streets.

"What about Paskovek and Digger?" Fireboy asked. "Shouldn't we tell them we're leaving? They've been real good to us. Doesn't seem right to just disappear."

"You don't think they'll try to stop us, Steam Brain?" Raven demanded.

"Why would they? They know we're friends."

"We're going to see Krimm, brother to the big bad Duke."

"How could they stop us?" Fireboy insisted.

"Don't be a dolt," she replied. "There's a deep canal right outside the door, a lot of big loose paving stones. Add a piece of rope, a handy cudgel, and *splash*, you're bottom muck."

"They wouldn't go that far," Carver said, "but they won't like it. It's best we slip away quietly." Seeing the look on Fireboy's face, he added, "We'll leave a note."

"What if they ask us where we've been tonight?"

"Tell them. Don't lie—Paskovek can still say truth well enough to spot a lie."

"Better yet, let me do the talking," Raven said.

Paskovek did ask, and they did tell him. Even Fireboy couldn't help interrupting to add details he thought were important.

Paskovek ran his fingers through his goatee, brooding. "Most peculiar," he said finally. He turned his deep gaze on Carver. "Your father must have had great talent."

Carver nodded, afraid to speak.

"Be careful," Paskovek told him. "Be very careful. Krimm sought out that mural for some arcane reason. Someday he may seek out you."

"Me?" Carver mumbled.

"You are your father's son," Paskovek said.

"I have no talent for painting," Carver protested.

"Krimm doesn't know that."

It was four days before Fireboy found a good boat. The next evening after work, Carver went from the paint house to the central canal but turned toward the river instead of the household. The avenue took him to the wharves. Fireboy and Raven were waiting for him, in an alley between two warehouses.

"Did you get it?" Carver asked Raven.

She pulled the linen-wrapped wand from under her topshirt. He took it with thanks and tucked it carefully under his own, with the end snug in his overshirt to hold it.

"Now, where to?" he asked Fireboy.

"Just a little ways down the quay." Fireboy whispered, even though no one was around.

Carver handed them each a limp fried roll he had purchased from a street vendor on the way over. "Eat," he said. "We may not get another chance for a while."

Fireboy grinned and held up a grease-stained sack. "Don't worry, nobody's going to starve on my boat. But that'll make a nice dinner." He took the roll and downed half in one bite. Raven looked at hers distastefully and nibbled a corner.

"Are you all right?" Carver asked.

She grimaced. "It smells like it's been dead awhile."

"You're no rosebud yourself." Fireboy mumbled, mouth full of his second half. He swallowed the lump and smacked his lips. "I'll take it if you don't want it."

She glared at him and kept nibbling.

Carver finished his own roll and licked his fingers. "We probably shouldn't loiter here. Let's walk around till dark."

Raven led them into the city, following the twists and turns of the side streets and alleyways, shortcuts she had scouted out as a courier. She walked briskly, as though she were on an important errand. As the gloom deepened and the crowds thinned, she avoided the streets with lights. Carver and Fireboy kept pace, and no one gave them a second glance.

When it was full night and darkness stretched from curb to curb, Raven led them back to the wharves. Fireboy pointed out one of the boats tied along the quay. It was a small open steam launch, the type that ferried passengers and light cargo.

There were lights here and there along the wharf, but all they did was darken the shadows. The three of them huddled against a warehouse wall, watching for any sign of life. They saw only one lean cat. The air got cooler and mist began to rise from the river. Soon, they saw a light moving up the quay. They lay flat behind a stack of empty barrels that smelled of old fish. The light swung closer, revealing two guarda. The men strolled by, shining their lantern this way and that. Carver winced as the beam fell across their hiding place, but the guarda moved on without pausing. When they were well up the wharf, Fireboy crawled out.

"Wait here," he whispered, then disappeared around the warehouse.

He was back in a few minutes, carrying a pair of oars. Beckoning, he scuttled across the wharf and dropped into the little boat. Carver and Raven were right behind him.

"I'll untie us," he whispered, handing each an oar. "You push off, then row."

Silently, they obeyed. Carver shoved the bow away, then swung the oar over the side and began to pull against the current, using one of the canopy poles to brace the oar. The boat seemed stuck, the water thick as mud. He heard Raven's oar splash lightly on the other side, heard her strain. Fireboy turned the wheel, steering them into the river.

Suddenly, there was a movement on the wharf.

"Pull!" Fireboy breathed. "Pull!"

Carver ducked his head to see beyond the canopy. Someone was standing on the edge of the wharf, backlit in the mist. Carver pulled harder, and the little boat moved beyond jumping distance. A light swung out, revealing the two guarda. They shone the light into the darkness, but the little boat was picking up speed, disappearing into the mist. Soon the guarda were just a spot of light on a gray mound spotted with other dim lights, all of it drawing farther away.

Fireboy told Carver to take the wheel and went back to the engine to build a fire and get up steam. Raven rowed slowly to help keep them pointed downstream. Carver watched the gray mass of the city drift by. It seemed to go on for leagues, larger than he had ever realized. It was still there when Fireboy turned a valve and put the engine in gear. Chuffing quietly, the boat began to pick up speed. Raven pulled in her oar, and Carver gave Fireboy the wheel.

They reached the harbor end of the city, marked by a black forest of masts. Then there was only riverbank, barely visible in the dark. The little boat began to lift and fall gently. All hint of land dropped away behind them.

At that moment, a quarter moon rose above the flat horizon, bleeding wan light through the mist. Behind them stretched a dimly seen shore; ahead lay a seemingly limitless stretch of sea.

"Where to?" Fireboy asked, voice tight with excitement and fatigue.

Raven pointed confidently. "That way," she said.

Fireboy stared into the darkness. "How do you know?" he asked.

"I can feel it," she said, and shivered.

Carver, too, could feel a strange pressure, like a breeze on his face, only there was no wind to ruffle the low swells. He nodded. "That's the way."

Fireboy looked from one to the other, frowning. "If you say so," he muttered.

They steamed through the moonlight. Carver kept the fire stoked, Raven navigated, Fireboy steered. Finally, they glimpsed a light in the distance.

"That's it," Raven said. Fireboy let out an audible sigh of relief and adjusted their heading.

As they approached, they could see that the light was high above the water. Then they noticed a dark mass looming to their right. Moonlight glinted on a white line of foam, and they heard the soft wash of calm waves against rock. Ahead on the other side, another tall shape loomed. An archipelago of high, straight-walled islands thrust up from the sea like grasping fingers. The light they were chasing shone high in the face of one farther on.

The boat's movement changed as they ran over a stretch of steep, short waves. Fireboy cut the wheel to the right to steer back onto smoother water.

"Ledge," he said shortly. "Not all these islands break the surface."

He slowed the boat, and they all peered ahead, watching for eddies and foam that would mark a dangerous shoal. The mist swirled confusingly over the surface.

"You're heading the wrong way," Raven said. She pointed at the light, now off to the side.

Fireboy turned the wheel and they went back to scanning the water. A few minutes later, Raven said, "You're aiming off again."

Again Fireboy shifted the wheel.

They went on for a while longer. The light grew closer, showing still higher above the surface. Then Carver noticed they were off course yet again.

"We'll watch for rocks," he said. "You steer."

But just a minute later, they were heading almost at right angles to the light. Fireboy swore and shifted the wheel. Almost immediately, the boat veered away. He swung it the other way, but the bow sheered past again. Hands clenched on the wheel, he fought to point them in the right direction. Raven added her strength. The boat veered sharply left and right, refusing to go toward the island. Carver could feel the faint breeze of magic pressing first one side of his cheek, then the other.

"Stop," he told them. "Let up and see what happens."

Raven snapped a curse and stepped away from the wheel. Fireboy held on with just one hand. The wheel didn't move, but the boat swung in a smooth arc, till it pointed directly away from the island.

"I guess we're not going to get there by boat," Carver said.

Fireboy eased the throttle back to a crawl. The little craft rolled uneasily in the swell. "What do we do?" he asked.

"I suppose we could try to swim," Carver said. "Maybe it's just the boat being blocked."

Raven shook her head. "That's a long stretch of cold, bumpy water, Monkey Boy."

"It's not that far."

"If I head off to one side, we can probably swing by closer," Fireboy said.

"You'll have to stay with the boat anyway. What do you think, Raven? Ready for a dip?"

She frowned and looked away. "I'd rather fly," she muttered.

"Well, that's why we're here," he said lamely. "So you can fly again."

She clicked her teeth. "Kah! I hate water, blast it! I'm a bird, not a fish!"

"We could wait till daylight," Fireboy offered. "Maybe if Krimm sees us circling around out here, he'll let us through."

"No," Raven muttered. "He knows we're here."

Carver realized she was right. The force on his cheek wasn't indifferent; it was cold and . . . "He's irritated. We're bothering him."

"Like a fly," Raven said. "Just a pesky bug."

Fireboy shivered. "You sure you want to get there?"

"Yes," Carver said, and Raven nodded reluctantly, glaring at the light.

They made a small float from two seat boards; then Fireboy steered them as close to the island as he could. As they swung near, Carver and Raven slipped over the side and began kicking toward the light, one at either end of the float. The pressure against them was still there, but they could make headway against it. Fireboy veered away to find a hiding place behind one of the other islands. He would steam back to the same place the next night and circle till near dawn, watching for a signal from them.

Almost immediately, the cold water began to weigh on Carver's arms and legs. He kept kicking in time with Raven, pushing steadily toward the looming dark face of the island. The light was high above them now and hard to see, but the mage breeze on their faces was a sure guide. Finally, he could hear the sound of waves lapping on the rocks. His hands were almost too numb to feel the seat board. Each kick was an effort.

"How are we going to get up that cliff?" Raven panted.

"There's got to be a wharf of some kind." He could hardly unclench his jaw to speak.

"Better hope it's on this side of the island, Monkey Boy."

It was, jutting from the sheer rock wall to meet them. It was only a few feet high, but it was smooth stone and they couldn't stretch their numb fingers high enough to grasp the edge. They struggled, trying to brace the float so one of them could scramble up and get a grip. Both kept falling into the freezing water. Each new attempt was harder than the last. Carver made one final try, flinging himself up as the small swell lifted him a few extra inches. His fingers caught the edge a moment, and he tried to swing his other arm up to get a second purchase. But there was a slick film of scum on the rocks and he felt himself slipping. He scrabbled against the rock, splashing his feet against the wharf, desperately searching for a toehold. Raven pushed against him and went under in a choking effort to hold him up. His fingers scratched vainly on the scummy rock as he slid back.

Suddenly, a hand gripped his wrist. A second grabbed his collar. He was hauled over the edge, then shoved on his belly into a dripping huddle on the wharf. He lay gasping, blinking salt from his eyes as the bulky form of his savior squatted down to haul Raven bodily from the water. She fell beside Carver, drenched and wretched and coughing up seawater.

Carver tried to say thank you, but the words caught in his throat. For the second time in a week, he found himself staring up at Uncle Piper.

Twenty-Two

"Follow me," Uncle Piper said. He turned and walked stiffly up the pier.

Carver stared at him, speechless. This was not a signboard; he moved and talked. But there was something odd about him. His motions were stiff. His voice was flat and emotionless. And his eyes showed no sign of recognition or any of the kindness that had made working as Uncle Piper's apprentice at all bearable.

Carver hauled himself up, then helped Raven. They were both soaked to the bone and shivering. Water ran down her miserable face.

"Wasn't that your uncle?" she asked.

Carver could only nod.

"Friendly lout, isn't he?"

They staggered after him.

The wharf ended at a natural crack in the rock face of the island. Uncle Piper led them under a stone arch and into a tunnel lit by glowing globes. The light was harsh and yellow. They passed through a door into a warmer space, and Carver paused to wring some of the water out of his clothes. Raven shook herself all over and raked back her dripping hair. Uncle Piper watched them incuriously, then continued without a word.

Carver stared after him. "He must be under some spell," he said. "It's like he has no mind of his own."

"I've never heard of a spell like that," Raven muttered. "You can't take away someone's will; you can't put any charm on them at all, unless they want you to."

Carver shook his head. "He would never want that."

They followed slowly. The stone hallway entered a stone room, also lit by the strange globes. Uncle Piper was sliding a gate back from a doorway at the far side. He stepped through and beckoned them to join him. Carver entered the little room hesitantly; the floor shook as he did. The walls were covered with stout bronze mesh a few inches out from the rock, like a cage set inside a cupboard. Raven held back, eyes darting from one side of the tiny space to the other.

"Not me," she said.

But Uncle Piper grabbed her arm and jerked her inside as though she weighed nothing. She squawked in surprise and tried to pull free. He held her tightly, with no apparent effort. As he slid shut the gate, trapping them all inside, Raven fought harder. Carver tried to calm her. Uncle Piper simply held her off and pushed a lever set into the wall. With a jerk and a rattle, the cage began to rise. The stone walls slid past. Carver looked up and saw they were in a shaft of rock. A rope stretched up into darkness, pulling them higher. The cage was a lift, just like those at the falls between the reaches. It bumped and rattled as it went, making Raven jump and struggle even harder. They passed several openings, each marked by a band of harsh light. Uncle Piper stared stolidly ahead, holding Raven away with one stiff arm. Finally, he pulled the lever back down and they rattled to a stop. He slid the gate back and let go of Raven. She darted out of the cage and crouched a few steps into the new room, panting. Carver hurried out and knelt beside her.

"We're out now," he said, touching her shoulder gently. She jerked and stared at him with wide, panicked eyes. "Don't be afraid. We're out."

She glared at him. "I'm not afraid, meathead! I . . . I couldn't breathe." She jerked up straight. "I'm fine." But her tone was shrill, and her eyes still stared wildly.

"If you're cold, come over here," a voice said.

For a moment, Carver thought Uncle Piper had spoken. The

voice had the same impersonal quality, but somehow it sounded more alive. He looked around. They were at the edge of a wide room that fanned out from the cage in a rough oval. On the far side was a broad window that looked out on darkness. The voice came again from the left.

"Come over here," it repeated. "Get in the light, where I can see you."

Carver and Raven stepped farther in. A man stood beside a metal stairway that spiraled up to a wide balcony in the arch of a high domed ceiling. He was dressed oddly in a gold-edged burgundy robe worn over breeches and sandals.

"Come on," he repeated a third time. A note of irritation sharpened his voice. "You spent all that effort to get here—don't dally now. I've got work to do."

Carver went closer, and Raven followed a couple of steps behind. The man watched their slow progress with growing impatience.

"I'm not going to blast you," he barked. "Come here!"

Carver took several quick steps forward before stopping himself just out of arm's reach. The man's face relaxed a little. He studied Carver from head to toe and back.

This was obviously Krimm. He had the same high cheekbones and sharp nose as his brother, the Duke, and the same blond-white hair, though his was thinning on top, making his forehead appear even higher. He wore wire-framed lenses like Scharl's, but behind them glinted the dark, deep-set eyes of his brother.

"You're soaked," he said, looking from one to the other. "You'd like to be dry, yes?"

Carver was taken aback by the mundane question. "Yes, sir," he replied.

"Good." Krimm's lips moved slightly. His left hand shifted, fingers tracing a vague pattern. Carver felt a strange tingle all over his skin. His clothes seemed to pull upward. All the water on him began to flow up through the fabric. He almost choked as it washed up past his nose and eyes, blinding him for an moment. Then it tugged up through his hair and coalesced into a huge inverted teardrop over his head. It merged with a similar blob from Raven and, bobbing like a soap bubble, drifted out the window on the far wall.

Carver was bone-dry. He felt warmed and chilled all at once and gave a last, violent shiver. "Thank you," he stammered.

Krimm grunted. He continued to study the two of them intently. It reminded Carver of Paskovek's searching look. He wondered if Krimm was a truth sayer on top of his other talents.

"I recognize you," Krimm said suddenly. "You're Painter's boy." He sounded surprised, and also strangely satisfied.

Carver suppressed another shiver and shifted away. But Krimm reached out his left hand again and muttered some low words. The locket stirred under Carver's tunic. Carver grabbed at it through the cloth, but it slid out of his grip. The chain flowed like water over his head and flew into Krimm's hand.

"That's mine!" Carver cried.

"Of course it is," Krimm snapped back. "You'll get it back." He flicked it open and studied the painting inside. "What's your name?"

"Carver."

Krimm raised his eyebrows. "Carver Painter? An odd name."

"It's Thomas Painter," Carver said sullenly. "I call myself Carver."

Krimm frowned. "Whatever you like. It's a painter I need. These are old already."

He gestured to his right, and Carver saw the mural from the tavern leaning against the wall, along with several other framed and unframed canvases and boards. They all held portraits painted by his father. Some of them he recognized as people from his village; others were strangers. All of them were worn and faded. Then something in the mural caught Carver's eye. The figure of Uncle Piper was gone from the center of the painting. In its place stood a gray silhouette with just the faintest hint of penciled detail, as if all the paint had been peeled away. As if the portrait of Uncle Piper had walked out of the painting.

Carver gasped and looked around for Uncle Piper. He was still standing by the lift cage, silent, stiff, and lifeless, like a painting on the wall.

Carver spun back to Krimm. The mage was watching him closely.

"You're quick, young Thomas. Very quick. You get that from your mother; she was the real light of that union. But your father was a genius, a mage in his own right. He had the talent I needed. Now here you are, with your mother's brains. I hope you also have your father's talent."

"I'm no painter," Carver said flatly.

Krimm's face stiffened. "You can't paint?" Once again his deep eyes searched Carver's face. "You can't paint," he said finally, and his disappointment was clear. "What are you, then?" The eyes probed. Carver felt as if his face were being peeled back. "Ah," Krimm said. "A wand."

Carver felt the wand shift. It was still wrapped in its linen sheath under his topshirt, and he grabbed and held it tightly.

Krimm grunted. "Keep it, boy, and this." He handed back the locket. "But know that a true mage doesn't need silly props."

"I'm not a mage." Carver gripped the locket. "I'm not a blasted painter. I'm a carver."

Krimm's eyebrows rose again. "Hence the odd name. Of course. Are you any good?"

Carver bristled. "I can carve as well as my father painted! If people would just let me."

Krimm smiled thinly. "I will be only too happy to let you. Carve something for me now."

Carver flushed, remembering his struggling efforts in Duns-gow. He slipped the locket into a pouch, hiding the cuts on his fingers. But Krimm's tone made him angry; that and the mention of his father. He wasn't going to back down now. "Carve what?" he asked.

"Just a sample. Something small to give me an idea of your talent."

"Anything I like?"

"Anything. Here's a piece of wood."

Carver jumped as Uncle Piper appeared silently beside him, holding a block of dark wood.

"You mean right now?"

"Why not?"

"Because we're tired and hungry, Glass Eyes." Raven stepped forward, hands on hips, and glared at Krimm. "We just swam a half a league to get through your blasted spell, we almost drowned, we've been up all night, and we're hungry."

His eyes narrowed. "You chose to make that swim; I didn't invite you. But I will be a good host. You will have plenty of time to rest later. As for food, I will arrange that as soon as Thom—" He caught himself with another thin smile. "As soon as *Carver* relieves my servant of that piece of wood."

Carver took the block from Uncle Piper's painting, which turned and went to the lift.

"He will return with your breakfast soon," Krimm continued, maintaining his smile. "As for you, my name-calling young mage, when you have eaten and rested, and when Carver has shown me what he can do, I will help you with your own problem."

"What problem?" Raven asked suspiciously.

"Your birdness," Krimm replied. "I can teach you how to be all that you can be, as both mage and bird." He turned back to Carver. "I can help you, too. You can become the carver you claim to be, not just a name. I can see you have real talent, perhaps even more than your father. All you need is someone who truly values your work. Carve something for me."

Carver looked at the block of wood in his hands. It was a rich brown, darker even than aged walnut, from some tree he didn't know. The grain was clear, with a subtle figure that swirled along the surface. It felt alive. Already he could sense a shape in it, begging to be released.

"All right," he said. "I'll carve something."

Raven glared at him but held her tongue.

"You can work here," Krimm said, indicating a bench and stool under the balcony. He walked over and cleared away some drawings and tools and pieces of metal. "My servant will bring your meal here. And a knife. You'll need a proper knife."

"I have one," Carver said, pulling Fireboy's clasp knife from his pouch.

Krimm frowned. "A steel blade? I do not allow iron here; it disagrees with me. You're a strong swimmer to get past my ward, with even a small bit like that. Ah, here comes the piper."

"Uncle Piper," Carver said. The lift gate slid back, and the animated painting carried a tray into the room.

Krimm's brows raised. "Your uncle? You know the people in the painting?"

"Yes."

"Good. You must tell me about them later. The more I know, the more life I can bring to the animations. I'm sorry your uncle is so stiff."

The animation walked over and put the tray on the workbench. It held two bowls of steaming soup, cups of hot cider, and a loaf of bread. Carver's mouth watered.

"Give your uncle that knife, Carver, and use this one instead."

Krimm lifted something from the tray and held it up. A blade glinted like gold in the yellow light.

Reluctantly, Carver handed Fireboy's knife to the animation and took the other from Krimm. The handle was white bone and fit his palm perfectly. The blade was small but sturdy, with a straight back, a fine point, and a curved edge as sharp as broken glass. He wondered if it really was gold.

"It's bronze," Krimm said, as though hearing his thoughts. "As

I said, I do not permit iron on my island. Now, there is one other thing, one other . . ." He studied Raven a moment, then asked, "What are you wearing around your neck?" She put her hand protectively to her throat. "Ah, a feather bauble. Let me guess: a gift from your mistress?" Raven nodded warily. "Interesting. It is iron underneath the enamel, but—" He lifted a hand, forestalling a remark from Raven. "But I will make an exception in this case," he finished, smiling slightly. "You may keep it. Now, please eat and rest, both of you. Then carve for me. . . . Carver? Good. Call me when you're done. I'll be working above."

He stepped onto the spiral stair, which immediately began to turn like a big screw, lifting him to the balcony. Carver and Raven watched, stepping farther and farther back, taking in more and more of the space above. It was filled with some great, glinting apparatus. Arms lifted and swung. Wheels of metal swirled. Pendulums oscillated. Balls twirled in eccentric orbits, some slow, some fast. A rack of light globes hung in the very peak of the dome, sending reflections of gold, silver, copper, and crystal dancing around the upper walls. Parts of it looked as if they came from a steam engine, others from a workhouse, others from no machine Carver had ever seen.

"What is it?" he gasped.

"No idea," Raven muttered. "And right now I don't really care. I'm too blasted hungry."

She went to the bench and drank half a cup of the cider, then tore off a chunk of bread.

Carver continued to watch the machine. Krimm studied some kind of gauge and made notes, occasionally glancing up to watch the twirling balls and arms. The light glinted off his lenses and his gold-trimmed robe, making him seem almost a part of the complex works. Carver watched, trying to match this odd, almost scholarly man to the tales they had heard of Krimm in Dunsgow. He was curt and demanding; highhanded, even. But somehow he didn't seem evil. Carver didn't know how he seemed. Elusive. Driven.

Maybe even a little crazy. But nothing like Carver had expected.

Again as though reading his thoughts, Krimm glanced down at Carver. He smiled thinly and light flashed on his lenses, making bright holes of his eyes, holes that showed nothing inside, only reflections of the whirling apparatus above him. Carver shivered and looked away. Through the big window across the hall, he could see the dim line of the horizon at the edge of the sea. Dawn was breaking. He wondered what Fireboy was doing, and how long his one sack of food would last. Then he joined Raven hungrily at the tray.

Twenty-three

Raven woke a few hours later, after a deep sleep in an alcove under the balcony. Daylight poured in through the big window. She rose and stretched out some of the aches from the long, cold swim. Carver's pallet was already empty. Probably trying to carve something, the stupid woodpecker. Krimm had said all the right words, that was for sure. She wondered if he really could restore her talent and finish her training. Even if he could, would he? And even if he did, what would it cost her? She had spent three years in service to Penalla. Penalla had been fickle, petty, and, Raven realized now, not very bright. But she had never been cruel or evil. Krimm was smart, serious, and cold. The thought of serving him made her stomach clench.

She got up and noticed the white-linen packet lying beside Carver's pallet. A sliver of green showed through a fold in the cloth. She stared at it for a moment in disbelief. Then she snatched it up and unwrapped the linen, revealing leaf after green leaf. The wand was whole again. She could feel the energy tingle against her palm. She waved it gently, thrilled to see a faint mist waft from the quivering leaves.

"Carver!" she called, trailing mist as she ran from the alcove.

He was seated at the workbench, hunched over the block of wood. Chips littered the floor around him.

"Hey, Carver!" She hurried over and held out the wand.

"Oh," he said. Then he blinked and looked again. "Oh. That's . . . wonderful."

She stared at him incredulously. "You don't sound like it's wonderful."

"I'm . . ." He shrugged and rubbed his bleary eyes with the back of his hand. The bronze knife glinted. "I'm kind of busy," he said. "Almost done."

"What? Have you been carving all night?"

"All morning, actually." He smiled, and his weariness fled for a moment. He held out the block of wood, transformed into a beautiful carved raven. "I can do it! It's like I never stopped. I picked up the knife and it felt like part of my hand. I looked at the wood and thought, I'll carve an eagle, like I did after Penalla died, I've done that before. But the wood wanted a different shape, and the knife heard it. I could see it then, carved before I even touched the wood. It was like—"

"Like magic," Raven said, trying to hide the bitterness in her voice. "Good work, Monkey Boy. You've got your knife, you've got your wand. I'm happy for you."

"Thanks," he said with a big, blind smile. "I'll just finish this now, right? Just a few more minutes." He was already shaving off a last bit here and there.

"Sure," Raven muttered. "Don't mind me, Chip Head."

She dropped the wand onto the workbench. Carver didn't even notice. All he cared about now was his carving. She wondered if Krimm had somehow enchanted him, if it was magic that made him so blind to everything else, even his own fatigue. Carver would probably welcome an enchantment like that.

Clenching her teeth, she turned and wandered around the hall. Uncle Piper's painting was slumped stiffly against the mural, as though drawn to its own world. Krimm was on the balcony with his apparatus. She could feel a faint pressure from the thing, like a gentle breeze stirred up by the spinning balls and waving arms. Fireboy would probably love it.

She went to the window, wondering where he was. She was high above the water, looking out through a hole in a sheer cliff. She could see the other islands scattered in the near distance. None was as tall as this one, but they were all wide enough to hide the little steamboat. Though she doubted it was hidden from Krimm. Much farther away, she could see the faint smudge of the mainland and the gap of the river mouth. She looked down and saw the small pier where they had nearly drowned. There was no sign of their float.

Kah! If she could only fly, she'd never touch open water again.

She heard something whir and turned back to the hall. Krimm was spiraling down the moving stairs. The Uncle Piper thing stirred, then went to the cage and descended out of sight. Carver turned from the workbench, holding the finished raven.

"Well," Krimm said, "you're certainly quick." He took the carving and turned it around, running his hand along the detailed ribs of the wooden feathers. He smiled. "Excellent. More than excellent." He turned his smile on Carver. "You are every bit as good as your father."

Raven grimaced as Carver blushed. The poor dolt was so easy, it was embarrassing.

"What are you going to do with it?" she asked, walking over to them.

"Do?" Krimm turned his glassy stare on her. The lenses made him look like an owl. A hunting owl.

"Do," she repeated. "We've seen the moving painting; your servant. Is that your plan with the carvings? More slaves?"

He actually laughed. "Can a painting be a slave? No, my doubtful friend, these are not people. They are only animations, and not very good at that. No better than machines. They don't really live."

"They look alive."

"But they aren't."

"They don't feel anything when you peel them off the canvas? When you make them fetch and carry for you?"

"They don't feel at all," he said. "Watch them closely. Their eyes never blink. They don't act on their own. They don't think. And that's the problem, isn't it? The ultimate problem: how to make them think. How to make them *alive*." His eyes flicked from her to Carver. "Come with me. I'll show you what I hope—no, what I *plan* to do with these carvings."

He stepped back onto the staircase and spiraled up to the balcony. After a moment's hesitation, Carver followed. Raven waited till he was all the way up, then stepped on herself, wishing she could simply fly there.

Krimm was threading his way through the lower mechanism of the apparatus. The globes and arms swung just over his head, but he ignored them. He reached a stationary shaft, pulled a lever, and waited while a broad, fluted cylinder rose from the floor. He placed the carved raven in the center, like a statue on a pedestal. Then he went to his bench. Raven expected him to twist a valve or pull another lever. Instead, he raised his hands and began to sketch the motions of a spell. His lips moved, silently speaking an incantation. The pedestal rose into the upper workings of the apparatus. The balls and arms whirled around it. Raven felt the pressure on her face increase. The balls spun faster. A hum began to tingle up her spine. It grew to an itch, then to a stinging needle dance. The apparatus blurred with speed.

There was a sizzling crack and a flash of violet light. For a moment, Raven went deaf. When her sight and hearing cleared, the apparatus was slowing down, lowering to a hum. The column descended. Raven stared at the carved bird. It seemed the same: dark wood swirled with subtly darker grain. But light glinted in its eye. It turned its head. It blinked.

"Ah!" Krimm exclaimed. "Did you see?"

He hurried through the mechanism, then bent forward, studying the raven. It croaked at him and stepped back.

"Yes!" he hissed. "So much better!" He held out his arm, and the once-wooden raven stepped onto it. He bore it back triumphantly. "So much better," he repeated. "Almost, almost alive." He held up the other hand and brushed the raven's head. "But not quite. You see? It's not breathing. And yet . . ." He turned his glassy stare on Raven. "You can guess what I plan to do, yes?" He turned to Carver. "With your help, yes? To bring these carvings to life."

He strode to the staircase and went down. The raven stood on his arm, turning its head. Despite the color, it looked completely alive at this distance. Raven and Carver glanced at each other and followed. As they reached the floor of the hall, Uncle Piper arrived in the lift with a birdcage. He stalked forward and held it open dumbly. Krimm placed the new raven inside, then took the cage and hung it on a hook under the balcony. He smiled at it smugly.

Raven looked at the raven. It looked back.

Idiot, she thought. You let him put you in a cage.

The raven blinked at her.

"Why?" she demanded.

"Why?" Krimm echoed. He stared at her as if she were stupid. "Why? I can give you a hundred reasons, my little birdbrain. Because it has never been done? Because it is simply beautiful? Because it is the ultimate magic? Because it is my greatest talent?"

"Because you need better servants?"

"Pah! I have plenty of servants. I can make all the servants I need from paintings."

"You said you were running out of paintings."

"Yes, they wear out. So what? This"—he gazed fondly at the raven—"this is what matters."

Raven clicked her teeth. "You still need servants to feed you while you play with your big machine. How do you get new ones?"

He glared at her in exasperation. "From new paintings. Where else?"

"Who paints them for you?" Krimm's glare hardened. His eyes flicked toward Carver. "You can't animate paintings unless they're good enough," she said. "Unless they're as good as Thomas Painter's. And no one else is that good, right, Glass Eyes?"

"You're very perceptive," he said coldly.

"So where's Thomas Painter?" she demanded.

"Under your feet. Just a few levels down, in a comfortable

chamber, where he and his wife have lived for the past ten years."

Carver went pale, eyes wide.

"With all the mages you had arrested?" Raven said.

Krimm sneered. "There is no comparison. Dunsgow's mages were useless fools, trapped in outdated ritual and superstition. Not one of them had a new idea, a power I couldn't wield better. They held me back. They fouled my spells with their nattering incantations. I silenced them. Thomas Painter had a talent beyond their crude magics. His art I cherished."

"Then why isn't he still painting for you?"

"He can't. Carver, your parents are here, but your father is blind. He stared too long at his paintings, and he went blind." Krimm reached out and laid a hand on Carver's shoulder. "I'm sorry to have to tell you. You're upset, yes? I was afraid you would be. You'd probably like to go see them now."

Carver stiffened and stepped back. "See them now?" he stammered. "I don't know." He glanced wildly at Raven. She remembered his fear at the tavern and glared at him. He looked away, fists clenched. "Not yet. Please."

Krimm's eyebrows rose. "Are you sure?"

"Yes," Carver said faintly. "It's been . . . I don't . . . I don't know what to say to them!"

"You could start with, 'Hello, I'm your son,'" Raven said.

"No," Krimm said. "I can see that it's all too much for you now. You need to rest. You hardly slept at all last night. Neither did I." He shepherded them back toward their alcove. "Later, Raven, after we've all rested, I will show you how to be a bird again."

"Why don't *I* go meet Carver's parents now?" she countered. "While he's sleeping. I can prepare them for the shock."

Krimm's eyes were cold behind his lenses, his lips thinned by vexation. "I keep underestimating you, little bird. You are as stubborn as you are talented."

With that he reached out and spoke a single word. The silver chain flew over Raven's head. Before she could even react, her feather pendant dangled from his fingers. He held it carefully at arm's length.

"Now for your lesson," he said, indicating the feather. "Your mistress—it would be Penalla, yes? It would seem she didn't trust you. Or maybe she was just jealous of your natural talent, which, I can assure you, is much greater than hers ever was. In any case, she gave you this, not to help you master that talent but to hold you down. It has a clever little spell on it, to limit you. To keep you in her control."

"Don't try to change the subject," Raven snapped. "What about Carver's parents?"

Krimm sighed. "I thought you wanted to be a bird mage. You are already, you know. All you needed was to get rid of this." He dangled the pendant. "And leave the spell around Dunsgow. Go on, say the words: change to a raven. Say them backwards and change back. You don't need Penalla to do it for you, or anyone else."

"What about Carver's parents?" she yelled.

Krimm's eyebrows rose. "All right. They're still here, as I said, a few levels farther down, where they have been since Painter gave up painting. Where you will join them, if Carver refuses to carve."

"In a pig's ear," Raven muttered. She moved her fingers, sketching the proper patterns of her spell. Silently, she mouthed the words that Penalla had taught her. She had no doubt it would work. From the moment the feather pendant had left her skin, she'd felt the old energy quivering in her heart, stronger than ever before. On the final syllable, a surge of power jolted through her, half pleasure and half pain. Her mouth pursed and stretched. Her gums ached. She dropped toward the floor as her legs shrank. Her clothes fell loose and baggy around her feet. She spread her arms and had wings. With a light bound, she cast off her clothing and lifted into the air. She hovered in front of Krimm.

"This is what a real raven acts like, Glass Eyes!" She jabbed her beak at his face.

But Krimm swung up his arm, batting her hard with the back of his hand. And suddenly the fake piper was there. He grabbed one wing and jerked her painfully from the air.

"No!" Carver yelled. He leaped toward the piper, but the thing slapped him aside with a heavy blow, and he sprawled against the wall.

Raven beat her wings madly, thrashing at the artificial man. She jabbed him with her beak, tore him with her talons. It was like slashing canvas. He didn't bleed, didn't even grimace. She poked at his eyes and tore one right out, but his face didn't change. He grabbed her other wing and squeezed her tightly to his chest.

Krimm reappeared, carrying the birdcage. He shooed out the false raven, which flew to the windowsill and sat there, blinking calmly at her. She raged and slashed at Krimm. He kept the cage in front of himself and advanced. The painting shoved her inside and slammed the door. Raven beat herself against the bars. They were bronze and didn't give an inch. Krimm produced a small lock from his robe and snapped it through the bars. Raven jabbed at his hand, but the bars were spaced too tightly. Her beak rebounded with a dull *clank*.

Krimm held the cage out and studied her. Then he carried it to the hook and hung it back up. The torn painting followed, dragging Carver along.

"There," Krimm said. "A bird in the cage is worth . . . everything." Raven croaked hoarsely and threw herself against the bars. He held up the feather pendant. "Quiet," he snapped, "or I will put this back on you in such a way that you will never get it off."

"You can't enchant me," she spat. "Not against my will, and you know it."

"I don't need to enchant you, little bird." Krimm dangled the pendant in front of her. "I'll simply enchant this." He hung it on another hook on the post, where she could see it clearly. "As for you," he said, turning to Carver, "I expect you to carve something rather special for me. It will be your masterpiece, I can assure you.

Under normal circumstances, I imagine you'd be happy to carve it for me. Now . . ." He smiled thinly at Raven. She hissed at him. "Now, I imagine you might try to refuse. Yes?"

Carver struggled against the animation. "You're blasted right I refuse!"

"Then I shall have to kill her."

Twenty-four

Carver slumped dejectedly on the stool as Krimm's animations dragged a man-sized block of wood from the lift and stood it by the workbench. There were three of them now: torn Uncle Piper, the mayor, and Silas Joynter. Krimm watched with satisfaction from his balcony. Raven huddled in her cage, sometimes watching with bright, mad eyes. Other times she ducked her head under her wing. Her body would shake then. Carver had to look away.

Krimm spiraled down the stairs.

"Is that good?" he asked Carver. "I can have them turn the piece however you'd like."

"It's fine," Carver said, hardly looking.

Krimm raised his eyebrows. "Show a little interest, or I can make it even more uncomfortable for your feathered friend."

Carver glanced at Raven, huddled in her cage, then heaved himself off the stool to look more closely at the massive block. It was basswood; honey colored, even grained, and perfect for carving. There were no checks or cracks, even through the heart. Amazingly, there were no knots in it. The tree must have been huge. Despite his anger, Carver grew excited at the thought of carving this perfect block.

"That's better," Krimm said. "Consumed by your talent. Just like your father."

Carver drew back from the wood. "Where is my father?" he demanded.

"Safely locked up below with your mother," Krimm replied. "She was the bird I used to snare him. Now he shares her cage."

"You didn't kill her?"

"He never gave me cause. I asked him to paint nine portraits for me, and he did. Every one a masterpiece." Krimm smiled ruefully. "Unfortunately, I misjudged the time it would take to finish my projects, and how quickly the paintings would age. Nine weren't enough."

"And then he refused to paint more," Carver declared, trying to feel braver at the thought.

"Not at all," Krimm said mildly. "Then it was too late. His eyesight was nearly gone."

"You're lying! He's not that old."

"It's more than time that ages a man. He wore, like his paintings. But that's neither here nor there. We are concerned with you and Raven and this block of wood."

Carver glared at him but finally had to drop his eyes. "What do you want me to carve?" he muttered.

"The Duke," Krimm said. "My erstwhile brother."

The three animations had carried over a tall, cloth-draped frame. Now Krimm pulled off the cloth to reveal a full-sized portrait of Duke Kovac. Carver recognized his father's workmanship immediately. But the painting was worn, much more than you'd expect after so few years.

"Your father put all his talent into nine of these," Krimm said. "This is the last. The others wore out. Life does that, I suppose, even near life. They become harder to animate, harder to make lifelike. And I need this one in particular to seem alive." He looked from the painting to Carver. His eyes gleamed. "Wood is closer to life than canvas. Round is easier to animate than flat. Think of it— you can help me create life from this piece of wood. Real life."

"Or you'll kill Raven."

Krimm eyed him as he would a backward apprentice. "If that's what it takes. I had hoped you'd see the beauty of the project, take it as a challenge to your skill."

Carver turned to the bench as though Krimm hadn't spoken.

"I'll need an adze or a hatchet to rough out the shape. Some chisels and gouges. A mallet." He picked up the knife in a clenched fist. "This isn't enough."

"You'll have whatever you need," Krimm said.

"A live model would help," Carver said, "but I imagine your brother's dead. Or is he simply locked up with my parents?"

"He drowned," Krimm said shortly. "The idiot. It made for an awkward year, until I could entice your father to come. However, if a live model will help, I can provide the next-best thing."

He rode upstairs to his apparatus. Meanwhile, the three animations went down in the lift. By the time they returned, bearing armfuls of bronze carving tools, Duke Kovac himself stood in front of the picture frame. The animation was almost flawless, but its skin looked checked and gray, like an old, dry painting.

"Where would you like me to stand?" it asked.

Carver couldn't sleep that night. Krimm had stayed up late, working at his apparatus and ledgers. Before going to sleep, he had put Kovac back into the painting, to save wear and tear. Then he locked Carver's tools into the cabinets above the bench. The other animations sagged against the mural. Raven muttered in her cage, dreaming.

Carver went to the window and stared out at the dark sea. The wind had picked up a little, making the reflection of the stars dance and shatter. He waited, watching, and finally spotted a patch of lighter gray on the gray of the water. As the moon rose, it took on shape: Fireboy in the launch, faithfully watching for them. Carver went to the alcove and brought back a blanket, then held his arms wide to shut out as much of the window as possible. He did it three times. A light flashed three times in reply. Carver watched until the little boat steamed back to its hiding place.

He went to the cage and whispered to Raven, "I just saw Fireboy. I'll get you out somehow. You can fly over and tell him what's happened."

"What about you?" Raven muttered.

"That's not important. I'm sorry, Raven. I don't know how I could have been so blind to Krimm. To his real plans."

"He enchanted you."

"How? I didn't want to be enchanted. I didn't really trust him. I don't think."

Raven croaked wryly. "He held out what you wanted—the chance to make the best carving in the world. You were easy, Chip Head."

"Not anymore."

"Then don't carve for him."

"I won't, as soon as I figure out how to get you out."

"I'm not leaving without you, Monkey Boy."

"Well, neither of us is going anywhere right now."

He squeezed a finger through the bars. She gripped it in her claw.

When Carver awoke the next morning, light was already streaming through the window. Krimm stood over him, frowning.

"Hurry up and eat," he said. "There's not much time."

"Why?" Carver asked blearily, but Krimm was already striding away, and Uncle Piper was handing him breakfast.

When he came out of the alcove, the Duke was already animated. Krimm held the adze, studying the shape Carver had roughed out. The slabs he had split off were stacked neatly beside the bench. The chips had been swept away. His tools were laid out and waiting.

"There's an event in the blasted city," Krimm said shortly. "It requires the Duke's presence. You'll have him for only a little while today. Can you continue without him?"

"I guess so," Carver said. "I could use one of the older paintings."

Krimm shook his head. "They're gone."

Carver looked from the Duke to Krimm. "I could use you for a model. For the body at least; you're built the same."

Krimm shook his head more slowly. "It takes all my attention to maintain the animation over that distance." He laughed humorlessly. "Today they will finally complete the chain around the city, which requires a ceremony, which requires the Duke. Except the chain makes it that much harder to maintain the animation. I won't be able to leave the apparatus as long as the Duke is in Dunsgow." His smile faded. "Ironic, isn't it? There's so much iron in the city now, so many machines and coins, I could have spelled them instead of wasting effort on all that chain. For that matter, I simply could have spelled the old wall. There was no real need to use iron, except that I had so much at hand and, unfortunately, the blasted stuff is an obsession of mine. Then, well, plans once started take on a life of their own." He paused, tapping the adze in his hand. "Can you work from sketches?" he asked suddenly.

"Yes," Carver replied.

"Your father did some. I'll have them brought up."

He handed Carver the adze and went to his staircase. "Use what time you have."

Less than an hour later, Krimm slowed the apparatus and opened his ward to let the Duke's boat through. Scharl himself came up the lift to escort the animation back to the city.

"We spotted a launch slipping behind another island," Scharl reported.

"Yes, a friend of theirs," Krimm said. "Ignore it. He's no threat."

Carver's heart sank even deeper.

The other animations stayed slumped by the mural until evening. Then only Silas Joynter stirred, to fetch Carver's meal. When he started to lock away the tools, Carver began sweeping up the day's chips. Carefully, he buried his knife in the pile and shoveled it up with the shavings, dropping everything into the bin by his bench. Joynter didn't notice. He locked up the other tools and shuffled back to his place at the mural.

The apparatus whirred and spun overhead. Krimm had

been there all day, making gestures and mouthing words Carver couldn't hear. His body was stiff, concentrated on his machine. The hum from the apparatus rose to an urgent pitch, and Carver wondered what the Duke was doing. Speaking to the crowd, perhaps. Meeting with the Barons. The crystal balls spun in dizzying patterns, but Krimm stood frozen, eyes closed behind his glinting lenses. Only his lips moved.

With a quick glance at the slumped paintings, Carver hurried to the bin and dug through the wood chips, shoveling the mass this way and that. Choking with dust and frustration, he tipped the bin over, then fell to his knees and swept his hands back and forth through the chips. Finally, with an echoing clatter, the knife bounced out and slid across the floor. Carver scooped it up and crouched, staring fearfully at the mural. The animations didn't move. The apparatus still hummed overhead.

Clutching the knife, Carver tiptoed to the birdcage. Raven was huddled inside, head down. Her wings twitched as she breathed.

"Raven!" he whispered.

She jerked awake and struck out blindly with her beak. It clanked on the bars.

"Hush!" he warned. "It's me." He held up the knife. "I'm going to get you out."

Her eyes fixed on the knife, then darted around the room. "Where's Glass Eyes?"

"Running the apparatus. Everything else is shut down. He can't keep any of the other animations alive. He's consumed by the Duke."

He grabbed the lock and tried to fit the point of the knife into the keyhole. It would hardly go in, but he pushed harder and twisted it this way and that. Raven pressed her face against the bars, staring at the lock with one wide eye.

"Hurry!" she snapped.

"I am," Carver muttered. He struggled with it some more, trying different angles.

"Blazing mages!" Raven croaked. "Who taught you how to pick locks?"

"No one!" Carver snapped back. "Not everyone has your great talents."

"Oaf! Let me!"

She tried to squeeze a claw through the bars. A talon dug into Carver's hand, and he dropped the knife with a yelp.

"Blast it, Raven! You can't reach it from inside."

"Just hurry, you stick-fingered git! I can't breathe in here!"

Carver gritted his teeth. He picked up the knife, took a deep breath, and reattacked the lock. The knife jammed. Cursing, he twisted and yanked. The blade snapped. He stared dumbly at the broken end, blocking the keyhole.

Raven shrieked and beat her wings against the bars.

"Hush!" Carver hissed. "Calm down!"

But he ignored his own command. Angrily, he stuck the broken blade through the hasp and tried to pry it open. The knife edge curled and chipped. The cage jerked back and forth on its ring. Raven squawked and cursed. Cursing with her, all thought of caution gone, Carver threw down the knife, grasped two of the bars, and yanked as hard as he could. The cage slipped from the hook and carried him to his knees. He knelt over it, tugging and jerking at the bars while Raven cursed him from inside.

Suddenly, with a startling creak and snap, the bars bent apart. One broke, cutting Carver's hand. He ignored the blood and pulled harder, bending back the ends of the broken bar, bowing the other more. He stood, put one foot against the next bar, and straightened his leg. The second bar broke. Carver tumbled back, kicking the cage across the floor. He went after it on hands and knees. Already Raven was forcing her head through the opening. He grabbed the bars on either side and pulled with all his might. Squeezing, jerking, cursing, she forced herself through. Carver fell back, with Raven clinging to the front of his jacket.

She stretched her wings to full width, then shook herself hard.

Loosened feathers swirled to the floor. She cocked her head and peered down at him.

"Thanks, Carver," she croaked.

"Sorry it took so long," he replied. "I'm not much of a mechanical."

He scrambled up and she flapped to his shoulder. He carried her to the window. There was no sign of Fireboy.

"Still too early," Carver whispered, "but I think he's hiding behind that island." He pointed at a dim spike against the sky.

Raven shook her head. "I can't see a thing at night. Where's the blasted moon?"

"It'll come up later. Fireboy will be out by then. You can follow his light."

"What about you?"

"Don't worry about me. Just go and tell Paskovek about the Duke and the chain."

Raven clacked her beak. "Dolt! I'm not leaving you with that madman. Come on."

She lifted from his shoulder and flapped toward the lift cage.

"It won't work," he called after her. "All Krimm's power is caught up in the apparatus."

But even as he said it, the globes flared to life, drenching the hall in harsh yellow light. Krimm stumbled to the rail of the balcony. He moved jerkily. His face was sallow, and there were dark circles around his eyes. Behind him, the apparatus whined as it slowed to its normal pace.

Krimm glared down at them. He raised a hand, and the three animations jerked upright. Immediately, they strode forward, reaching for Carver. Raven flew at them, cawing harshly. Uncle Piper stumbled and ducked. Joynter spun and swung hard, catching her wing. Feathers flew loose as she careened away. Carver ran toward the window.

"Go, Raven!" he cried. "Go! Don't try to fight them."

She ignored him, soaring up to take another dive at the animations. Suddenly, a second raven dropped on her from the glare above the apparatus. It was the carving. In a flurry of black and brown wings, the two birds tumbled toward the floor. Joynter and the rest ran toward them. One bird croaked in pain, then pulled free inches above the stone and struggled for height. The other was too slow. It hit with a thump, and Uncle Piper grabbed it by the legs.

"Not that one!" Krimm yelled. The animation went stiff and the fake bird pulled free.

Carver yelled to Raven, pointing toward the neighboring island. "That light! It's Fireboy!"

She swooped toward him and landed heavily on the windowsill. "What about you?"

"Go!" He shoved her off the sill. Joynter lunged, but missed her and nearly fell out the window.

"Go!" Carver yelled again, as the animated raven soared past his head in pursuit. Then the mayor slapped a hand over his mouth. It tasted like dust and pine spirits. Carver struggled, but Uncle Piper grabbed his legs, and they lifted him off the ground.

Krimm strode up and stared out at Raven, rapidly beating toward the light from the launch. The false raven was flying jerkily, falling behind. Krimm took a deep breath. He looked tired; his shoulders slumped. But his eyes flashed with anger. He straightened himself and raised a hand. Joynter scurried to the workbench to fetch the wand. Krimm took it, studied it a moment, then swung it through the air.

Carver bit the mayor's hand and shouted, "No!"

Krimm gave a strained smile. "There are times when a wand can be useful. It helps focus your thoughts when you're tired. Or using unfamiliar talent. Watch and learn, boy."

He swung the wand back and forth, studying the mist that formed on the leaf tips. Satisfied, he pointed it at the sky and mumbled a few words. Instantly, a knot of cloud blew in from seaward. Raven was just visible in the growing moonlight, halfway to the dim hull of the launch, flying fast. The animation followed jerkily in dogged pursuit.

The clouds were faster than either. Krimm's smile grew. With a few sharp strokes, he twitched the clouds into a massive thunderhead. It overtook the animation, then Raven, far short of the launch. Krimm snapped the wand, and lightning snapped from the cloud to the sea. The false raven flared in a blue corona, then shattered like a lightning-struck tree. The crack of thunder slapped Carver's ears hard enough to sting, and with it came a blast of wind. Raven twirled up and down in the raging gusts.

No! Carver screamed inside. He jerked his hand from the mayor's dry grip and grabbed for the clouds. Without a wand, without even thinking, he hooked his fingers and felt the fabric of mist and rain catch under his nails. With all his strength, he squeezed. The wand twitched in Krimm's hand. The dark massing thunderhead squeezed in on itself. Carver pulled, clutching his hands to his chest. The wind lessened and almost veered out to sea. Raven regained her wings and flapped frantically toward the launch. Desperately, Carver poured his will at the cloud. He flailed his arms, hacking off bits, squeezing it more.

Krimm spun and struck him viciously on the ear. The pain shattered his thoughts. He clutched the side of his head, blinded by tears. Then the mayor had both his hands again, and Joynter held his head, making him look.

Krimm turned back to the window. With two quick waves of the wand, he reshaped the towering cloud and called back the wind. The darkness bore down on Raven. Krimm snapped the wand, and another bolt of lightning seared the sky. Dark images of Raven twisted on the backs of Carver's eyes. He blinked away tears, then was blinded again by a blast of rain. It poured like an avalanche from the black, swollen cloud, dashing Raven toward the water. She disappeared in the curtain of rain. It slashed the sea like a knife. The next gust of wind struck the launch, laying its beam into the sudden waves. Then the wall of rain struck, blotting out everything.

Carver lay still in the grasp of the animations, staring desperately into the storm. The rain went on for long minutes, drowning the moonlight and all sight of the sea. Finally, Krimm lowered the wand and wearily swept it sideways. The clouds were slow to obey, moving in fits and starts toward the mainland. Leaving behind a barren tract of water.

Twenty-five

After raising the storm, Krimm watched silently, grim faced and haggard, as his animations chained Carver to his workbench with bronze manacles. Then he took the wand up to the balcony, only to return without it a minute later. He gave Carver a last cold look before stumbling to his alcove and collapsing into sleep. Carver dozed fitfully, too bruised inside and out to rest. When the animations stirred late the next morning, he was still huddled against the bench, staring out the window at a bit of empty sky. The mayor brought breakfast, but Carver ignored it. Then Krimm appeared from his alcove, looking rested and satisfied. He came over and stood above Carver, eyes hidden behind the reflections in his lenses.

"You have an odd collection of talents," Krimm said finally. He sat on the stool, leaning on his elbows, eye to eye with Carver. "Most mages have one, if that. In fact, most people who call themselves mages have less than a glimmer of talent. Your mother, for example. Yet here you are, from the same family, with so much more."

"I'm no seer," Carver said.

"You're not a painter, either. I'll bet you can't even stand the smell of it, yes? Well, my family were blacksmiths, but I have absolutely no skill with iron. Oh, it has its uses: machinery, money, chains. But I can't abide it. It makes me clumsy and dulls my talent—not that I had any as a smith. Did you notice?" He held up his left hand, and Carver was startled to see that the little finger was missing. "I burned that off when I was half your age," Krimm said. He regarded the smooth stump with a faint smile. "My parents despaired. My father was, after all, the master of his guild. He owned a brace of foundries. Never mind that I had a brother to carry on the family honor. Never mind there was no reason for me to work with iron. They insisted I was born to the forge. I *would* become a smith. Sound familiar?"

Carver looked out the window.

"I had different talents, Carver, but I had to decide to use them. That choice was mine, and no one else's. And you see what it's got me; I still have most of my fingers." He chuckled, a sound so unexpected that Carver looked up at him. Krimm grew serious again. "Carver, I have the skills of a dozen mages. I have skills other mages can't even imagine. My talent *is* imagination. I am a seer, but I don't see the future. I see truths that aren't yet real. I create the future. Other mages merely manipulate nature. I learn its secrets, and then I change it."

"For the worse."

Krimm stood suddenly, knocking the stool back. Carver flinched.

"How can you say that?" Krimm exclaimed. He gestured, and the manacles fell from Carver's wrists. He pulled Carver to the window and pointed to the haze that hovered over Dunsgow.

"Think of all the new ways of making and doing and living you saw in Dunsgow. You're from upriver, Carver; you know what I mean. And it's not just the steam and the coal gas and the commerce. People are free in Dunsgow. They aren't marked by their names to live a life that doesn't suit them. There are no apprenticeships to labor through, no bonds to pay off in order to live and work as they please."

He turned to gaze up at the apparatus, still spinning slowly in the vault of the ceiling. "It's not perfect yet," he went on quietly, and Carver wondered if he was referring to his machine or to Dunsgow or both. "There is a great deal more work needed, to push new ideas upriver, to civilize the upper reaches. Think of that, Carver: steamboats on the upper reach. Coal gas. Organized workhouses instead of inefficient trade shops and guilds. Real industry."

Carver's head was spinning, trying to keep up with Krimm's grand pronouncements. "I thought you didn't want that," he said. "I thought you were blocking ideas from spreading. The spell on the chain . . ."

"The spell blocks magic, Carver, not thought."

Carver started to argue, but Krimm was caught up in his own designs. "There is some other force, some magic that holds back progress at the falls. Magic is stronger on the high reach, Carver. For years I've studied it, the force of magic. Pushed and prodded it. Built this"—he gestured at the elaborate machine above them—"to understand and control it. To overcome it, and force progress beyond the barriers of the falls. My apparatus channels energy, Carver, enough energy to change all the reaches. And why? To capture that energy in return. As I have with Dunsgow. So that here . . ." He gripped Carver's shoulder. "Here I can master the real challenge, to go beyond mere animation. To control life." He took a deep breath and seemed to see the room again. "With your help, Carver."

He studied Carver from behind his thick lenses. "You have a choice to make now—to use your talents or not. To see the future or to keep peering through the veils of the past."

Carver glared at him, jaw clenched. He couldn't believe this. Not after last night. Did Krimm really think he would forget everything—Raven, Fireboy, his parents?

"My parents—" he said.

Krimm cut him off. "Your parents! A seer and a painter, and yet they had no vision! I thought your mother at least would see. She seemed to. She brought your father to me, so he and I could work together. But even she lacked the imagination to carry through."

"She brought my father to you?" Carver couldn't believe that either.

"Of course!" Krimm snapped. "I searched the five rivers for someone with your father's genius. He was just the person I needed to carry on after Kovac died." Krimm sneered. "But your father was a peasant, perfectly content to dabble in rustic portraits

216

in your dingy little village, glued to his reach by the same force that fights the spread of ideas upriver. It was your mother who realized the future lay with me. Cramped up in Wanting with her chickens, jealous of your father's talent. Oh, yes, she loved him, but she also envied him. Greatly. I offered her a talent of her own, and she took it. I helped her see that her future was here, and she brought your father with her."

"But not me," Carver said bitterly.

Krimm studied him again. "She refused to bring you."

"She refused?"

"Refused. Insisted that she'd seen a different future for you. And I didn't insist otherwise. I was shortsighted, Carver, and I'm sorry. I let her leave you there, branded with your father's name. Forced into the image of Thomas Painter. When what you really are is a carver. And a weather mage. And a seeker, like myself. And how much more, Carver? Imagine how much more." Krimm faced him, took both shoulders in his hands. "You took off your old name. Now take off the mask and show the world your true face. Choose your own life. With me."

Carver stared back at Krimm's earnest smile. Half of what he said made sense. The other half turned Carver's stomach. His mind darted from one side to the other, looking for something solid to land on. His father hadn't wanted to leave. His mother had refused to bring him; she had seen a different future. He glanced at the mural. At himself in the shadows, holding a wand: his father's painting of her vision of him now. But what did it mean?

And then he noticed, soaring in the sky high above the crowd in the mural: a raven.

He turned back to Krimm. He stood up straight and shrugged off the mage's hands.

"No," he said. "I already made my choice. I'm not my father. I won't be your tool."

Krimm stepped back, eyes narrowed. Once again Carver thought the mage would hit him. Instead, he took a deep breath and slowly let it out. Something moved in the reflections in his lenses. Carver started to turn but was grabbed from behind by Joynter and the mayor.

"You can kill me if you want," he said, trying hard not to sound frightened. "I still won't carve your statue."

"It's not you who'll die," Krimm said.

"You've already killed all my friends," Carver said.

"I can kill your parents, too."

"They're already dead," Carver snapped. He no longer believed anything from Krimm.

"No, they're quite alive," Krimm replied.

"You're lying."

"Am I?" Krimm raised his eyebrows. "That's another decision you'll have to make."

"Show me!" Carver demanded. "Take me to them!"

Krimm shook his head. "No."

"Because you can't. Because they're dead!"

"No. Because they'd tell you not to help me, to go ahead and let me kill them." Carver blinked, brought up short by the unexpected response. "You're going to have to decide this one on faith, Carver. If I'm lying, then go ahead and refuse, and nothing lost. If I'm telling the truth, their deaths will be on your head for the rest of your life. And, I assure you, I will keep you alive a long, long time. The choice is yours."

Carver struggled to see through Krimm's ruse, searching for some way to outsmart him. "They abandoned me," he muttered.

Krimm nodded. "A serious crime."

"I don't even like them."

Krimm shrugged. "Well, if you hate them that much . . ."

Carver sagged. He didn't hate them. He didn't know how he felt now, not after everything Krimm had just said. And even if he did hate them, he couldn't kill them. That would be no better than what they had done to him. Worse.

"All right," he said. "I'll finish your blasted statue."

Twenty-six

Krimm posed for an hour or two. He was a fidgety subject, but it was all Carver could do to lift the adze anyway. He couldn't get his mind off Raven and Fireboy. His eyes kept blurring with tears. He wiped them furiously, turning away from Krimm. Beneath his sorrow lay a great bed of anger. He couldn't think of anything but grief and hate.

Later, when Krimm had finally had enough and spiraled up to his balcony, Carver was able to clear his mind. He went over everything Krimm had said about his parents, trying to tell if the mage was lying. It was all so contrary to what he'd believed: his mother lured by Krimm, his father merely a pawn, both still alive. He tried to see the lie in it. But he wasn't a truth sayer; he couldn't be sure.

He pulled the locket from under his shirt and studied the faces of his father and mother. What should I do? he asked them. They smiled back, mute. He turned to the mural, wishing he could conjure an answer in the faces there. His eyes went to Aunt Zarah, with her hens, and suddenly he remembered her seeing: Mistress, Mage, Mother. The rune spoken by a wooden rooster he had carved. He turned to the roughed-out statue. Tried to imagine it speaking, performing Krimm's will. Was this what Zarah had seen? He clenched his fists, ready to refuse again. Then sagged as he thought of his parents. Mother. And father.

He shut the locket and slipped it back under his shirt. There must be some way, he thought. Some way to keep this statue from coming to life. And then he remembered another thing Krimm had said, about a veil and about a mask. It gave him an idea, a vague hope that he could spoil Krimm's vision of the future.

Sometime later, Scharl returned with the Duke, and the next day Carver worked from the unanimated painting. It was his own suggestion, to save wear. He knew the animations could somehow communicate with Krimm; having the Duke as a model would give him no privacy at all. As it was, the other animations watched fixedly, as though they were interested. Only their unblinking eyes gave them away. Carver wondered if he would be able to put his plan into effect.

That evening, he swept up the shavings as usual, and a chisel with them. Soon after dinner, the animations slumped against their mural, and Carver knew Krimm had fallen asleep. He counted another hundred heartbeats, then quietly went to the bin and dug out the chisel. He selected one of the slabs he had split off earlier when roughing out the contour of the statue's body. He clamped it on the bench and began to carve.

For the next four days, he worked on the statue when Krimm was awake, then worked on his own carving when the mage was asleep. During the day, he focused completely on his carving and his parents. The result was a turmoil of pleasure and confusion that he hoped would hide all thought of his nighttime activities from Krimm. It seemed to work, and Krimm noticed the new energy Carver put into the statue.

"I know you hate me, Carver," he said. "Even so, you can't bring yourself to do a bad job. I won't forget that when you've finished."

Carver gritted his teeth and kept working. He had most of the body done. Only the hands and face still needed work. And when he was finished . . . what *would* Krimm do then? Free him and his parents? Demand another carving? Or simply kill them all? Assuming his parents were even alive.

That night, Carver left the alcove for the first time since Krimm had blasted Raven and Fireboy in the storm. He crept to the lift and slowly opened the gate, then closed it just as carefully. Krimm slept; nothing stirred. Carver pulled the lever down, holding his breath as the cage began to descend. He stopped at the next level and began to search.

The following night, he searched the next level below, and then the next. He found bedrooms and a kitchen, a pantry and closets, a workroom furnished with tools made of bronze, silver, and even gold. He didn't find his parents. And he didn't dare spend too much time, because he still had his own carving to finish. But he didn't know how many levels the island had, so he slowed his work on the statue, pretending to put special effort into the Duke's face.

Krimm grew impatient. On the fourth day after Carver had begun his nightly explorations, as he was adding the finest bit of detail to the Duke's eyebrows, Krimm came down from the balcony and strode into the alcove. He watched Carver for a minute, then snapped, "That's good enough."

"It needs to be perfect," Carver said, still working. "It has to look so much alive—"

"I'll give it the life it needs," Krimm said. "Just get it done."

Carver glanced up. Krimm was frowning, his lips a tight line. His eyes glinted. Carver looked away, suddenly afraid Krimm could see right into his mind.

"A few more hours," he said. "Tomorrow at the latest. And then the painting."

"Painting?"

"Unless the wood color will change when you animate it." Krimm shifted his gaze to the statue, and Carver almost laughed. The great mage had forgotten that little detail. "My father . . . ," Carver suggested.

"Your father is blind!" Krimm glared at him. "You've had some training with paints."

Carver shook his head. "I'm hopeless. Like you with iron."

"You'll be good enough," Krimm said, and he smiled mirthlessly. "The Barons are used to a sickly Duke. I'll have paints brought up. And brushes. Your father's, in fact. Maybe they will inspire some latent talent in you."

They didn't. Mixing the colors was easy enough. The hard part was picking up his father's brush the first time. But it was just a brush; it gave him nothing, not even memories.

Krimm watched him paint late into the night, then spent more time at his apparatus. Carver, suddenly feeling the effects of his sleepless nights, didn't even try to sneak away when Krimm finally went to bed. He fell into an exhausted doze, troubled by dreams.

The next day, he painted the Duke's hands. It seemed easy enough; there was no need to paint on highlights and shadows, because the veins and creases were carved in place. But skin is not a single, smooth color. Carver spent hours trying to get the proper shades and texture. Finally, Krimm stopped him. Once again, he said it was good enough. So Carver started on the head, with its skin and hair and eyes. He saved the eyes for last.

"I'll be able to finish them tomorrow," he told Krimm late that night, wiping his own eyes wearily. "If I try now, I'll botch it and have to clean them off and start all over."

Krimm regarded him from behind his lenses. Finally, he nodded. "All right, sleep. Sleep well. Tomorrow will be a remarkable day."

As soon as Krimm himself was asleep, Carver went to the lift and held the lever down until the cage reached bottom. He went out onto the stone pier where he and Raven had first arrived. He looked up at the stars and down at the slowly moving sea and felt an almost overpowering urge to jump in and swim as far as his arms would take him. But that wouldn't stop Krimm, or save his parents. If they were even alive. He went back in to search.

He found two alcoves flanking the entry and a small barracks with several bunks. All of them were dusty and unused. There were no stairs, up or down. If there was a dungeon, it had to be somewhere in the two levels he had skipped. But the next level was a single storeroom that stretched the full width of the island. Scattered globes cast harsh light on barrels and boxes and the squat columns that supported the ceiling. Raw ingots of silver and gold were piled near the door, as though they were no more important than any other supplies.

Heart pounding, Carver went up again, to the only level he hadn't searched.

The cage opened onto an anteroom with three doors. All of them were shut and blank, but one was marked by a strange portent: a slot cut into the bottom of the door. Piled before the threshold was an untidy heap of trays with plates and bowls and spoons. Some were empty, but most held the dried remains of food that had lain so long, it was unrecognizable. Scattered among the debris were the tiny black droppings of mice. A film of dust covered everything.

Carver's heart chilled. He felt lightheaded. He knew what he would find inside. The door was secured with a pair of sturdy bronze bolts. He slid them back, pushed the door open, and stepped over the pile.

Inside, a single globe flickered feebly from the center of the ceiling. The air was damp; a cool sea breeze came in through a barred window. There was a table and chairs, a cupboard, a washstand. Carver stepped farther in and saw a bed in the far corner. Something lay on it. In the flickering light, it appeared to breathe.

Trembling, Carver stepped softly to the bedside. The illusion of life died; two skeletons lay in a tangle of moldering clothes. They were brown with age. A little hair still clung to one skull: long, fair hair falling in brittle strands across the remains of a woman's dress. The other wore a man's topshirt. Carver's mind raced. It can't be them, he thought. It can't be. It's two mages from Dunsgow. Two servants. Two—

The flickering light glinted on something gold resting in the cage of the woman's hand. It was a locket, twin to the one he wore. Carver swallowed bile. Krimm had lied.

He reached for the locket, hesitated as his fingers neared his mother's bones, then pushed them open. They were cool and smooth and hard, like the gold shell of the locket.

He turned the locket in his hand, feeling the design. He opened the cover and held it close in the flickering light. Inside was a beautiful miniature portrait. Himself. And not the toddler they had left behind. It was Carver now, a boy nearing manhood. He was smiling. Carver wondered what he could ever be happy about. He let the locket fall and watched it bounce and rattle on the stone floor.

The bitter taste seemed to fill his whole head. He had known all along they were dead—had been grieving for them all his life, in fact—but still had hoped against hope he might find them. Hoped so much that he'd let it cloud every choice he made. So much that he'd yielded to Krimm. Despite Raven and Fireboy. He had used his talent for a lie.

The bitterness turned to burning rage. He dashed tears from his eyes with the back of a fist. He turned for the door, bumped into the table in his blind hurry, and heaved it over with a crash. He kicked through the piled dishes, sending them smashing into the walls as he strode to the lift. He slammed the gate shut and jammed the lever so hard, it hurt his palm. He counted the levels, willing the cage to rise faster, banging the thick bronze mesh again and again with his fist. He yanked down the lever before the cage was flush with the opening and crashed through the gate, half tripping on the lip of the floor.

"Krimm!" he yelled.

He stumbled to his workbench and grabbed his hidden chisel from the bin.

"Krimm!" he yelled again, attacking the lock on the tool cabinet with a fury that sent slivers of metal flying into his own face. The lock split open. He threw the chisel aside, wrenched open the doors, and grabbed the hatchet. He spun, panting, looking for Krimm, fist clenched on the handle.

The mage was standing in the center of the hall. He looked completely at ease. Light glinted on his lenses.

"I see you found your parents," he said.

Carver snarled and charged, swinging the hatchet with all his might.

Suddenly, the Duke's painting stepped from behind his frame and blocked Carver's swing. The hatchet dug into the Duke's arm with a strange tearing sound. The Duke didn't even grimace. He jerked back, making Carver stumble. The hatchet tore free and clattered to the floor by the spiral stairs. Carver scrambled to his feet, flailing at the Duke's grasping arm. More figures came from all sides of the hall: the mayor, Joynter, Miller, Baker. And Piper and Singer and even Aunt Zarah. Carver was grabbed by a dozen hands and hoisted into the air, helpless. The animations carried him to Krimm and stood him upright, pinned tight amid their cold, dry bodies.

"I'm surprised you care so much for your parents," Krimm said.

Carver tried to kick him, but even his legs were pinned.

Krimm raised an eyebrow. "Revenge is a waste of time, Carver. There's nothing you can do to change the past, or the immediate future."

"I will not finish your blasted statue," Carver spat.

Krimm merely looked irked. "I expected that, but I have another Painter at hand."

Uncle Piper left the crowd surrounding Carver and went over to the bench. Woodenly, the animation took white paint and a brush and filled in the statue's eyes. Then he added circles of pale gray and dots of black. The result was a puppet's stare.

"That won't fool anyone," Carver sneered. "Even I could do better than that."

Krimm smiled thinly. "It's quite good enough. I will give it all the life it needs."

Piper and the Duke took hold of the statue. The Duke's half-severed forearm dangled uselessly. Several new animations joined them. They carried the statue to the stairway.

Carver struggled, but his captors dragged him after the statue, up to the balcony. Krimm came last. He went immediately to his control bench and began his spells. The apparatus sped up. The animations carried the statue into the workings and placed it on the column where Krimm had animated the raven. It rose into the center of the spinning arms and spheres. Carver struggled harder, but it was no use. The animations squeezed his arms till they went numb. He could only watch in despair.

The spheres began to glow, weaving bright patterns across the vault of the ceiling. The levers lifted and fell; arms spun, glinting. The hum grew to a whine, then a cry, then a shriek. And the statue shifted. For a moment, Carver thought it was going to topple from the column. He willed it to fall. Instead, it seemed to grow. The skin shone. A hand twitched. The chest lifted.

Krimm gave a choked exhalation. He gestured, and the column lowered even before the apparatus began to slow. He rushed toward the statue as it settled on the ground. Carver strained forward, staring desperately. The statue stumbled off the column, struggling to breathe. It shook its head. It groped at its face with its hands. Carver felt hope bloom in his chest.

Krimm peered into the statue's eyes. They were blank. Then the statue grabbed the sides of its head. It dug its fingers into the flesh, pulling, jerking. With a sudden snap, its whole face came free.

Carver laughed. Krimm turned, surprised, then spun back to stare anxiously at his creation. The statue man lowered his hands. They held a mask, a mask of the Duke's face that grimaced and twitched, half alive, half wood and paint. The statue man took a deep breath and turned to Krimm. The mage recoiled. The statue's face—the real, unpainted face that had been hidden under the mask Carver had made for it—was Carver's father, Thomas Painter.

Krimm stared a moment, then wrenched the grimacing mask from the statue's hands. He strode from under the spheres and arms, holding the mask like a sacrifice. He stood before Carver, eyes blazing, panting with rage. He shoved the mask at Carver's face.

"You did this," he grated. "You ruined it. My statue. My work."

Carver smiled.

Krimm stared at him for three breaths. With a snarl, he lifted the mask high in both hands, ready to smash it on Carver's head. Carver flinched, then tried to stand tall and defiant. Suddenly, a harsh, inhuman cry filled the room. Krimm, already striking, jerked at the sound. Carver twisted sideways. The mask missed. It brushed past his ear and came down hard on the figure of Silas Joynter, crushing his head like a clot of old plaster. He fell, crumbling.

Another cry filled the hall, then a dozen more, the shrill calling of birds. Carver tore free and spun away from Krimm. All around him, the room was filled with soaring, diving birds: gulls and ducks, terns and gannets, a twisting cloud of white and gray. And at their head was a black shape, stooping like a hawk at Krimm.

Raven.

Twenty-seven

Raven dove at Krimm's face. More than anything, she wanted to rip off his stupid lenses and sink her talons into his eyes. He stared at her like a half-wit, completely surprised. She cawed in triumph.

At just the last second, he ducked and threw something in her path. She rolled sharply, catching a wild glimpse of a painted face that grimaced as it twirled past. It clipped her wingtip. She veered and suddenly was flying through the middle of the apparatus. Heavy arms swung past, rods shot up in front of her. She looped and turned, dodging spheres. A gull to her left wasn't quick enough. One of the crystal globes caught him from behind and smashed him to the floor in a spray of feathers.

Raven snarled in rage and swooped below the blasted mechanics of the thing. Then she was in the clear beyond the balcony. She turned, searching for Krimm. But he had left the unprotected railing and fled back to his control panel, shielded by the flailing arms of his machine. He watched the melee in the room, mouthing incantations. Raven flew higher, looking for an opening, but he had her spotted. Every time she started to drop on him, the apparatus spun faster, flashing metal into her path.

She resisted the impulse to ignore the machine and dive straight at him. Impulses like that had nearly gotten her drowned. She circled at the height of the vault instead, marshaling her flock. The gulls had created mayhem among Krimm's animations, but no real damage. Even as she watched, the rest of the figures in the mural were heaving themselves off the plaster. She searched the crowd for Carver. He was still on the balcony, kicking and struggling in the hands of the carved Duke. With a shock, she saw that it wasn't the Duke after all; Carver had given it some other face. But it was Krimm's tool anyway. It had Carver in a chokehold that was turning him blue.

Raven sent all of her flock against the statue, but they couldn't hurt it. When they cut its skin, it didn't bleed or show pain. So she sent them at its eyes. It shook its head wildly, then finally let go of Carver to beat at them with its hands. Two of them went down, but the rest managed to back it against the railing. Carver regained his feet and lunged at the thing's chest. Arms flailing, it tipped over the railing and fell heavily to the stone floor.

Raven crowed. "Good shove, Monkey Boy!"

Carver turned toward her. His eyes were red with tears. Then two more of the blasted animations came at him. He took one look and leaped over the railing after the fallen statue. Raven dove on the paintings to keep them from following. She clipped one hard on the head, and it stumbled into the rail. The other swung at her and nearly hit home. The swish of his blow ruffled her tail feathers as she yawed away.

She had a glimpse of the statue, heaving itself up. Its head was split as far as its nose, but it was still acting alive. The blasted animations seemed indestructible. Once again, she soared high and directed the fight, sending the gulls in teams at the faces of Krimm's puppets. And always looking for some way to get to Krimm.

But he was safe under the arms of his machine. The apparatus spun faster, and now Raven could feel the wind it created, not the soft brush of air but the cold brush of magic. It pushed on her wings, making them heavy. The gulls slowed. They fought her control. And Carver was backed into a corner by his workbench. He had a hatchet and was swinging hard at any figure that came near. Two of them lay nearby, their legs sliced almost through. Another had lost its head and crumpled like a crushed pot. But there were still enough left to win. And the wind from Krimm's machine was blowing stronger and stronger.

"Carver!" she croaked. "Go for the window. Run for it!" She dove at the figures attacking him, pulling a cluster of gulls reluctantly along. He took another swipe at the leading figure, the hen woman from his village. Now tears were streaming down his face. Suddenly, there were two Carvers by the bench. The one from the mural had pulled itself free. Gray with the shadow in which it had been painted, it advanced on Carver, waving the painted wand.

Carver, the real Carver, screamed in rage and swung the hatchet with all his might. The animation's arm flew off. The wand went with it, both crumbling to scatter across the floor. That didn't stop the animation. It struck at Carver with the stump. He backed against the wall.

But the other figures were confused by the double. They slowed, and some of them even attacked it. The fight turned into a free-for-all.

Raven dove into the midst again, landing a solid blow on a child who had latched onto Carver's leg. Carver shook it off.

"Go, Guano Brain!" she yelled. "Krimm's machine is too strong!"

"We've got to stop it!" he yelled back.

"How?" she snapped.

"Break something!" he cried, waving his hatchet threateningly at an advancing line of the blasted paintings. "Jam the gears!"

"With what, blockhead? A feather?"

He looked at her excitedly. Then he threw his hatchet at the nearest figure and darted to the side. He snatched something from the post by his workbench and threw it toward her.

"Use this!" he cried exultantly. "There's iron in it! He can't abide iron!"

She swooped toward it, extending her talons to snag the thing just above the reaching arms of the animations. At the last minute, she realized what it was: Penalla's black feather.

At once, she felt the drag it had on her power; Penalla's spell still clung to it. Raven began to lose control of the gulls. Half of them flew in bewildered circles, crying like a bunch of idiots. The wind from Krimm's machine seemed to double in strength, or it doubled Penalla's spell. Her wings felt like lead, hands and fingers trying to break through her enchantment. The chain almost slipped from her grasp. Then she saw Krimm's face, eyes gleaming behind his ugly lenses as he watched her struggle. He smiled and traced patterns in the air, working on her through the pendant.

"Not on your life, Glass Eyes!" she muttered.

With a furious effort, she gripped the chain and labored to the peak of the ceiling. She hung there a moment, looking for the thickest collection of gears.

I wish Fireboy could see this, she thought. He'd know where to put this blasted thing.

Then she plummeted into the swirling machine. Backwash from the slicing arms buffeted her. A gold sphere clipped her tail and knocked her into a dizzying spin. The unnatural shriek rang through her body. But she held her course for the center of the whole spinning works. At the last minute, she dropped the feather into an apex of rods and gears, then flattened her dive and aimed straight at Krimm, her body once more all raven. His eyes widened in disbelief as she dodged the spinning arms. He ducked. She missed his eyes but came out with his lenses hooked in her talons.

At that instant, a great clank and wail of metal rang through the hall as the tiny feather jammed between two gears. The bright spheres in the apparatus jolted to a ragged halt, bending arms and rods into hard angles. The feather slipped, then caught again, then slipped. The machine swung and jerked. A crystal ball broke loose and slammed into the control panel, shattering against the levers and gauges. Sharp fragments flew everywhere. A rain of quicksilver sprayed over the rail of the balcony onto the milling animations.

"Hurry!" Carver yelled. He was standing by the window, waving madly.

"Jump, you dolt!" She dropped the lenses and began beating hard for the window. "I'm right behind you!"

Carver turned and put one foot up on the window ledge. Then he hesitated, staring down the seven high levels to the sea. Gulls flew past him to escape the noise and flying metal.

"Jump!" she cried again, flapping furiously toward him. The animations stumbled and flopped like shreds of canvas. Behind her the apparatus groaned. The remaining arms and globes spun in widely erratic orbits. They clattered and cracked into each other. Shards of bronze flew past her, shattering the rock wall right beside Carver.

He climbed up on the ledge and tensed but still couldn't jump.

"Chicken guts!" She slammed into the back of his head, toppling him out. She tumbled with him, gaining control only at the last second. She pulled out of her fall; Carver kept going. He hit the cold, gray water like a sack of flour, feet first, at least, but with a splash that wet her as badly as a heavy rain. She swerved away, cursing and blinking salt from her eyes. When she looked again, he was floating facedown, dead still.

"Blast!" she croaked. "Not again!"

Seething with disgust, she dropped to the water and changed back to a girl. The cold made her gasp, but she flipped Carver over and began towing him away from the island. Fireboy was already rowing toward them in the wooden wherry they had commandeered to slip through Krimm's iron-blocking spell. He shipped his oars and heaved Carver into the boat. She splashed in after, grabbing for the second pair of oars. They rowed away as hard as they could. Above them, metal tore and shattered. Raven felt magic prickle her face in sharp gusts. She could almost see it rippling from the high window. Then there was a heart-shaking rumble as something heavy shook the stone walls of Krimm's hall. Dust blew through the window. The entire cap of the island settled by a man's height. Boulders tumbled into the sea, splashing water high up the sheer sides. Waves rocked their little boat. Then everything went silent.

"Wait." It was Carver, coughing out water as he pulled himself upright between the thwarts. "Wait. Can you feel it?"

Raven and Fireboy stopped rowing.

"What is it?" Fireboy asked.

Raven felt the change. "The magic wind has stopped."

Fireboy looked from her to Carver, then up at the dark, sagging window. He shook his head and pulled again at his oars.

Twenty-eight

arver was shivering so violently, Fireboy and Raven had to help him aboard the launch. Raven gave him her top-shirt, then turned her back and dressed while he changed out of his soaked clothes. He draped them around the firebox and shoveled in a couple of scoops of coal to get warmer. Then the two of them joined Fireboy at the wheel. He was steaming away from the island as fast as the little boat would go.

"Where to?" he asked.

"The high reach," Raven said.

Fireboy chuckled. "She's a good little boat, but she won't make it up First Falls."

"Just get me close to it, Steam Brain. I'll fly the rest of the way."

Carver laughed. He couldn't help himself. He laughed and threw his arms around their shoulders. Fireboy laughed right back, and even Raven smiled.

"How did you do it?" Carver asked. "I thought . . ." He shrugged.

Fireboy grimaced. "Don't ever want to go through that again. When that wind hit . . ." He shook his head. "Lucky Raven made it first. It took both of us on the wheel to dig the rail out of the water. Then bail? You should have seen her bail. She saved us, all right."

"It wasn't me," Raven said. "Boat mage here charmed us through."

Fireboy patted the wheel. "No, we just had the right boat. But even she couldn't fight that kind of wind. Pushed us all the way to land. By then we needed coal anyway. And food."

"We came back as soon as we could," Raven finished.

"Thank you," Carver said. They shrugged, embarrassed.

"Well, where do we go now?" Fireboy asked again.

"Someplace dry," Raven said. "Just as long as it isn't that stinking city."

"No, we have to go back," Carver said. "We have to tell Paskovek."

"You don't think he knows already?"

"Not about the chain. It's like Penalla's feather, Raven. The spell isn't gone just because Krimm is." He flexed his hands and shoulders, feeling the pain and stiffness from the days of hard work, the fighting, the brutal fall into the water. He was weary from the nights of carving and searching, still angry, still grieving. "We have to finish it," he said. "We have to tell Paskovek and help him break the spell."

"How?" Raven demanded. "It's Krimm's spell. Unless we find a stronger mage . . ."

"I don't know," Carver replied. "But we have to try."

Carver tended the fire. By the time they left the high islands behind, he was starting to feel warm again. When they could clearly make out the river mouth, he changed back into his damp clothes and returned Raven's topshirt. He still didn't know how they were going to deal with the chain, and that made him feel cold again.

When they entered the river, the motion of the boat changed. Carver's stomach felt sour as they slopped through the jumbled current around the first string of shifting, scrub-covered islands that blocked their view of the city. Through a gap, he spotted another boat steaming out on the other side of the islands.

"There's the Duke's boat," he said.

"With a squad of guarda," Raven added. "What do you think? Heading out to check on Krimm?"

The afternoon sunlight flashed on a pair of lenses. "I guess so," Carver replied. "Scharl's on board."

Raven smiled grimly. "He's in for a pleasant surprise." Then the other boat began to turn. "Blast! He spotted us."

Fireboy twisted a valve. Their little boat churned harder against the current. "They're going to have to work to catch us," he said.

Carver watched the larger boat fall back. Then the islands hid it. But a moment later, it steamed through the gap and turned in pursuit. He had a sudden, awful memory of their mad flight down the River Slow. He hoped this race would end differently.

At first they outraced the Duke's boat. Carver could make out Scharl by the glint of his lenses. He stood in the very bow, flanked by the bright uniforms of his guarda. Then they swept past the last of the islands, and Carver looked ahead. The gray wall of Dunsgow loomed beyond the ships and wharves of the harbor. A faint breeze blew the stench of the city at them, and Carver almost gagged. He had forgotten how vile it was. He stared through the growing haze and could easily make out the dark line of chain at the top of the wall. He still had no idea how to break the spell.

A shot rang out from behind. He turned and saw a wisp of white smoke drifting away from the Duke's boat. It was gaining on them. Another shot came, and he saw it splash in their wake.

"We're still out of range," Raven said. "Can you beat them to the wharf, Fireboy?"

"I think so. Take the wheel." He ran back and added coal to the fire.

Carver followed. "I can do that."

He heard another shot; something whined past his head and struck the boiler with a shrill clang. Carver flinched and turned to stare at the Duke's boat. It didn't look any closer, but the guarda had found the range. He turned back to Fireboy and found him leaning against the rail, clutching his forearm. His face was twisted in pain.

"What is it?" Carver cried.

"Splinter." Fireboy moaned. "Shot bounced into the coaming.

Tore it up. It's not bad," he added quickly when Carver reached for his arm. "Just hurts."

"Get up front," Carver ordered. "I'll tend the fire."

Another shot whizzed past, splashing into the water to their left.

"Fire's okay for now," Fireboy said. "You come with me."

They scrambled into the relative safety in front of the smoke-stack. Raven looked at Fireboy's arm and cursed. Carver tore a strip from his shirt and bound it around the wound, trying to ignore Fireboy's stifled moan.

"Raven, go on ahead and find Paskovek. Tell him about the chain."

She looked from him to Fireboy and back. "Right," she said. "As soon as you land, lose yourself in the alleys. I'll find you in the Old City."

"Just help Paskovek."

She started stripping off clothing. Before she was even done, she was changed. A moment later, she was in the air. More shots rang out, but Raven flew low, directly ahead of the boat. As she neared the moored ships in the harbor, she flew higher, weaving between the masts. Then she topped them and approached the wall.

Suddenly, she started to sink. Her body seemed to grow, her wings to shrink. She beat them frantically, still lumbering toward the wall.

"What's the matter?" Fireboy said. "Did she get shot?"

"It's the chain," Carver said. "She's in the spell."

They watched numbly as Raven struggled to stay aloft, to stay a bird. Her shape bulged and shrank. She sank and rose and sank again. Finally, with a last effort they could see even at that distance, she threw herself forward. Her head changed as she arched downward. Then her feet. Her wings jerked upward and suddenly were arms, grabbing at the sky. She plummeted out of sight behind the wall.

Fireboy beat the wheel with his good hand. Carver cursed. Another shot clanged against the stack and tore splinters from the planking. They both ducked. Fireboy twisted the throttle valve as far as it would go, but the little boat was already at top speed. Carver crawled aft and crouched by the firebox, shoveling in a little more coal, trying to shape the fire just a little better, trying to ignore the whining shots.

He scrambled back to the wheel. They steamed into the midst of the moored ships. Fireboy headed straight for the still-distant wharf, skimming close by the tall hulls. The shots kept coming.

Then Carver felt the chain, a hint of dullness, as though the city's haze had been made into lenses and forced over his eyes. He looked behind. Shots splashed into the water all around them. He looked ahead. The wharf seemed leagues away. The spell grew heavier, weighing on him like a damp cloak. He shook his head blindly, trying to clear the sullen sense of failure and weakness washing over him. If only he could fight back somehow. He didn't have a firearm, didn't even have a knife anymore. In a moment, he wouldn't have the talent left to use a knife. Or a wand of any kind. At least on the River Slow he'd had a wand. If only he still had it . . .

"Blast!" he shouted.

Fireboy jumped. "What? Are you shot?"

"No! I'm an idiot! Veer off! Quick, get me away from the wall!"

"But what about—"

"Veer off! It's our only chance!"

Fireboy swung the wheel, and they churned around the bow of one of the moored vessels, barely missing its anchor chain. The Duke's boat swerved to cut them off. The guarda took aim.

"Duck!" Fireboy yelled, yanking Carver down below the coaming. Shots tore into the wood, sending splinters against the boiler and stack.

"Have you got a knife?" Carver asked.

"What?"

"Have you got a knife? I need one."

"You already lost the last one I gave you?" Fireboy muttered, but he pulled a new folder out of his pocket and handed it over.

"Thanks," Carver said. He peered over the coaming, then scuttled around to the other side. Using the dented smokestack as a shield, he stood and opened the knife. They were drawing steadily away from the wall. Already he could feel the spell lifting from his shoulders. His vision cleared. The knife felt alive in his hands. He raised it over his head and sliced through the air.

Immediately, the wind picked up. Fog streamed from the end of the knife. Small clouds appeared as if from nowhere.

A wand could be useful, Krimm had said. When you're tired, or using an unfamiliar talent. Or, Carver added, when you're fighting for your life, and those of your friends.

As Fireboy wove among the moored ships and back into the open river, Carver sliced again, drawing the knife along as though he were slicing a smooth curve into a block of hardwood. Using his strongest talent to strengthen the other. The wind strengthened too, raising whitecaps on the water. More clouds began to spiral in above him. A shot whined off the boiler, but he ignored it. He spread his feet to brace against the choppy motion of the boat and began to carve on the sky.

He felt the texture of the air, the grain made by breezes and mist, flowing like the figure in the heart of a tree. He carved and sliced, shaping a bowl of wind and cloud, a dark well that sucked at the plumes of smoke and haze rising above the city. Lightning flared at its edges. It spread over Dunsgow, scattering showers of rain that pebbled the river and the rooftops. Some he caught before it reached the ground, swirling it back up to deepen the growing pool.

"They're gaining again," Fireboy said softly, and the shooting increased.

Carver nodded. That was good. He sliced again, carving more cloud.

"They're getting pretty close," Fireboy said. His voice was tight.

Carver smiled grimly. "Almost done."

With a final sweep of his arm, he slashed the knife downward from cloud to river, and rain poured down after it, a dark, raging fall of water outlined by lightning. It hit the water beside the Duke's boat, blasting a wave of spray over the side. The boat reeled onto the opposite beam. Then the circle of falling water centered on the boat. Carver held the knife pointed directly at Scharl, twirling just the tip. His forearm ached with the fine pressure needed to confine the rainfall. The Duke's boat settled. The starboard railing went under, then the port. Men were foundering, abandoning their heavy firearms to keep their heads above water, to find air in the drowning rain. The top of the smokestack disappeared below the surface, and there was nothing left but struggling men and a few loose boards swirling on the churning river.

Carver flicked the knife sideways, and the downpour shattered into a fitful, gusty shower. He felt weak, even a little sick. Fireboy was shouting, pounding his arm. "Not done yet," Carver said wearily.

Blinking his eyes clear, he turned to face the wall. The chain showed clearly, a black, uneven line that looked solid and massive even at this distance. Once more he raised the knife and worked on the sky. He carved thunderheads from the remaining cloud and rain, drew in more smoke from the city. He made the clouds as black and massive as the chain, feeling the power build under his blade, build to the point of explosion. Once more he slashed down. Lightning blasted from the sky, searing bolts that struck the chain. They struck again. And again, not once but many times in the same places. Till the chain was melted and broken along all the length of the wall he could see.

Exhausted, Carver lowered the knife. Its tip was blackened. His hand ached. He had to use his other hand to force his fingers open so he could let the knife go. He sank onto the seat and watched numbly while Fireboy steered them back toward the wharf. And there was Raven soaring into view above the shattered wall top. She winged toward them, cawing in exultation.

Twenty-nine

Carver shouldered his bundle and quietly let himself out. There were not many people at the table to take notice, no longer a guard at the door. Most of the household had moved with Paskovek to a large, bright house near the Plaza. Only a few remained here with Digger, to seek out the poor and homeless and help them find work. With the Duke gone and his workhouses shut down, there were beggars back on the streets. Merchants and fabricants, who had grumbled when the goods from the Duke's houses cut into their profits, now grumbled about the beggars. Some even hinted that workhouses were not such a bad idea after all.

Carver sighed as he made his way through the alley to the street. It had been like that for the past two months: constant bickering between the different factions who wanted to control the low reach now that Kovac and Krimm were gone. The Barons were one faction, the merchants another. Then there were the mages. Paskovek had tried to act as a mediator in the councils that followed the breaking of the chain, but other mages had appeared in the city, drawn from hiding places along the coast or up on the middle reach. They flexed their newly restored talents and chose sides. Very few of them had Paskovek's honesty. They all claimed true sight or foresight to back a list of outrageous demands. Carver shrugged off the destinies they foresaw. He knew now that the future changed with every choice a person made.

The truth seemed to change too. Everyone in the city *knew* Carver had drowned Scharl and ten boatloads of guarda with a tame tornado, and sliced the chain with a flaming sword. Most claimed to have seen it with their own eyes. And the stories of his battle with Krimm had become so fantastic, he could hardly recognize them. In the latest version, Raven was a dragon leading a hundred avenging eagles. Strangely, the apparatus had disappeared from the tale. Instead, Krimm controlled an army of stone ghouls with a crystal staff, and Carver shot him with a silver firearm.

With that kind of reputation, every faction wanted him on its side. Or wanted him gone. Even Paskovek, who was happy enough to be seen with Carver when he wanted to remind people of the power of magic, was also happy to stay at arm's length. He seemed in awe of Carver, almost a little afraid.

So Carver was leaving. He didn't like being known as the boy hero, the mage killer, the bringer of lightning and storms. And he wasn't going to be the muscleman for any faction. All he wanted to do was carve. But whenever he picked up a knife, people suddenly grew quiet. They watched him from the corners of their eyes and quickly found business elsewhere. Just in case. Even now, simply walking down the street, he created a pocket of space in the crowd. Oh, people smiled and nodded, and some bold ones even said hello, but that was because his hands were empty. If he reached into his pocket, they'd flinch. He could imagine the effect if he carried a wand, or even a crude stick. He couldn't help but grin at the thought. Half the mages were all show and flourish. A few had even started to carry staffs and wear lenses over their eyes. Maybe, when people discovered what fakes they were, the myths about him and Krimm would start to fade.

But Carver wasn't going to wait around for that. He didn't belong in Dunsgow anyway. The chain might be gone, but the workhouses still ran from dawn till dusk, and many through the night. Krimm had claimed that people in Dunsgow were free to do as they pleased; no apprenticeships, no bond servitude. Instead, they got to choose which workhouse or counting house to serve. Meanwhile, the merchants and fabricants still swung their bulk importantly through the streets like little barons, cursing the beggars. The water still stank, the air still burned his eyes and throat. And he itched to carve.

He came to a main avenue, crossed the bridge over the canal, and went down the steps to the quay. He had money in his pouches for the fare at least, real copper and silver coins that he could use on the upper reaches, and even here these days. There were several wherries waiting at the quay, and he started toward the nearest.

"Hoy! Carver!" It was Fireboy, waving from his own boat, the very launch that had carried them safely to Krimm's island and back. Now it had carved nameboards at the bow: *Little Sprite.* The owner had presented it to Carver in the first days after the breaking of the chain. He suspected the merchants had paid the man off. It had been like that at first, everyone friendly and working together to clean up the remnants of Krimm's misrule. Gifts and tributes for the hero. Carver had given most of it away, keeping only a small set of chisels and knives and a little money to travel on. The launch he had given to Fireboy. One person at least in this city could do what he really wanted. It gave Carver the hope that there were others.

He walked down to the *Little Sprite.* "Hoy, boatman," he said. "I thought you'd be busy overcharging a boatload of passengers by now."

Fireboy flashed his bright grin. "They're onto me. Competition's tough, you know."

"How has business been? Are you making out?"

"It's up and down," Fireboy allowed, "but I'm doing fine. I'm sleeping on board to save rent. If the council will just leave taxes alone, I'll have enough in a year."

"I've got more than I need," Carver began.

Fireboy shook his head. "You paid your share. I'll do the rest."

"The rest" was enough to pay off the bond on his family.

"Then I'd better let you get on with it," Carver said.

"Oh, I'm waiting for a special fare."

"Who's that?"

"You. I hear you need passage to the lift at First Falls."

"How did you hear that?" Carver demanded.

"A little bird told me."

Carver laughed. "Good. I'd much rather pay a friend for a boat ride, even if he does overcharge." He stepped into the cockpit and dropped his bundle on the seat. "Besides, I'm going to miss tending fire for you." He picked up the shovel and used it to open the firebox. Peering inside, he put on a critical frown. "Whoever laid this fire doesn't know his ash from his elbow. Who's your fireboy, Fireboy?"

Fireboy laughed. "That's me, Fireboy and Boatman, both. That's why I like this little launch—I can handle it all by myself. I don't need to pay for help."

"I'll be your fireboy this trip," Carver said, carefully spreading a layer of coal. "And I'll still pay the fare."

"We can talk about that when we get there," Fireboy said.

The trip upriver raised Carver's spirits. As they left the canals and the factories behind, they also left the stench and foul water. The haze thinned with each league. The cool autumn sunlight grew stronger. A weight lifted from Carver's shoulders; he was leaving the bickering factions behind too, and his distorted reputation.

"Which river will you take?" Fireboy asked, as he nosed the *Little Sprite* to a gentle stop at the landing below the great cliff.

Carver watched the lifts rise and fall. "The River Slow," he said.

"You sure? You'll have to get past Cutter. You cost him a boat and a bondservant. He's proud. He won't forget."

"I noticed him glaring at me in the council," Carver said wryly. "But he won't dare touch me now. I have a reputation."

"More than reputation," Fireboy said.

Carver shrugged. "My family needs to know what happened to my parents. Besides, I promised the mayor a good rainfall. After that . . ." He shrugged again.

"You know you can always come back here."

"Thanks."

Carver held out his hand, but Fireboy threw his arms around him, and they embraced for a moment. Then Carver picked up his bundle and stepped off the boat. Fireboy refused to take his fare, but Carver had left some coins hidden by the coal bin where he knew Fireboy would find them, along with the coal carving of the original *Water Sprite,* finally finished. Wordlessly, they shook hands one last time. Then, blinking hard, Carver turned and headed for the lifts. Behind him, Fireboy blew two long blasts on the whistle.

There was a line of people and piles of goods waiting for the lift. More were going up than used to, now that you didn't need a pass from the Duke. More than that, something in the recent events had loosened the bonds at the falls. The magic blockage that Krimm had fought against had lessened. Soon pedalers and steam power would spread along all the reaches, and there were people in line wearing long, loose breeches and topshirts with sewn-in pouches. Fashions would change, then all of life. He wasn't sure they were ready for it up there, but the flow had started. Like the river, there was no stopping it now.

He paid his fare and got on with the rest but stood by himself at the railing. As they rose above the rooftops, his eyes followed the line of the river. He picked out the *Little Sprite* steaming briskly downstream, the smoke from its stack rising into the yellow air above the river. As more and more of the reach spread out before him, Carver realized that the haze from Dunsgow washed right up against the cliff face, like a slowly climbing tide that never turned. He could taste the foul stench of it at the back of his throat.

At the top, Carver stepped off the lift and stared around like all the other newcomers. It looked the same as he remembered— guarda and baronsmen, porters and wagons and stacks of produce and raw materials. But somehow it was all new and strange. He walked along the rim, looking at the middle reach and the broad, clean lake, and also looking down at the low reach and the blot that was Dunsgow at the river mouth. Farther out, almost on the horizon, he could see the tall teeth of the archipelago that held Krimm's island, though he couldn't tell which one it was. He could see birds soaring below him too, but none were ravens. He wondered where she was. She had become an envoy for Paskovek, carrying messages to members of the council and even flying up and down the reach to seek out mages who might have escaped Krimm.

Carver took a last look at Dunsgow. The city's haze hung dirty and yellow in the thin sunlight. The brown outflow from its canals stained the river and the sea far from shore. He drew in a deep breath of clean air and thanked the stars that he was leaving all that behind. You couldn't even see the stars at night from Dunsgow. People down there worked long, hard hours inside, then spent the rest of their time in a cell of haze.

Carver started to turn. Then paused. He studied the filthy city far below. He reached into his pouch and took out Fireboy's folding knife with its blackened tip. He had promised himself he wouldn't use his weather talent again till he was on the upper reach, far from Dunsgow. But now he snapped the knife open and cradled it in his palm, feeling energy flow easily into the blade. Here, far above the city, it felt more powerful than ever. With a frown of concentration, he considered his first cut. Then he lifted the knife and carved the sky.

He kept his hand low, his motions small, and no one noticed what he was doing. He was just a young man, hardly more than a boy, taking in the view. Soon, everyone was too distracted to notice him anyway. They were hypnotized by the strange storm that swept in below and drenched the low reach. First came wind. It blew steadily, apparently right from the cliff face, pushing at the edges of the haze over Dunsgow. Then came clouds. They rolled in like ocean swells, shedding a drenching rain from the cliff to the river mouth. Wave after wave, they washed over the city. Strangely, they seemed drawn to the smokestacks above the workhouses. They paused, pouring rain directly down the tall brick and stone and iron tubes, until the fires went out and the smoke went white and dribbled to a stop. But still it rained, till the streets ran gray with dirty water sluicing down the cobbles and into the canals. And the canals swelled, washing everything into the river, merging with the rain-stoked current, flooding out to sea.

Then the storm passed. Sunlight glinted on wet roofs and shining streets. Not a single scrap of haze marred the sky.

Carver stretched, then closed his knife and dropped it back into his pouch.

"It won't do any good, Monkey Boy." Raven was perched on the railing beside him.

He smiled. "You don't think?"

"The stinkards are used to it."

"No. They've just forgotten it can be different. Maybe they'll decide they like this better."

She croaked a curt laugh. "Maybe. But it takes a lot to make a monkey change its ways. And monkeys are messy. By nature."

He shrugged. "It's worth trying."

They looked out at the city for a moment longer; then Carver turned to Raven. "Isn't the council meeting today? Paskovek will be needing you."

"I do my part before the meetings. Peck, peck, peck. By the time the greedy shrikes meet, they're so glad to be quit of me, they'll agree to anything goat beard proposes."

"You're getting to be a real schemer."

"Ravens are."

"Don't get your hopes up. I'm told it takes a lot to make a monkey change its ways."

She clacked her beak. "I've heard it's worth trying."

They laughed, and Raven hopped onto Carver's shoulder. "Where now?"

He started toward the waterfront. "Find a boat upriver."

"You could fly, you know."

He peered around at her. "Really?"

"No problem," she said. "Of course, you'd have to leave that bundle behind. And all your clothes."

He chuckled. "And you'd have to come to turn me back into a monkey boy. Still, it would be fun."

"Maybe next time."

He nodded. "Sometime."

"Soon!" she croaked, and nipped his ear.

He yelped and gently cuffed her head. "All right! Soon."

"Promise!"

"Right, right."

She lifted off then, brushing his face with her wings as she went. In a few hard beats she had risen high above him. Then she rolled smoothly and swooped, flashing right by his face.

"Don't forget, Monkey Boy!"

She dipped past the railing and swept down in a long, graceful arc toward the wet, glistening chimneys of Dunsgow.

Carver watched till she was a tiny black dot in the sky.

"I promise," he said.

Then he turned and began his journey upriver.